COMING of AGE...
AGAIN

a novel

CAROL MIZRAHI

ISBN-13: 9781466337435
ISBN-10: 1466337435

*Dedicated to all those who have the courage, the spirit,
the guts, and whatever else it takes
to come of age again ... and again... and again.*

Acknowledgments

Thanks to my progenitors (the Brusiloffs, the Baderacks, the Moskovitzes, and the Finders) who made my being here possible.

Thanks to my husband, Yoram, who supported me through the highs, the lows, and all the in-betweens.

Thanks to my children, Michael and Todd, who now know more about Irene, Sylvia, Barbara, and Rochelle than they do about me.

Thanks to Carol Somberg, more than a fine book designer: a good (and patient) friend.

Thanks to Nancy Coffey, who has no idea how her belief in *Coming of Age . . . Again* provided me with a much-needed shot in the arm over the years.

Prologue

*"Friendship is almost always the union of a part of one mind
with the part of another; people are friends in spots."*

George Santayana

IT is quite possible that if Miss Thompson had been an altogether different kind of person, Irene, Sylvia, Barbara, and Rochelle would not have become lifelong friends. One can only guess about that, but what we do know is that the kindergarten teacher's autocratic style and stern demeanor brought them together and created a bond that lasted for over fifty years. At the root of Miss Thompson's pathological need to control everyone and everything in her path was her diminutive size, which explained why she taught kindergarten. By fifth grade, most children had outgrown her.

That year—1952—as Miss Thompson watched the children come through the door, clinging to their mothers for dear life, she felt very positive. It was the first time in ten years of teaching that the number of children had "come out even." She had exactly twenty-four children on the roster, which meant there would be four and only four children at each of the six round classroom tables. Such precision, she believed, augured in a year of peace, symmetry, and absolute control.

As each mother and child made their tearful good-byes, Miss Thompson pinned a tag with his or her first name onto their shirts and blouses. Then she took hold of their cold, sticky hands and led them one by one to a pre-determined table while whispering reassuringly, "There, there," and "Now, now. It's going to be all right." When all twenty-four children were seated, Miss Thompson closed the classroom door, marched to front-center of the room, and introduced herself.

1

"Hello. My name is Miss Thompson, and I'm your teacher. The first thing I want you to see is that at the center of each table there is a cutout of a jungle animal ..."

That was as far as she got. The door opened, and Mr. Pintar, the school principal entered. With him was a pretty, dark-haired child who, unlike the others, did not look frightened. She looked past Miss Thompson to the other children and busily searched their faces, as if expecting to find an old friend—or make a new one.

"This is Irene," Mr. Pintar said. "Her family just enrolled her, and she's been assigned to your class."

"There must be a mistake. I have twenty-four children, *exactly* twenty-four children."

"It's no mistake." He handed her the updated roster.

"But I only have twenty-four chairs."

Wordlessly, Mr. Pintar left the room, returning minutes later with Miss Thompson's twenty-fifth chair. He set it down at the Zebra's Table, directed the twenty-fifth child to sit, and exited. The perfect symmetry of Miss Thompson's classroom had been destroyed, and with it, her composure. She began to hyperventilate. *Do not let one little girl destroy your year,* she told herself. *Do not, do not, do not!* She glared at Irene, who, instead of looking apologetic for the imbalance she had created, was waving a glad hand to the other children. *You will not destroy my year, little girl. You will not,* she told herself.

Suddenly, the one lone boy at the Zebra's Table let out a scream. "Idonwannabewithgirlsonly!"

Before Miss Thompson could stop him, he had dragged his chair to the Tiger Table, where two boys and girls were sitting. Miss Thompson immediately noted this transfer onto her roster.

"Now that *that's* settled," she said, waving her yardstick through the air, "I will continue. As I was saying, you will notice that at the center of each table is a jungle animal. The table you are sitting at will be your table for the year. You might like to think of it as your home away from home." She smiled insipidly at the children, who were mostly too cowed by their first day to respond to anything. "Those sitting at the Zebra table will be called The Zebras. Children at the Elephant table will be The Elephants—the same for the monkeys, the hippos, tigers, and lions. So now, let's say hello to our new family."

Irene, the twenty-fifth child, was the first to bray. Sylvia, Barbara, and Rochelle responded in kind, and all the other children followed suit: elephants trumpeted, monkeys howled, hippos bellowed, tigers growled, and lions roared, culminating in a thunderous and unpleasant cacophony of clamor. Miss Thompson felt another panic attack coming on. She closed her eyes, inhaled and exhaled deeply while rocking from one foot to the other. The children quieted, fascinated by their teacher's peculiar behavior. After a minute, Miss Thompson opened her eyes, grabbed her yardstick and pointing it ahead of her like a dowsing rod, descended upon the Zebra's Table. And Irene.

"You started it," she said. "With your braying."

"But that's how zebras say hello," Irene explained, opening her mouth wide, preparing to repeat her performance. Miss Thompson smacked her yardstick against the edge of the table.

"There are rules in life and in school," she began. "The first rule is that we never speak unless we're called upon. And to be called on, you must first raise your hand. Do you understand?" She paused to examine the four upturned faces. No four little girls could look more different from each another, she thought: Irene was dark-haired and dark-eyed, Rochelle, blonde with blue eyes, Barbara had red hair and freckles, and the fourth one, Sylvia—there was no one good feature to describe her kindly. She was, in total, a singularly unattractive child. "I repeat," Miss Thompson continued. "You must raise your hand and be called upon before you speak; otherwise, you can imagine what it would be like if twenty-four children . . ." She stopped herself. " . . .if twenty-*five* children all spoke at once."

Irene raised her hand. Miss Thompson ignored her. Irene jumped to her feet and waved her hands frantically overhead, miming the words: "Call on me. Call on me."

"Yes. What *is* it?" Miss Thompson finally asked, unable to ignore Irene any longer.

"No, I can't."

"No, you can't *what*?"

"Can't magine if twenty-five all talked at once."

"Irene, that wasn't a real question. It's what we call a rhetorical question, which means I didn't expect an answer."

"Then why'd you ask?"

Miss Thompson jabbed her yardstick at Irene, like a fencing foil.

"Sit down right now, and remember what I said about speaking out of turn. That includes laughing. If there is ever an outburst like that again, I will have to speak to your parents, and you know what *that* means."

Twenty-four ashen-faced children sat quietly. Irene raised her hand.

"*Now* what?" Miss Thompson screamed at her.

"I don't know."

"You don't know *what*?"

"What it means if you speak to our parents."

"You, Irene, are a troublemaker who is taking time away from my teaching. I want you to apologize to the other children. Right now." Irene was silent. "I said now!"

Irene looked around the classroom. "Soreee," she whispered.

"We can't hear you."

"Sor-reeeeeeeeeee!" she screamed.

The classroom door opened, and Miss Thompson was signaled out into the hall.

"Don't forget!" she said, leaving the room. "No talking while I'm gone."

The door closed shut.

"I don't like her!" Irene said to the other Zebras.

Rochelle's baby blue eyes opened wide. "Don't we *have to* like her? She's our teacher."

"I don't have to like anyone I don't like," Irene shouted. The children at the other tables giggled.

"You're going to get in big trouble," Barbara warned.

Sylvia, already jealous of the attention Irene was getting, jumped into the fray. "Who's afraid of trouble? I'm not!"

Miss Thompson returned to the classroom.

"Let's begin our first lesson, which is about organization, leadership, and government. Every political unit has a leader. The president runs the country. The state has a governor. Your mother and father are the head of your home. The school has a principal, your classroom a teacher, and now each table will have a leader. We will vote."

Barbara raised her hand.

"Yes, Barbara. What's your question?"

"What's a vote?"

"You pick someone at your table to be the leader. Everyone picks one person, and the child with the most votes becomes the leader of that group." Sylvia raised her hand. "Yes?"

"Can we vote for ourselves?"

"You wouldn't want to do that. That wouldn't be very friendly, and we all want to make friends, don't we? So let's begin."

Barbara voted for Irene. Irene voted for Barbara. Sylvia voted for herself, and Rochelle refused to vote because voting was the same as choosing, and whenever she chose, it came out wrong. If she refused to chose, she'd learned, eventually some grown- up would decide for her, like her mother or father. Maybe teachers did in schools what parents did at home.

"You didn't vote," Barbara said to Rochelle.

"I don't want to."

"You have to," Sylvia said. "Vote for me."

"No. Vote for Irene," Barbara argued. "She'll be a good leader."

"I'll be better," Sylvia said, pulling on Rochelle's arm.

Rochelle shrugged off Sylvia's hand and tucked her delicate neck down deep into her chest. "I'm not and you can't make me!"

Miss Thompson tapped the large wall clock behind her with her yardstick. "One minute to go."

Barbara whispered in Irene's ear: "If you vote for you, and I vote for you, you'll have two votes and win."

And that's how Irene became leader of the Zebras.

Later in the morning, when the children went outside for recess, they circled the Zebras, asking to play with them.

"We're poplar," Barbara later explained.

"What's 'poplar'?" they asked.

"Children want to play with us. They like us. That's poplar."

Sylvia wanted to know what "poplar" was good for. The question puzzled Barbara. "It's just good. Everyone knows that."

"Name me one thing it's good for," Sylvia demanded.

"It's good for everything!"

"Then let's always be poplar together," Irene suggested. The others nodded in excited agreement. "We have to do something to make it forever. That's what they do in movies. Let me think what." They waited for their leader. "Let's pinch each other but not very hard."

"Who does the pinching?" Sylvia asked, suspiciously.

"We all do. We stand in a circle, and we pinch the person next to us one time until everyone's been pinched."

That first day of school had other firsts for the Zebras: Irene enjoyed her first political win; Barbara experienced her first success as a political strategist; and Rochelle learned that indecisiveness worked as well at school as it did at home. As for Sylvia, she decided that "poplar" was something she wasn't, and the closest she would get to it would be a pinch away from someone who was.

* * *

For the next six years, the Zebras remained inseparable friends, but by seventh grade, Barbara and Irene were anxious to break away from the pack. All that stood in their way was guilt. "We'll still be best friends forever," Irene explained to Sylvia and Rochelle. "But there's not going to be any more Zebras."

Tears welled up in Rochelle's eyes, and Sylvia clenched her fists so tightly her nails dug into her palms and made them bleed. "We'll still see each other," Barbara assured them, "but this is so much healthier," she added, repeating her mother's words.

Rochelle and Sylvia were afraid that without Irene and Barbara's proximity, they would be friendless. That is, essentially, what happened to Sylvia, but Rochelle, whose beauty outweighed her passivity and indecisiveness, was not forgotten. Sylvia saw very little of her three best and only friends and became despondent. Her English teacher noticed and counseled her. "You're too smart to care about being popular. Use that good brain God gave you, and I guarantee you one day you'll be a star, while all those silly girls will be doing housework and changing diapers."

Sylvia thought about it, long and hard. What was the worst thing that could happen to her if she became known as a "brain"? Boys wouldn't like her because boys didn't like smart girls, which was why girls worked hard *not* to get A's. They also didn't want C's because C's could keep them out of a good college where they expected to go to find the right kind of husband. B, therefore, was the grades of choice, but no boy was going to like her no matter what grade she got, so why not study hard and make something of herself?

Six years later Sylvia graduated high school salutatorian and won a four-year scholarship to the University of Chicago. Unfortunately, she never got there.

Barbara and Irene started college at the University of Illinois, and Rochelle enrolled at the Chicago Art Institute. Rochelle was the first to marry. She married Mark because—unlike the other men she had dated—he didn't ask. He told her. He also told her to quit art school, where she was not only winning awards but beginning to sell her paintings. Then he told her to stay home and raise their children, and after forty years of marriage, he told her he wanted a divorce.

Barbara married Richard, a law school graduate her mother approved of. "Say yes to this one," she advised. "He's going somewhere." Her mother had been right, and because the marriage gave Barbara what she needed most in life—financial security and social status— she had been willing to "look the other way" during Richard's many short-lived and non-threatening affairs.

Irene married Phil two weeks after she graduated from college. Their happy thirty-year marriage ended in 1998 when Phil was killed by a drunken driver. Since that time, Irene has been searching for "the perfect man." She thought Mel was the one, but that was before he moved in—before the "up" toilet seats, the Metamucil-coated glasses, and the water stains on her wood furniture.

Sylvia was the last to marry. She was in her late twenties when she met Morris Mazol, a quiet, gentle man ten years older than she, and although she felt none of the excitement her friends had displayed, she was happy: happy to quit her job, happy to be married, happy to have a child, but most happy to join her three best friends once a week for a (usually) friendly game of mahjongg.

CHAPTER ONE

Mahjongg at Sylvia's

*"Habit: Chains that are too small to be felt till
they are too strong to be broken."*

Samuel Johnson

THIS week's mahjongg game was at Sylvia's home in Wicker Park. Sylvia and Morris had bought their 1930's home thirty-four years earlier, when Sylvia was pregnant with Mary. They converted the one-family two-story residence into two flats. The Mazol family lived downstairs, while the upstairs unit was rented.

Since Morris' death twenty years earlier, Sylvia's life and habits had barely changed. Her daughter Mary still lived at home. The 1970s shag carpeting still covered the wood floors, the phones were rotary, the appliances gold, and the wallpaper flocked. Only the TV had seen upgrades. Sylvia now owned a 48" plasma screen with high definition. Her friends called her cheap, but she considered herself "frugal, a lost virtue in a world of people with throwaway mentality," she liked to say.

"Rochelle, make a move already. We're not going to live forever," Irene said.

Of the four of them, Rochelle should have been the confident one. She was the only one to sail gracefully from childhood into womanhood, going to sleep one night and waking the next morning beautiful and bountiful. She needed no training bra, no braces, and no nose job. She never saw a zit, her hair didn't frizz, and she was a perfect ten. She had been a true princess in body, mind, and spirit, but as the only child of middle-class, middle-aged parents, she had been over-indulged and over-protected. Their hovering led to her insecurities, which led to her indecisiveness, which led to her neediness, which led to her dullness, which led to her divorce.

"Rochelle, please," Sylvia begged. "Make a move."

Although now almost sixty-three, Rochelle is still blonde and beautiful and, it seems, indecisive.

"Rochelle!"

Rochelle selected a tile from her wall, studied it, and put it back.

Irene touched the gem-studded initial pin on Barbara's jacket. "I don't remember seeing this before," she said. "Is it new?"

"No, Richard bought it for me last year, when he was shtupping one of his bank tellers. It's a Buccarelli original." They shrugged, as if to say, who's Buccarelli and who gives a rat's damn? "Buccarelli is a very famous Italian jewelry designer."

Barbara hadn't changed much either. She was still a size eight and her hair red, though now she colored it. As for the freckles, they had faded over the years.

"Rochelle, please," Irene pleaded. "I have a meeting at ten tomorrow morning. I don't want to be late!"

Rochelle pulled a tile from her rack and threw it. "Six dot."

"I'll take it." As Irene reached for the tile, she grimaced at the sight of her prominent veins, rising high off the back of her hand, the beginning of old lady's hands. She'd been botoxed, collagened, and juvidermed. Most recently, she had had her eyebrows tattooed. She colored her hair and worked out on a treadmill three days a week, and if it weren't for her hands, she thought, she could pass for fifty. "Did you know there's a new procedure for extracting fat from your ass and injecting it into the backs of your hands? To plump them up?"

"You going to do that too? On top of everything else?" Sylvia asked.

"Four bam!" Irene flicked the tile in Sylvia's direction.

Whereas Barbara, Irene, and Rochelle all looked ten years younger than their age, Sylvia looked ten years older, but that was an improvement. When they were in their thirties and forties, Sylvia looked twenty years older than her age. She had gray curly hair that resembled an aging floor mop, but instead of following her friends' recommendations and paying for a good hair stylist, she continued to go to Hair Today, Gone Tomorrow, which cost her $9.99.

Sylvia pulled a tile from the wall, set it on her rack, and threw an eight crack. It was Rochelle's turn again. They waited. And waited.

"Any new jokes?" Barbara asked Irene.

Irene was their jokester and story teller. Not only did she hear more jokes than they—possibly because she was the only one who had a forty-hour a week job—but she remembered and told them well.

"Did I tell you the one about Abie and Sara in Florida?" She hadn't. "Abie and Sara are in their eighties, living in Florida. Abie calls his son in New York and tells him he and Sara are getting divorced. The son tells him not to do anything until he has a chance to talk to his sister. He calls his sister, who calls her father and tells him not to do anything; that she and her brother are flying to Florida first thing in the morning. Abie hangs up the phone and says to Sara: That takes care of Rosh Hashanna. What'll we do for Passover?'"

They didn't laugh.

"That's the way it is," Barbara said, throwing in a tile. "For the first fifteen years they need us. The next fifteen, we're inconvenient, and in the end—irrelevant."

"God, how I *wish* I were irrelevant," Rochelle whined.

"You would be if you put your mouth where your money is," Sylvia snapped. She was referring to the half a dozen different therapies and therapists Rochelle had engaged since her divorce from Mark. Despite the time and money spent, she continued to be accommodating and compliant.

"It's hard to break old habits, especially when you've been rewarded all your life for deferring to others," she answered, in her own defense.

"If you try to please everyone, you can never please yourself," Irene advised, picking a tile from the wall. "Four dot."

Sylvia took a tile, added it to her rack, and discarded. "Six crack."

When it was just her and Mark, Rochelle thought, he had been happy. Then the children came. He said she went overboard, catering to their every demand. He wasn't happy. When the children left home and were on their own, Mark was happy again. Then the grandchildren were born, and their daughters made her their nanny, errand girl, and back-up cook. Mark wasn't happy. He complained that they rarely had a weekend without toddlers underfoot. He suggested they sell their home and buy a condo downtown, "far away from the children and grandchildren." He began looking at properties. When Bette and Amy got wind of it, they threw tizzy fits. Hadn't they bought their homes where they did so the grandchildren could bond with their grandparents? Didn't their parents love their grandchildren? Amy, an assistant professor of sociology at Northeastern Illinois University, quoted the latest research: "Small children who have the opportunity to bond with their grandparents grow up with stronger and healthier egos." Later, she repeated Amy's treatise to Mark. "*Our* parents didn't help raise *our* children," Mark countered, "and just look at the size of their egos!"

"Rochelle! It's your move!"

Things came to an ugly head when Bette and Amy suggested she install an elaborate children's playground in their backyard.

"It'll make your life so much easier," Bette reasoned. "When the children come to play, you can just open the back door and let them out."

"And if you decide at anytime within the first thirty days that you don't want the set, the manufacturer promises to remove it within twenty-four hours," Amy added.

Mark continued to object. "They're already here too much, and with Disneyland operating in our backyard, they'll never go home. Why don't you install these fun stations in your own backyards?" he asked his daughters. They explained that the really nice systems were too expensive for one family plus their backyards were too small. Their parents' was ideal.

Rochelle pleaded their daughters' case. After several weeks of "no," Mark changed his tactics. "I've spent our entire marriage making decisions for the two of us. I'm going to leave this one up to you."

Two weeks later when Mark came home from work, he found a metropolis of tunnels, bridges, slides, and swings installed in their yard and his prized $1,000 Platinum Weber grill relocated to the side of the house. Within twenty-four hours he had packed, moved out of his house of thirty years and in with his secretary.

Neither Bette nor Amy took any responsibility. Their father had set her up, they said. He knew she was a rotten decision maker. He had counted on her to make the wrong choice; after all, didn't he move in immediately with his secretary? The playground was an excuse, not a reason.

After Mark left her, she went to bed and stayed there for days. Irene, Sylvia, and Barbara made her an appointment with the then-celebrity therapist Dr. Mervin Merkin. When Dr. Merkin's hand grazed her, she wasn't sure. And when he brushed the front of her blouse, she was sure but reluctant to confront, but when his mouth clamped down on hers and his tongue found its way past her teeth, she fled his office.

She joined T.M., which promised her a "life-changing" experience. They asked her to drop out at the end of the first week. They'd caught her sleeping. Next she signed up for yoga. On her first day of class, while laying on the guru's floor, bent into the dog position, a giant cockroach waddled towards her. She never went back. EST gave her a headache and Rational Thinking bored her. A fellow docent at the art museum told her about Madame Savansky. "She's a brilliant advisor and clairvoyant. I highly recommend her."

"Rochelle?" Irene tapped her on her head. "Yoo hoo. You in there?"

Irene was right, Rochelle thought. During all those years, of catering to others, she had done nothing for herself. "I'm sorry." She blindly discarded a tile.

"What was it?" Barbara asked.

"Six crack."

"And that Gypsy woman you've been seeing. I don't think she's doing you one bit of good," Barbara remarked.

"First of all, they're called *Roms*, not Gypsies, and, two, I *am* making progress." They were not convinced. "Tomorrow morning I'm converting Adam's old bedroom into a studio for myself, and in the afternoon, I have an appointment at the Art Institute. I'm signing up for summer classes."

They raised their glasses in sincere tribute.

"Ching, ching, skol, and l'chaim," they said.

That's when Rochelle's cell phone rang. She read the caller I.D. and flinched.

"You don't have to answer it," Sylvia counseled.

"It's Bette," she said, in a tone that implied she had no choice. "Hello."

"Hi, Mom. You busy?"

"Yes, I'm with the girls. We're in the middle of mahjongg."

"What are you doing tomorrow?"

"I'm setting up my home studio in the morning, and I have an appointment in the afternoon," she said, softly.

"You haven't forgotten that I'm bringing Jonathan over Thursday morning, have you?"

"No, of course not."

"Have you cleaned up the backyard yet?"

"Don't worry. It'll be done by Thursday."

"But if you're busy all day tomorrow, how will you have time to clean the yard before eight in the morning Thursday?" Rochelle didn't answer. "We were just plain lucky that Jonathan and Emily weren't seriously hurt last week." When Rochelle still didn't answer, Bette moved in for the kill. "Personally, I think you've got your priorities confused. It would be wiser for you to clean the yard in the morning before you do anything else. You'd never forgive yourself if something happened to one of the children, right?"

"Yes, I suppose so," she whimpered. The girls rolled their eyes at each other.

"I knew you'd understand. I have to go now. See you Thursday."

"Some progress," Irene commented.

"Jonathan fell over a ground root last week and twisted his ankle, and Emily cut herself on a rusty bottle cap in the sandbox," Rochelle explained, anxious to defend herself.

"Your daughters should be cleaning your yard. Not you! They're half your age," Barbara said.

"Or they can pay someone else to do it with the money they save not paying you one red cent for child care," Sylvia added.

"And what about your studio?" Irene asked. "When will you do that?"

"What's another day or two?"

"Nothing when you're thirty, but maybe a lifetime at sixty-two."

Rochelle fled the room, in tears.

"When is she going to stop covering up for her children?" Barbara asked.

"When are we?" Irene answered.

"Hers don't deserve it."

"Neither do ours."

While they waited for Rochelle to return, Irene dropped bits of pretzel on the decades old shag carpet beneath her feet. She watched the carpet fibers part, like the Red Sea, and the pretzel pieces disappear from sight. For fifteen years, once a month, when Sylvia was mahjongg hostess, she had been feeding bits of this and that to the microscopic creatures (whom she named The Shags) living at the base of Sylvia's carpet. "If it weren't for me," she repeatedly told her granddaughter, Maya, who had been raised on Shag stories, "they would have died out years ago. We're the only company Sylvia gets in a month."

The part about the mahjongg group being Sylvia's only company was almost true. Three to four times a year, when Mary had a new love interest, Sylvia would invite them home for dinner, but they generally left before dessert.

Irene's Shag stories grew in number and sophistication over the years, mostly in response to Maya's developing inquisitiveness: "How come the Shags don't get sucked up and out when Sylvia vacuums?" They've been able to survive over the years, Irene explained, because of Darwinian adaptation. They now have wiry feet, and when they hear the Super Deluxe Dynamo Vacuum approaching, they wrap their feet tightly around the base of the carpet fibers. "How do they make babies?" led to other Shag stories. She now had over two dozen tales at various stages of development. She had originally planned to finish and publish them in another two years when her pension kicked in and she could afford to retire, but after she met Mel and was certain that he was "the one," she began to consider the possibility of retiring earlier . . . but that was before he moved in.

"Have you ever thought of replacing your carpet?" Irene asked Sylvia, throwing the Shags another crushed pretzel.

"Why would I? It's as good as new."

"But the color."

"What's wrong with citrus green?"

"Don't you think its gotten greener over the years? It's more of a pea-green now."

"What I think is that you need to curb your imagination."

"Is Mary out with Eric?" Barbara asked Sylvia. Eric was Mary's current boyfriend. Sylvia ignored the question, apparently absorbed by the act of ferreting the almonds out of the bowl of mixed nuts. "I said," Barbara repeated, "Is Mary out with Eric?"

"She's not seeing him anymore," she whispered.

This was Mary's third break-up with a man since January, and it was only April.

"Wasn't he just here for dinner Friday night?" Barbara pursued. Sylvia downed the almonds. "Has anyone else noticed that Mary's relationships with men always end right after Sylvia invites them home for dinner?"

"What are you feeding them, Sylvia?" Irene asked. "Shrapnel?"

"One day she'll meet a man of substance."

"What does that mean?"

"Eric was a wuss."

"In other words, not a man worth dying for." Irene and Barbara grinned at each other.

"That's right. I don't mind dying for a good cause, but I don't think a wussy son-in-law is a good cause for dying. Even *my* pathetic life is worth more than that."

Sylvia was convinced that she had a fatal swallowing disorder called the Chasanov Choking Syndrome (CCS), named after her mother's family. Curiously, no reference to CCS could be found in any medical text—not the *PDR*, *Merck*, or *The New England Journal of Medicine*. Google searches produced only trombone players and family trees, and Wikipedia, for the first time ever, had nothing to say on the subject.

"Sylvia, dear Sylvia, you have to give this up. It's a *bubbameisse*," Irene said. "You do not have a swallowing or choking problem. Tonight, for example, you single-handedly finished all the almonds in the nut mix and never, not once, did you hick, hock or hoke."

"What's more," Barbara added, "in all the years we've known each other, you have never choked in our company."

"I only choke when I'm stressed, and yes I did. Don't you remember? It was at Morris' funeral when his whore showed up, and if it hadn't been for my cousin Albert, I would've choked to death."

"OK, that was it. One time, and it had nothing to do with a structural problem. You were simply fried out," Irene insisted.

Sylvia marched into the kitchen, removed the magnetized glass frame from the refrigerator door, and returned to the living room. She waved it at them—show and tell style.

"Remember this? It's my mother's autopsy report. Cause of death: CHOKING. Did you forget they found a piece of carrot lodged in her windpipe?" Sylvia recanted the story of her mother's death on the average of four times a year. They made an effort not to interrupt her, having decided years earlier that these quarterly regurgitations were cathartically beneficial. "Vera and Al were in Los Angeles visiting Clara, and I hadn't talked to Mama for two or three days, which wasn't unusual. She was only sixty and in good health, with a lot of friends in her building she was always visiting so when I called and she didn't answer, I didn't think there was any reason to worry. It wasn't until the neighbors smelled her decomposing flesh that they called the police." They grimaced. "I'll never forget the stench of her rotting body. She deserved better than that, and so do I!"

"Her death was tragic, of course," Barbara agreed, "but it was an accident; not the result of any swallowing disorder."

"When your mother and your mother's mother and your mother's grandmother all choke to death, it's no accident. My mother might still be alive today if she hadn't been living alone."

"It's not fair to keep Mary here at home with you, no matter how afraid you are," Irene said, trying to be as gentle as possible.

"I have never used my disability to influence Mary. I encourage her to date. I want her to meet some nice young man, get married, and move out, but until she does, why shouldn't she live here with me and extend my life?"

Silence followed.

"Rochelle?" Sylvia yelled. "We're waiting for you." They heard the toilet flush.

"How's your new assistant working out?" Barbara asked Irene, anxious to change the subject.

"Best employee I've had in a decade. Would you believe there are mornings when she gets to work before me and is still there when I leave? She's almost too good to be true."

"Then she probably is," Sylvia quipped. "In fact, she sounds a lot like Heather on *Days of our Lives*, in which case she could be after your job."

Sylvia saw conspiracies and betrayals behind every door, both open and closed.

"That's ridiculous. Why would anyone in her right mind want my job? It's boring, non-creative, and doesn't pay very well."

"That's what you think at sixty-two, but to an ambitious thirty-something, it might look like the best job in the world or the best job in the world on the way to the *next* best job in the world."

"She can have it when I retire."

"What if she doesn't want to wait? What if she wants it now? Two years can seem like a lifetime to the young," Sylvia argued.

And to the middle-aged, Irene thought.

"You need to get out more," Barbara advised. "You watch too much TV."

Rochelle returned from the bathroom and took her seat at the table.

"Whose turn is it anyway?" Irene asked.

"Who else?" Sylvia answered.

In one fell swoop, Rochelle knocked over the four tile racks. "Game's over," she announced.

It was so unlike Rochelle that they applauded her. She had unilaterally made a decision.

"What if we had still wanted to play?" Barbara jibed.

"I don't care."

"What if we won't love you anymore?" Irene asked.

"Your love is the only dependable love I know."

"In that case, dessert time. Meet you all in the dining room." Sylvia left for the kitchen.

Barbara's cell phone rang.

"Richard," she explained, before taking the call. "Yes, I'm here with the girls. We're just having dessert." She looked at her watch. "That late? No, I won't. I'll see you in the morning." She turned off her phone.

It wasn't *what* Barbara said but *how* she said it.

"Richard up to his young tricks again?" Irene asked.

"You need to confront him," Rochelle said.

She shrugged with practiced indifference. For twenty-five years she had treated her husband's infidelities like so much falderal because there was a predictable and non-threatening pattern to them, and what she needed most in life, she knew, was security and constancy. Say what one might, Richard's inconstancies had been constant.

First there would be a short run of evening business meetings and one or two out-of-town consults, accompanied by a sudden personality change. He would go from his usual indifferent demeanor to that of an overly solicitous husband, agreeing with everything she said and did, no matter how foolish it was. Most out of character was his short term generosity, usually expressed in the form of an expensive piece of jewelry, like the one she was wearing tonight.

Fine jewelry had been only one of her rewards. The second was that during these flings, he made no sexual demands on her. She had to admit that she enjoyed these short respites from Richard's clumsy and selfish lovemaking. Yes, that's how it had been, she thought, but this time it was different.

"I couldn't live like that," Irene said.

"I don't believe it's worth starting a war and changing an attractive lifestyle for a few dozen thrusts, plunges, grunts, and groans," Barbara answered.

"Definitely not," Irene agreed. "Not when you put it that way."

Sylvia entered the dining room, carrying her famous rum trifle. She served and joined them at the table.

"Talking about the men in our lives, how's it going with Mel?" Barbara asked Irene. When she didn't answer, they guessed: Irene had already soured on Mel. They had lost count of the number of times Irene had announced she had finally found "the one," only to hear her confess a few weeks later that so and so wasn't the one.

"He's not the one?" Sylvia teased.

"Go ahead and laugh. I deserve it, but I really thought Mel was the one, and he was, right up until the minute he moved in. Before that we had fun together. We did things. We went out, but all he wants to do now is sit in front of the TV and watch sitcoms. It's like the Mel I dated and the one I'm living with are two different people."

"We told you to take your time," Rochelle reminded her, "but you were in a big hurry."

Yes, she *had* been in a hurry, she thought. She had met Mel only a few days after she discovered that her once-beautiful legs had turned into two jiggling containers of cellulite. She had been at work, walking between the elevator and her office when she felt a strange chafing between her thighs. She went into the bathroom, stood in front of the full length mirror, pulled up her skirt, pulled down her knee-highs, and looked. She wasn't sure what she expected to find—maybe a used dryer sheet stuck between her thighs; instead she saw that her once firm inner thighs—having had no previous contact with each other—had turned to fat and flab and were rubbing against each other. She wondered if anything else had gone wrong.

Her eyes traveled down her legs to the loose folds of skin covering her knees. She squeezed together the excess skin of one knee and calculated that she had enough superfluous material to cover a second knee and maybe even a third. It was gross, she thought. And embarrassing. She could never wear a bathing suit in public again! Or shorts. She pulled up her knee-highs and stretched out her arms. The skin of her underarms hung down like twin bats. That's when the bathroom door opened and a tight-skinned thirty-something year old entered and stared at her. She dropped her arms.

"What are you looking at?" she growled. "If you live long enough, your body will fail you, too. One morning you'll wake up and find that you've got enough extra skin on your body to cover another 5'8" woman!"

Soon after that she began to notice other changes—like the bald spots in her eyebrows. She paid a tattoo artist $350 to fill in the blanks. A week later she found long, dark hairs growing out of her ear lobes. The electrolysis cost her $200. She was in a panic, which had less to do with vanity and more to do with the message she was getting: time is running out.

"Yes, I *was* in a hurry," she admitted. "I should have taken my time."

"But now that he's moved in you should try to make it work," Barbara advised. "Trust me when I tell you that a good man is hard to find, and Mel seems like a good, decent person. There is no perfection."

"Phil was perfect," Irene answered.

"Only after he died," Sylvia reminded her. "You have a short memory."

"We all make our compromises," Barbara added. "God knows I've made mine."

Mel in the abstract was not the issue, Irene thought. She could rationalize and compromise with the best of them, but when they were sharing a space, all rational thinking went out the window. "The truth is," she said, throwing herself on the mercy of the court, "his habits are driving me crazy."

"Of course, they are," Sylvia agreed. "He's a man."

"Did you forget your mother's mantra?" Rochelle asked. "All men need retraining." They smiled at each other. Who could forget those printed note cards she had inserted in their shower and bridal gifts. No "Best wishes" or "Here's to a lifetime of happiness," but "You have one year in which to train him. After that, what you got is what you're stuck with."

Ironically enough, Irene thought, her mother had been a failure in training her own husband. She was still working on him the day he died, more accurately, up until the hour he died. They'd been watching TV. Her father had gone to the kitchen for a drink before going upstairs to bed. Minutes later, when her mother went into the kitchen, she found the lights on. "Gerald!" she screamed, standing at the bottom of the stairs. "Gerald!" He came out of their bedroom and looked over the railing. "What is it, Dora?" Her mother answered, "Are you never going to learn to turn off the lights when you leave a room? Come down right now and turn off the kitchen light!" Down he came, looking old and tired. He obediently turned off the kitchen light, closed his eyes, and slumped to the floor. Dead.

That was when she decided that retraining was not only impossible, it was morally wrong to marry someone with the intent of changing him.

The front door opened and closed. Mary entered, still dressed in her nurse's uniform. She circled the dining room table, giving them all a kiss hello. She was her father's daughter: tall and thin and built like a model. She had thick auburn hair, honey olive skin, and high cheekbones. A classic American Beauty if not for her ethnic nose. Most Jewish parents, anxious for Yankee Doodle children, encouraged their daughters to "fix" their noses, but not Sylvia. She had raised Mary on a litany of adages, such as handsome is as handsome does, rarely do great beauty and intelligence go together; most beautiful things are useless, and a pretty woman never knows what a man wants from her, all intended to discourage her from becoming any more attractive than she already was and consequently finding a man worth her mother's "dying for."

Mary joined them at the table.

"Been shopping?" Irene asked.

"Yes, a new good luck piece." She held up the gray stone, hanging on a silver chain around her neck. "It's a Lodestone. Lodestones contain magnetite, which is supposed to attract good luck."

Irene, Barbara, and Rochelle felt personally responsible for Mary's twenty-year obsession with lucky charms. They had given her her first amulet on her thirteenth birthday, soon after her father's death. She had changed from a happy and outgoing child to a withdrawn and moody adolescent. They had hoped the good luck piece would give her something to believe in—until she believed in herself again.

Mary wore the *yad* for several months, waiting for her luck to change: for her father to return from the dead and her mother to love her, but when neither happened, she concluded that not all amulets were lucky for all people. What she needed to do, she decided, was to retire the failed charm and buy another . . .and another . . .and another . . . until she found her designated lucky piece.

She began frequenting antique shops, psychic storefronts, and church and temple gift shops. She ordered amulets from catalogues and magazines, and by the time she was twenty-five and had graduated from nursing school, she had collected eighty-five amulets and was still living at home with Sylvia. That's when she realized her second mistake: in a world filled with millions of good luck pieces, it would take an inordinate amount of good luck to find the one piece intended just for you, and anyone who had that kind of luck, didn't need a good luck piece. The joke was on her.

"You don't still believe in that stuff, do you?" Barbara asked.

"Of course not. I collect out of habit—not belief." She turned. "I'm off to bed. Please say hello to the children for me."

Minutes later they heard a scraping noise, followed by a loud bang from the back of the house. It shook the dining room walls, misaligning Sylvia's carefully arranged gallery of family photos (minus any of her father or dead husband).

"What was that?" Irene asked.

"The upstairs renters. They must be moving furniture again."

"That wasn't from upstairs. It was from the back of the house, where the bedrooms are."

"It was from upstairs," Sylvia repeated, bringing an end to the discussion.

CHAPTER TWO

Irene and Mel

"Maturity is the ability to live in someone else's world."

Oren Arnold

As soon as Irene entered the foyer, she heard Mel snoring. It would be another long night, she thought. There were dirty dishes in the living room, a milk-coated drinking glass on the kitchen counter, and the toilet seat was "up." She shuddered at the sight of two pubic hairs on the toilet rim, glued in urine drippings. She started to wipe them off with a piece of toilet paper but stopped herself, echoes of her mother's second favorite war cry ringing in her ears: "The more you do, the more they have you do." She slammed the toilet seat down on the pubic hairs. Mel's snoring stopped for a moment and then resumed, full throttle.

It wasn't that he was stupid, she thought. He had a bachelor's degree in accounting from Penn State, an MBA from Wharton, and for the past thirty years had been an actuary with Metropolitan Life. Yet despite repeated complaints, he continued to leave the toilet seat up.

On the bathroom floor near the waste basket lay a bloody string of dental floss. She looked skyward and called out plaintively to anyone who would listen that there was apparently no end to it—the number and variety of Mel's nasty and irritating personal habits. "Just when I think I've seen it all, he comes up with something new!" No one answered. "There's no way I can retrain Mel in a year. What's more, I don't want to try. Maybe you can invest a year when you're thirty-something, but at sixty-three, one year is a dog's year, which means I could be dead before the experiment ends!"

She washed and creamed her face, studying her reflection in the mirror. She had just finishing paying off the tattoo artist who did her eyebrows, and now there was something else going on. It looked like the shape of her face was changing, maybe even sinking. She looked thinner, even gaunt. Could that really happen, she asked herself? Did people lose bone? Or fat? She puffed air into her cheeks and held her breath. Yes, that looked more like her, the way she'd always looked, but she certainly couldn't spend the rest of her life puffing air into her cheeks. She turned off the bathroom light and told herself she needed to be more patient with Mel.

He was lying on his back, snoring so thunderously the bed vibrated. She pushed him gently in the shoulder. "Mel?" The snoring stopped—but only for a moment. She shoved him harder. He turned from his right side to his left. Now he was snoring in her face instead of away from her. She trembled with irrational hate.

"Shut the hell up!" she shouted, but he didn't. She shook the headboard. Hard. And harder.

He woke up, opened his eyes, and smiled at her, lovingly.

"Hi Renie. Have a nice evening?"

"Very nice."

"Did you quit the game?"

"No."

He slipped out of bed and staggered towards the bathroom. She turned off the light, hoping that in the three minutes it took him to empty his bladder, she could fall asleep, but the sound of his urine dripping slowly from his enlarged prostate into the toilet bowl unnerved her as she imagined more pubies joining the first two. And then it was quiet.

"Mel! Lower the toilet seat!"

He didn't. He returned to the bedroom, adjusting his boxer shorts. Her heart raced uncomfortably. It was crazy to let something as inanimate and benign as boxer shorts make you shake with loathing. After all, half the men in the world probably wore boxer shorts and half the women certainly weren't getting heart palpitations over it. Yes, Phil had worn BVDs, but ... Mel got into bed.

"Mel, have you ever thought about wearing BVDs?"

"Yeah, tried them once, but they strangled my nuts. Night, Renie. Love you."

The snoring began again. She stuffed bits of Kleenex into her ears and punched her pillow, viciously.

CHAPTER THREE

Sylvia and Mary

"To have a grievance is to have a purpose in life."

Alan Coren, *The Sanity Inspector*

S YLVIA knocked on Mary's bedroom door.

"You up?"

"Yes."

She tried to push the door open, but it was still blocked from the night before.

"Move the dresser!" she ordered. She heard the dresser scrape across the wooden floor. Sylvia opened the door and looked in. It was odd, she thought, how nothing ever changed. The extra blanket was always neatly folded at the foot of Mary's bed. The throw pillows never moved, and her collection of Nancy Ann Storybook dolls, standing on bookshelves, never changed position. Day after day, year after year, nothing new was added and nothing old was subtracted. It was almost as though Mary didn't live here, Sylvia thought, wiping a finger across the dusty dresser top.

"Breakfast will be ready in ten minutes."

Sylvia was unloading the pantry shelves when Mary entered the kitchen. Cans, boxes, and bags of foodstuffs were piled high on the kitchen counters. Mary poured herself a cup of coffee, sat down at the kitchen table, and turned Sylvia's Rolodex cleaning file to April 20.

"It says here you're supposed to be cleaning the front closet today. And didn't you just do the pantry?"

"Yes, but I have a new philosophy about food organization since then. Goods should be shelved according to frequency of use, not by food groups, most-used products on the middle three shelves, least-used on top, and all the bags—grocery, gift, high and low-density plastic—on the bottom shelf. What do you think?"

"Sounds like a plan," Mary answered, buttering a piece of dry toast.

"What do you think of my signage?"

Sylvia had used file folder labels to tag the shelves: CANNED GOODS, CEREAL, BAKING PRODUCTS.

"There's a visual conflict between your professional organization and your amateurish handwriting. What you need is one of those electronic label makers."

"And your bedroom is thick with dust, Sylvia answered. "When are you going to clean it?"

"You clean where you belong. I don't belong here."

"I don't think living with a mother who has a serious medical disability until Mr. Right comes along is too much to ask from one's only child."

"There will be no Mr. Rights. You'll see to that."

"I'm not the one Eric ran away from. It was you, letting your mother choke to death."

"You weren't choking. You were laughing your guts out."

"You didn't have to invite him for dinner. Or any of the others for that matter."

Mary put down her coffee cup. "You better eat and fast cause I'm leaving for work in five minutes."

"You know why you invite them? So I can test them for you, and if they fail, I've done your dirty work. You're rid of them, and you can blame me." Mary left the kitchen with Sylvia in pursuit. "He wasn't good enough for you! You can see that now, can't you?"

"What I see is an angry, fearful woman who's concocted a swallowing disorder so she won't have to live alone," she answered, before leaving the house.

Sylvia watched Mary walk away, down the front steps and up the street, in the direction of the El. She stayed there at the window, as she did every morning, until Mary was out of sight. The phone was ringing when she returned to the kitchen.

"Hello."

It was her sister, Vera. For every call Vera made to her, she made ten to Vera. That was because Vera didn't need her for anything, and she needed Vera for what little social life she had. Her low status, she believed, was predicated on two factors: she didn't have a husband or a college degree, and Vera had both. Of course Vera wouldn't have had that degree if not for her . . . not that Vera had ever thanked her. It did her heart good to see how her sister Clara, who lived in California, treated Vera, not that she was treated any differently. Clara never visited and rarely called them. "She thinks she's better than us because she's married to a doctor and lives next door to Goldie Hawn," Vera once explained.

"What's up?" she asked.

"Elaine's decided it's medieval to wait until the baby is born to buy her clothes and things. She says she's going to do it today, and I was hoping." She hesitated. "I was thinking maybe you'd like to join us."

She feigned indifference. "I'm cleaning the pantry today."

"You can clean the pantry anytime. And I haven't seen you in a long time." Vera did not want to be alone with her razor-tongued daughter, she thought, but before she said yes, Vera would have to up the ante. "And after the shopping, we'll do lunch." She waited. "My treat, of course."

"Well, I suppose I could finish the pantry tomorrow. What time and where?"

She hung up and wrote on her wall calendar in Wednesday's empty white square: SHOPPING, WATER TOWER, in capital letters. She didn't need a calendar for her few social engagements but because her friends had calendars in their kitchens, all their squares packed with names, she had to have one, too. And once a month, before she hosted the weekly mahjongg game, she made sure all her blanks were filled—with fictitious names and places—in case someone read her calendar, the way she read theirs.

After Morris died, she had tried organizational and volunteer work but quickly alienated her co-workers. After a number of such failures, she gave up trying and retreated to the safety of her living room. She was the winner, she decided. The people on TV were far more interesting than anyone she had met volunteering.

She ran her Super Deluxe Dynamo Vacuum over the living room and dining room carpets, noting, as she always did after the girls had come for mahjongg, there would be a curious collection of food droppings on the floor around Irene's chair.

CHAPTER FOUR

Barbara and Richard

"Adolescence is the stage between infancy and adultery."

Anonymous

B ARBARA beat three eggs, one-quarter cup of milk, and a teaspoon of pure vanilla extract together in a bowl while she watched two women through her kitchen window, teeing off at the fifth hole. The blonde was annoying, she thought, the way she repeatedly threw back her long, thick hair, as though the weight of it was more than a person could bear. If it really were, she reasoned, the woman would either cut it off or pull it back into a pony tail. Her behavior was nothing but an obvious pubescent affectation.

She prided herself on how much she could discern about people by studying their body language and listening closely to what they said. She credited these powers of observation on decades of reading mystery writers.

The blonde turned, and for a moment, they made eye contact. She didn't like what she saw: the kewpie doll lips puffed up on Botox, the pug nose, and the tall, thin body. She was an aging example of Richard's preferred type, she thought, and for all she knew, this slut might have been one of Richard's two-week shtups twenty years ago . . . until he dumped her . . . whereupon, she hypothesized, the blonde found some other man who would—someone who was willing to dump his wife, a wife, like her, who had done everything right: had joined all the right organizations, made all the right kinds of friends, and entertained all the right people, the kind of people her husband had wanted for clients.

She knew that Irene, Sylvia, and Rochelle did not believe in her bank teller theory—that most of the women working in banks were there to meet men with deep pockets. If they weren't, she'd argue, they would never take a job that made you sit in a narrow window six hours a day and paid you minimum wage. They could easily go down the street to Best Buy, have freedom of movement, earn a higher hourly salary and get commissions. "Answer me that." They couldn't. "It's because at the bank you have access to everyone's account balances with one simple keystroke. That's all the foreplay these women need." What she didn't say was that for Richard, who'd never heard of foreplay, they were a perfect match.

The sound of water running through the pipes stopped. Richard had finished his shower. She put a tablespoon of butter in the frying pan, dipped bread slices into the batter, and transferred them to the pan. When Richard entered the kitchen, his French Toast and fresh coffee were waiting for him. He gave her a kiss—the kind of careful kiss you give your maiden aunt with a mustache—and sat down at the table. He looked good for sixty-five; she thought, except for the developing paunch.

"What time did you get in?" She hadn't meant to ask, but she couldn't stop herself.

"Not late," he answered.

"What's not late?"

Richard tapped the side of the sugar bowl.

"What's that?" he asked.

She looked. "What's what? I don't see anything."

He dipped his spoon into the bowl and waved it under her nose. "Can you see it now?"

An ant leaped from the spoon and fell onto the kitchen table.

"You mean the ant?"

"Of course, I mean the ant. How did it get in here?"

"He must've walked. Ants don't fly."

Richard dragged his index finger over the leather placemat. "My placemat is sticky." She pretended not to hear. "I don't know how to tell you this, Barbara, but I'm very disappointed in you. You used to be such a meticulous housekeeper."

I'm very disappointed in you had controlled her for decades . . . and still intimidated her son, she feared.

"About next week's dinner party," she said, changing the subject. "I'd like you to look over this guest list." She handed him a notepad. "The ones with the asterisks are people we owe. The ones without are people we don't owe but we haven't seen in a while. Is there anyone you want to add or subtract?"

He scanned the names without touching the paper. "Seems all right—except, I don't see Phyllis on here."

"Phyllis who?"

"For God's sakes! How many Phyllises do you know?" They were about to have another argument over something else that didn't matter, she realized. Everything about Richard's behavior this time was different. "I don't get it. Before Alex died, we saw a lot of the Wexlers. Now Phyllis has become *persona non gratis.*"

"That's not true. I intend to invite Phyllis. I'm just waiting until I have someone for her."

"What does that mean? That you're getting her someone to keep?"

"You know what I mean. It means I'd like to pair her off with someone for the evening so the table will come out even."

"I see. If Phyllis doesn't have a partner, the table legs will be different lengths."

He was going out of his way to make her look foolish, she thought. His new lay must be something else. "You know exactly what I mean; that I want to wait until I have someone appropriate to seat her with. It makes for better table talk."

"I've been eating dinner with Phyllis for twenty years, and she's always seemed perfectly capable of sitting and talking on her own. I've even seen her talk to people across the table from her. She's very clever that way."

She couldn't count the number of times Richard had complained after someone else's dinner party that the evening had been deadly; yet, he was oblivious to the variables that went into creating a successful evening. "There's a science to picking your guests and where you seat them," she explained. "You don't seem to understand that. It can make or break the evening."

"I want you to invite Phyllis to the party. No, forget that. I *insist* you invite her." If Richard had been the one who died, and she was the widow, Phyllis would exclude her without thinking twice. "If you don't know where to put her, seat her next to me. I'll talk to her." He paused, and she could see it coming again. "I'm very disappointed in you, Barbara. You've become a major snob."

"I'm a snob? I've got news for you. I've always been a snob, which is why you married me. The truth is you're a snob, too, but I'm an honest one."

His face bloated red with anger. "I won't be home for dinner tonight. I have a lot of paper work at the office. Don't wait up."

"Did you forget? We're meeting Beverly and Gene at the club for dinner."

"Cancel it!" He got up from the table. "Oh, by the way . . ." He softened his tone, which meant he was about to ask her for something. "My dark blue suit needs cleaning. It's on the valet upstairs."

After the garage door closed, she went upstairs to their bedroom, took a 400-power hand-held magnifying glass and a pair of tweezers from her night table drawer and carried Richard's suit jacket to the east window. She plucked human hairs off the jacket and examined them under the magnifying glass. These were not the non-threatening long and cheaply bleached blonde hairs of Richard's previous short-term whores. These medium-length hairs were colored a smart golden-brown and had gray roots. Richard's latest slut, she concluded, was older than the others, in which case she might also be shrewder and more determined, pressured by the knowledge that time was running out on her.

She sniffed his jacket and blanched. While the other bitches had worn cheap Walgreen perfumes, she was almost positive this scent was Coco Chanel, which sold for $400 an ounce. If she was right, Richard's latest whore might be different enough to destroy everything she had spent a lifetime building.

CHAPTER FIVE

Irene and Mel

"Familiarity is a relation into which fools are providentially drawn for their mutual destruction."

Ambrose Bierce

MEL bent over the sleeping Irene and kissed her tenderly on the cheek. "I hate to wake you," he said, apologetically. "You look so darn beautiful when you're sleeping."

Irene opened her eyes. The first thing she saw was Mel's paisley print silk robe. It reminded her of the fabric used to line funeral caskets. She closed her eyes again. "Don't go back to sleep. Breakfast is ready." The whistling of his robe leaving the room was like nails dragged across a blackboard. It sent shivers up and down her spine. She opened her eyes again and stared at the picture of her mother, sitting on her dresser, framed in silver. Doris' lips moved. "So what if you don't like his robe or underwear? He's good-natured, caring, and has money in the bank. You're not getting any younger, Irene," she warned. "You're lucky to have him. Will you never learn to compromise?"

Her mother was right, she thought. It was unreasonable to think she could live with Mel—or anyone else for that matter—the same way she lived alone. She needed to be more patient, she told herself, getting out of bed and going to the bathroom, where now—instead of two pubic hairs glued to the toilet rim—there were four. She started to hyperventilate, but the sound of Mel's happy whistling in the kitchen as he made them breakfast cut through her anger, and she quietly lowered the toilet seat.

Concentrate on his strengths, not his weaknesses, she told herself. Concentrate on his strengths, not his weaknesses, she repeated, turning on the shower. Be creative. Find new and different ways to encourage him to curb his disgusting habits; otherwise, you'll have to return to the meat market, where pickings are slim and getting slimmer by the day for women your age.

She stepped into the shower and was pelted by water daggers.

"Goddamnit! If you're going to change the setting from gentle to needles, remember to put it back where you found it!" she screamed. She changed the setting and picked up the shower soap, now decorated with pubic hairs.

"Renie, you OK?" She could see Mel on the other side of the frosted glass door. "I heard you scream."

"Yes, yes, everything is fine."

"Breakfast is almost ready."

I'm a shit, she thought. So he changed the shower setting. No big deal, but what *is* a big deal is that he worries about me; that he makes me breakfast every morning, and that he's always happy to see me.

She sat down at the kitchen table. Mel kissed the nape of her neck.

"Toasted your bagel medium, just the way you like it, and I made you a vegetarian omelet." He slid the omelet onto her plate and brought a bowl of Fiber One to the table for himself. She tried not to look at his robe but that meant not looking at Mel. Yesterday she calculated that Mel wore his robe 80% of their waking time together. Looking at him in it made her feel like an inmate at a long-term care facility, living with geriatric patients. "And that's low fat cream cheese," he said, pointing to the container on the table. She nodded. "What time did you get in?"

"Around 10:30. You were sleeping."

"I tried to stay awake, but I couldn't keep my eyes open. How's the omelet?"

"Perfect. But you gave me enough for two. Want some?"

"No way! My last cholesterol check was 280, my triglycerides were over 400, and my LDL was too high to count." Please, dear God, she prayed. Spare me from another one of Mel's morning medical rounds. "I need fiber to keep things moving. You do, too," he advised. Fiber, she thought, tasted like cardboard. "Can you even *remember* taking a dump before you were fifty? Back then, we just did it without a second thought. Kerplunk. Kerplunk. Right? Like it was our God-given right." She put down her fork and pushed her plate towards the center of the kitchen table. "We should have appreciated what we could do when we could do it."

"Sleep OK?" Irene asked.

"Not really. I had to get up to go to the john three times. My prostate gets larger by the minute. It's probably time to see an urologist." It was her opinion that when you asked someone how they slept the night before, it was only a social convention. It was not to be taken as a literal invitation to discuss your bowel and bladder movements. "The first two times I went right back to sleep, but the third time I had acid indigestion and had to take bicarbonate of soda. By then I was wide awake." If he had left the glass of bicarbonate on wood, there would now be a white ringed stain on some piece of furniture, a stain that would never come out, she reasoned. "I sat up in bed for about a half hour waiting for the big belch. When it finally came, it was so loud I was afraid it would wake you." She thought back again to the months they had dated—before Mel moved in—and was positive he had never, not once, mentioned his bodily functions. "Nature calls," he said, getting up from the kitchen table. "It's like an orgasm—not something you want to miss."

Her mother's spirit took over Mel's empty chair.

"You're a romantic fool," she heard her say. "If Phil were alive today, you can be sure he'd be complaining about his BMs and high cholesterol."

Yes, she had to remember that Phil died at fifty-five, when all his organs and orifices were functioning well, and he looked as good to her as he did the day they met. It was during her senior year of college. Kathy, the only other senior in the dorm besides her, had gotten engaged the night before. As Kathy flashed her two-carat marquis-cut diamond to the underclassmen on the floor, she got the unmistakable feeling they were all staring at her, pitying her because she was a senior, not engaged and not even dating anyone seriously.

They were right to pity her. In less than six months she would graduate and be expected to return to her parents' home because no single women—at least no respectable single women—would live alone. And when her parents' friends came to the house to play bridge, they would probably send her upstairs to hide in her room. She was, after all, a failure, a pariah and a source of embarrassment. She had spent four years at college and what did she have to show for it? No husband. No fiancée. Nothing but a rotten bachelor's degree. Worse yet, she would be expected to teach elementary school, and she hated teaching. She had only majored in education because her mother had convinced her that that was what nice Jewish girls did because then— if your husband died—you had a profession to fall back on. She had given in to the family pressure because she never believed it would come to such a sad end—that she would graduate from college.

She had returned to her dorm room and thrown herself across the second bed in the room, vacated two months earlier by an upperclassman who had dropped out of school to get married. After an hour of self-pitying sobs, she got up, looked in the mirror and said: "It's a free world. The Constitution guarantees me the right to life, liberty, and the pursuit of happiness. I don't have to live at home and no one can make me, and I will not teach school to a gaggle of geese. But what will I do, she had wondered. "I have to do something, and I'm trained to do nothing."

She walked to the college bookstore and poured over the few books on vocations, imagining herself doing this thing or that thing. That's when she saw him—Phil—standing behind a glass counter, helping a customer. His skin was olive-toned, his hair jet black, and he was cute, maybe the cutest guy she'd ever seen. He looked up and smiled at her, and she thought she'd die. After he finished the sale and the customer left, she approached him, ready to buy whatever it was he was selling. He stood maybe four inches taller than her, just the right height for the ballyhooed Hollywood kiss. She prayed to God he was available . . . and Jewish.

Mel returned to the kitchen and reheated his coffee in the microwave.

"I forgot to ask," he said. "Did you tell the girls you're quitting mahjongg?"

"No, I didn't because I'm not."

"But you promised," he whined. She didn't answer. "You're afraid of them." She didn't deny it. It took too much effort. "Someone would think they were the Mafia instead of three sixty-five year old Hadassah women."

"Sixty-two," she corrected, opening the morning paper. "But let's just pretend that I had quit. What would we do then on Tuesday nights?" He looked at her, confused. He didn't get it. "You know. Since I wouldn't be playing mahjongg, what would we do instead of?" It still did not compute. "You and me, Mel. What would we do together on Tuesday nights?"

"Why would he have to do something? We'd be together, like we are now; like all the other nights."

She turned a page of the *Tribune*. "There's a class in Tai Chi starting at the Y on Tuesday nights. How would you like to join?"

He laughed. "Tai Chi? At *our* age? This isn't the age of Tai Chi."

"What is it the age of then? Bingo?" She turned to another page of the paper. "And I see that the public library is offering a course on the Great Books Tuesday and Thursday nights. We could take that."

"Tuesdays and Thursdays?" Mel wailed. "Jeez, Renie. Some of my favorite sitcoms are on Tuesday and Thursday nights."

If Mel weren't living with her, she thought, she wouldn't need to seek consensus or ask permission. She would simply sign up for whatever and go—not that she was opposed to the courtesies that went with living with another person because she wasn't, but there had to be an equitable trade-off between what you gave and what you got. "How about a class on the opera?" she asked.

"Opera? Are you kidding?"

She set down the paper. "Mel, remember how it was *before* you moved in? We went to plays and concerts, and . . ."

"Yeah, and let me be the first to tell you that it was wearing me out. I don't know how much longer I could've kept up that pace. It's a good thing I moved in when I did."

"Are you saying you moved in because you were tired?"

"No, not exactly, but you have to admit all that running around isn't normal. That's not how people live."

"What were we doing then, if not living?"

"We were courting. I mean, it was fun and all that, but once two people are living together, life has to take on a slower, more sustainable pace. You know what I mean."

The phone rang. She read the caller I.D.

"It's Susan," she said.

"You're not going to answer it?"

She shrugged. "She just wants money. That's almost the only time she calls, and now with her wedding coming up."

"You should do what I do with my sons. Keep your wallet open and your mouth shut."

"I can't afford your philosophy so I keep my mouth open and my wallet shut." The phone continued to ring.

"I'll be glad to help," Mel offered. "I can afford to, you know."

"Thanks, but no thanks. I really appreciate the offer, but she's my daughter, and my problem."

She was a terrible person, she thought, asking Mel to make changes when he made no similar demands on her. He didn't ask her to give up her cotton briefs for bikinis or thongs. And he never complained about the way she did things around the house. And he was good and generous and she was lucky to have him, and when she was sick and old, she could depend on him, which was more than you could say for most men.

They kissed good-bye outside the building. Mel walked towards the El station, and she boarded the Number Ten bus to the Tribune. She scoped out the other passengers before taking the empty seat next to an elderly white woman. Old white women, she thought, were wiser than old white men. Old Asian women, on the other hand, were wiser than old white women, and old Black women were the smartest of all. She turned to her traveling companion.

"I think one of the best parts of living with a man is having some-one to say good-bye to in the morning and hello to in the evening," she confessed.

"If that's all you want a man for, I suggest you get a dog. They're cheaper, more obedient and loyal, and far less trouble than any man I ever knew."

The bus stopped, and the old white woman got off.

"Dear God, please make me an old wise woman before I die," she prayed.

CHAPTER SIX

Rochelle and the Butterfly

"Confidence is a plant of slow growth in an aged bosom."
William Pitt

AFTER an hour of cutting off low-lying branches, Rochelle sat, exhausted, on the edge of the sandbox. The ground roots would have to wait for another day, she thought, sifting through the sand and removing bits of metal and plastic. A large monarch butterfly landed on a side of the sandbox, no more than a foot away, and stared at her with unflinching black eyes.

"Women my age are not supposed to be taking care of small children," she said to the butterfly. "That's why God invented menopause." The butterfly inched closer. "But I have only myself to blame. If I had listened to Mark and sold the house, we would still be married; not that my daughters think much of my loss. They've let me know that they think I'm better off without him. *I* don't think I am, but they certainly are." The butterfly hopped closer. "With Mark out of the picture, I have far fewer social invitations, which means I have more time for them, time to baby sit with their children." She threw a rusty bottle cap into a bucket. "You know that expression about you only go around once? Well, it's a lie. This is my second time around."

She reached for the butterfly, expecting it to fly away; instead, it flew into her palm and sat, motionless, staring at her with unblinking eyes.

"You probably didn't see my mother's butterfly garden because butterflies don't live that long, but if you had, you would have loved it. It was magnificent, planted with all kinds of weeds and bushes, thistles, and flowers, the kinds that attract caterpillars and butterflies. Community groups used the garden for fundraisers. My mother would lead visitors down the slated walk and name the plants and the varieties of butterflies swooping overhead. I loved that garden. When I was a child, I'd lie on the grass, look skyward, and wait for the butterflies to fly past me, tickling me with their velvety wings."

Rochelle drew the butterfly ever closer.

"Why haven't you flown away? Did someone send you to me?" The butterfly flew onto her shoulder. "My mother promised that if there were a way back, she'd return, but she never said what form she'd take. Maybe a butterfly. She was, after all, a butterfly herself—beautiful and fragile and powerless against my overbearing and controlling father." She checked her watch. "I've got to go now. I have an appointment in less than an hour. Maybe we can meet again some time."

The butterfly flew ahead of her, and when she opened the back door, it flew inside the house. She made a fast sweep through the downstairs, searching for it. When she couldn't find it, she set a bowl of sugar water on the kitchen table and went upstairs to wash and dress. She had decided to wear her black cotton summer suit to the interview, but it wasn't in her closet. She thought back. She had picked it up from the cleaners on Monday, but had she taken it upstairs? She couldn't remember, but what she did remember was that Bette was at the house on Monday, when she brought Jonathan for her to baby sit.

She picked up the phone and put it down again. Bette's orders were never to call her at work; unless, of course, something had happened to Jonathan. Madame Savansky advised otherwise. "Vat ees zee verst ting dat could happen to you eeef you defy zee order? Vould you die?" Of course she wouldn't, she said. "Vould they forbid you to take care of zer children?" If only they would, she prayed. "Eeet ees time to take charge of your life!"

She called Bette.

"It's Mother," she started.

"My God! Is Jonathan all right?"

When she heard the panic in Bette's voice, she was sorry she had called. "Yes, he's fine. I'm calling about something else—my black cotton suit. I can't find it, and I wondered if maybe you took it."

"You called me at work to ask me about a piece of clothing?" Madame Savansky's words echoed. No, she wouldn't die. Yes, they would still leave their children with her. "This piece of clothing is the suit with the mandarin collar and gold buttons that you asked me to give you when I get tired of it, or will to you when I die, whichever comes first, you said."

"Oh, *that* suit!" Bette laughed. "As a matter of fact, I did borrow it. I guess I forgot to bring it back."

"That's all you have to say?"

"How about thanks?"

"Thanks is what you say when you take something with permission. You say 'I'm sorry' when you take something without."

"You're out of control, Mom. It's not like you don't have a hundred other things to wear. I'll bring it tomorrow when I come over with Jonathan."

You have rights, Madame Savansky repeatedly said. You have rights but you've given them away. When will you take them back?"

"No! You'll bring it over tonight when you get home from work."

"That's impossible, and you're being unreasonable. I won't get home until late. Then I have to make dinner, put Jonathan to sleep, and prepare for a new client. I'll bring it tomorrow when I come over, and that's final. I have to go now. People are waiting."

The phone went dead. The butterfly flew into the bedroom and perched itself on her dresser top.

"What's unreasonable," she said to the butterfly, "is that my children take my clothes, my food, and anything else they want from my home without asking, and what's even more unreasonable is that I let them." She approached the butterfly. "And you know whose fault it is that I'm such a coward? My parents. What I learned from them is that I'm incapable of making smart choices for myself." The butterfly suddenly—and curiously—Rochelle thought, flew out of the room. She picked up the phone and called Mark. It was the first time she'd called him at work since their divorce the year before.

"You OK?" he asked. He sounded concerned.

"Yes, fine. I have a quick question for you. If my mother were to come back to life as an animal, which one would she be?"

"A deer."

"Not an animal then. Say an insect."

"A butterfly."

"And if I hadn't agreed to let the girls install Disney World in our backyard, would you have left me, or were you planning to leave me anyway, and I just made it easier for you?" She hadn't intended to ask. It simply tumbled out.

"This isn't a good time, Rochelle. Can I call you back later?"

She started to say yes but stopped herself. "Can I call you back later?" was a question with a choice of answers. Just because she had been raised to be agreeable and give people what they wanted, didn't mean she had to. "The sky wouldn't fall," as Madame Savansky put it. "No, you can't call me back because I won't be here. I'm leaving the house now for a meeting." And she hung up.

She was in her car, backing out of the driveway, when her younger daughter, Amy, pulled in behind her and stopped. Amy got out of her car, her granddaughter in tow.

"What are you doing here, and why isn't Emily in school?"

"They had a fire, the school is closed for the rest of the day, and I have to teach in an hour. Your line was busy so I knew you were here, and I thought . . ."

Rochelle cut her off. "You thought wrong. I have an appointment at the Art Institute in a half hour. I was just leaving."

"You can take Emily with you. She's never a bother," and before she could stop her, Amy had strapped Emily into one of the children's seats in the back of her car. "Thanks, Mom. See you in a few hours."

First she called Madame Savansky. Then she rescheduled her appointment at the Art Institute.

CHAPTER SEVEN

Irene and Bambi

"All we do is done with an eye to something else."

Aristotle

WHEN Irene entered her office that morning, she found Bambi going through her private files. "What are you looking for?" she asked, puzzled.

"Oh, hi! I didn't hear you come in. I was looking for . . ." She groped. ". . .hard copies of last month's Macy's ads. You know, the ones with the sectional leather couches."

It wasn't what Bambi said, Irene thought, but the way she said it that raised her suspicions. "Did you forget? Current year's ads are kept in the main room, in the blue books."

Bambi laughed, falsetto. "Oh, jeez, you're right. I'm sorry. I don't know what I was thinking."

Through her large window wall, she watched Bambi return to her cubicle, call someone on her cell phone, and minutes later leave the department. She decided to follow. Bambi took a down elevator. She took the next "down," arriving in the lobby just in time to see Bambi exit the building with Charles Williams, the newspaper's CFO. Sylvia could be right, she thought. Bambi might really be after her job. Why else would a lithesome thirty-something year old with firm skin and no belly fat make friends with a loathsome old man like Charles?

Her cell phone rang. It was her daughter Nancy.

"It's Susan," Nancy began. "I told her I'd give her a wedding shower but that it had to be in our home. We can't afford a fancy hotel or restaurant, which is what she wants, and you know what she answered me?"

"Yes. She said, 'If you *really* loved me.'"

"That's right, and then she hung up on me."

"You did the right thing."

"I know, but I always get that sick feeling in my stomach. Sometimes when I hear her voice, I break out in a cold sweat. You have no idea!" Yes, she did. Once upon a time, Susan's temper had controlled her, too; if not, she would never have co-signed that bank loan with her, a loan that took her two years to pay off when Susan fled the country with some Moldovian poet she'd met. That's when she realized that if she didn't protect herself from her daughter, she could end up on the streets in her old age. "I told Benjamin that I would try to find an inexpensive restaurant for the shower, and he said if I did, he wasn't going to the wedding."

"He's right, of course. You know what you can afford; furthermore, if you give into her now, it'll never stop. Do not let Susan cause problems in your marriage." Nancy started to cry. "Hey! What are you crying for? I'm the one who gave birth to her, and do you hear me crying? Listen, I've got to go now. I'll call you back later. Give Maya a hug from me and tell her I have a new Shag story."

She hung up and called Mel at work. "I have an idea," she started. "Let's meet for dinner tonight after work, like we used to do before you moved in."

"Tonight?" he groaned. "There's a special on the Discovery Channel. How about later in the week?"

"You can tape the program, and watch it later."

"There's something about tapes. It never feels quite the same."

CHAPTER EIGHT

Barbara and Rhonda

"Luxury corrupts at once rich and poor, the rich by possession and the poor by covetousness."

Rousseau, *The Social Contract*

B ARBARA entered the bank wearing jeans, a t-shirt, a painter's cap, and large, dark sunglasses. From her hiding place behind a large ficus, she perused the lineup of tellers. Three of the four were look-alikes, all clones of Richard's preferred bank slut. They were wearing low-cut blouses, but not so low that they couldn't pass the bank's dress code. Those three, she knew, were not her problem. It was the fourth teller, the one unlike the others, who spelled trouble with a capital T.

She gerrymandered her way into the line. When she got closer, she could read the name plate on the window: MS. BERGER. Ms. Berger was wearing an expensive business suit with a designer scarf draped over her shoulders. Pinned to Berger's scarf was an elegant pin, the initial "R" studded with diamonds. It was a Buccarelli original.

"Beautiful, isn't it?" Berger asked, following her gaze. "My boyfriend had it commissioned for me by that famous Italian designer Botticelli." Berger's smile exposed four of the longest and sharpest canine teeth she'd ever seen.

"R?" she asked.

"For Rhonda. Now what can I do for you?"

She handed Rhonda Berger a hundred dollar bill and while Rhonda counted out her five twenties, Barbara examined her face.

Yes, Berger was running out of time. Lines were developing around her mouth, furrows forming between her eyes, and there was a hint of a developing double chin. Rhonda needed to land her big kahuna and soon. Her time was running out.

Barbara sniffed. "Is that Coco Chanel you're wearing?" she asked.

"Yes. How observant of you!"

Rhonda Berger winked at her, as if to say that the two of them were members of the same exclusive club, restricted to those who shared their exquisite and expensive tastes. Not on my money, Barbara thought, returning her wallet to her purse. Ten-dollar trinkets were one thing. Buccarelli jewelry at a thousand dollars minimum was quite another!

CHAPTER NINE

Rochelle and
Madame Savansky

"Hope deceives more men than cunning does."

Vauvenargues

I T was too quiet in the back of the car. "What are you doing?" Rochelle asked Emily when she stopped for a red light.

"Just coloring. One day I'm going to be an artist, like you used to be, Grandma, but right now I'm painting on glass."

She whipped around. The window next to Emily had been opaqued with a rainbow of crayons. She grabbed whatever crayons she could reach and threw them under the front seat. Cars honked at her. The light had changed. She moved into traffic.

"I want my Mommy!" Emily screamed.

"So do I!" She found a parking place in front of Madame Savansky's shop, put an hour's worth of coins in the meter, and unstrapped the screaming Emily from her car seat. "Behave yourself! We're going to visit a friend of mine, and you have to be very quiet. She doesn't like noise."

A bell screwed to the door of Madame Savansky's storefront jingled as they entered. A dozen or so candles—both wax and electric—were lit, and on the walls of the semi-dark room hung photographs of Madame Savansky's family—or so she said. Sometimes the psychic would point to the men and women in the photos and name them, but Rochelle had the feeling that the names changed from time to time. In the center of the room stood a large square table, guarded on all four sides by heavy arm chairs. She seated Emily before taking her usual place.

"Don't forget what I told you," she said. "Absolutely no talking."

The vinyl curtain that separated the parlor from the living quarters was pushed aside, and Madame Savansky stepped into the room. The black sleeveless dress she was wearing exposed two tattoos— one on each upper arm. On the right arm was the Empress, and on the left, the High Priestess, both images from the Rider-Waite tarot deck. Madame Savansky's thick black hair was pulled off her hawkish face into one long braid. Large gold hoop earrings weighed down her earlobes. The madame stared—and not too kindly— at Emily.

"I wanna go home!" Emily screamed.

"Quiet," Rochelle said to Emily, and to Madame Savansky, she explained. "This is my granddaughter. I didn't know I'd have to bring her. Sorry."

Madame took the empty seat across from Rochelle and removed a card deck from a colorful silk scarf.

"I wanna go home!" Emily repeated. "You can't make me stay here! She's a witch!"

Madame Savansky pointed an expensively manicured fingernail at Emily. "Leeetle girl, you veel keep quiet or elz." She turned to Rochelle. "I can zee vie eeet vas so urgent to zee me today. You do not dee-serve such a burden een life, my dear."

"Didn't your Mommy tell you that tattoos poison your skin and make you die?" Emily asked the Gypsy.

Rochelle felt a measure of pride. Emily would not be like her, afraid to confront the world. On the other hand, one day the world might be afraid to confront Emily!

"Tell zee child to piss off, or I veel charge you double."

"Emily, we're not going to be here very long. If you sit quietly for just a few minutes, I'll buy you an ice cream later."

"What flavor?"

"Whatever you want."

"What size?"

"We'll discuss it later."

Madame Savansky shuffled the cards and set the deck in front of Rochelle. "Vee do not half much time zo deevide zee deck eeento three piles." Rochelle divided them. Madame removed the top card from each stack and laid them on the table, face up. Emily lunged for one of the cards, but Madame was faster and grabbed her hand in midair. "Don't touch!"

"She's a witch!" Emily screamed.

"Leeetle girl. Thees eees my houz, and eeen my houz, I make zee rules! Now quiet zo I can concentrate."

The room was suddenly quiet. Madame studied the three cards, slowly and deliberately. After some minutes, she lifted her head, stared into Rochelle's eyes, and said, without an accent, "Listen carefully, my dear. You will never have a life of your own if you don't get rid of your grandchildren."

"Does my Mommy know I'm here?" Emily shrieked.

Madame Savansky pointed at the second card. "And you will never get rid of the grandchildren until you get rid of the children."

"I'm going to tell on you," Emily threatened.

Madame Savansky pointed to the third card, the Tower. "And you will never get rid of the grandchildren or the children until you get rid of the house. Then and only then will the princess be freed from the monsters!" Madame looked at Rochelle sternly. "Do you understand what I'm saying? Sell your house, and the rest will take care of itself! And one more thing." She pointed to the letters on the pillars of the Empress card. "You see the B and J? Look for someone with these initials. He or she will show you the way. Be sure to follow."

She gathered up her cards and returned them to the scarf.

"But I don't know any B.J. or J.B."

"Then you soon will. Be on the lookout."

She rubbed her fingers together, making the universal sign for money. "That will be $50."

"Fifty dollars? But I've been here less than ten minutes," Rochelle protested.

The Gypsy smiled at her. "I am very proud of you, my dear. That is progress. A month ago you would never have challenged my price. Right?" She rubbed her fingers together again, less patient now. "Fifty dollars." Rochelle pulled a fifty dollar bill from her wallet and set it on the table. "And one more thing. Never come here again with that or any other child!"

CHAPTER TEN

Sylvia, Vera, and Molly

*"The Family! Home of all social evils, a charitable institution
for indolent women, a prison workshop for the slaving breadwinner,
and a hell for children."*

Strindberg

SYLVIA pushed her way onto the crowded El. There were no empty
seats. She reached for the overhead strap and surveyed the seated
passengers. Seventy-five percent of them were at least thirty years
younger than she, she noted. When she was their age she would have
given up her seat to a sixty-two year old woman. It was her opinion that when civilities went out the window, so did civilization. The
country was on the decline. Take the Boy Scouts, for instance, with
a tradition of honor and service. Where were they? She hadn't seen
a Boy Scout in a decade or more. And what about Girl Scouts? Or
Brownies or Cub Scouts for that matter? Had they all disappeared
off the face of the earth, or were they dressing in plain clothes, fearful
of public ridicule?

The car lurched, and she was pushed into the knees of a young
girl with olive-dark skin, lovely brown eyes, and coal black hair.

"I'm sorry," Sylvia said.

The girl smiled at her, sweetly. "Would you like my seat?"

"How very thoughtful of you. Yes, thank you." The girl got up,
and Sylvia quickly sat down. They smiled at each other, warmly. "Are
you a Brownie?" she asked.

The girl broke into tears and fled to the back of the car.

The woman next to her jumped up from her seat. "Racist pig!" she shouted, before heading in the same direction as the little girl.

Sylvia wept inwardly. She had never intended to offend the child, but that was what always happened to her when she stepped outside her home, herself, and her small group of friends. She invariably put her foot in her mouth. Either her brain or her tongue were miswired. Maybe both. She considered trying to find the girl, but decided that would serve no purpose. The damage was done.

* * *

When Sylvia reached the infants department at Macy's, her sister and niece were already there—and arguing.

"It's mauve!" Elaine insisted, shaking a baby blanket in her mother's face.

"Sweetheart, that's pink," Vera answered.

Vera had always let Elaine have her way, Sylvia thought, so why now when Elaine was eight months pregnant was she bothering to contradict her?

"It's mauve! Mauve! Mauve! Mauve!" Elaine thundered.

Elaine's once-bouncy golden ringlets hung limp and dull around her bloated face. She was at least fifty pounds overweight, and her complexion had gone from clear to blotchy. She was the exception to the rule that all pregnant women are beautiful.

"That blanket's as pink as pink can be, *Sweetheart,*" Vera argued.

"Any fool can see that it's mauve, and don't patronize me by calling me Sweetheart." Elaine saw Sylvia then, hiding behind a display. "Sylvia! Tell my mother what color this blanket is. Mauve or pink?"

Sylvia hesitated. She did not want to become the target of her niece's acidic tongue. "It's on the cusp."

Elaine's eyes—already half-lost from sight inside her puffy cheeks—dilated.

"On the cusp, huh? My aunt, the color maven, thinks this mauve blanket is 'on the cusp'? You know what *I* think? I think I need to have my brain examined for agreeing to go shopping with the colorblind sisters."

Shoppers stopped to watch and listen. Vera, embarrassed by the wrong kind of attention, tried to explain.

"It's the hormonal swing," she explained to the onlookers. "Once the baby is born, she'll be back to her usual sweet self."

"How *dare* you talk about me like I'm not here! Maybe that's where Paul learned it—from my family." Elaine threw the blanket on a display table and waddled away. Vera and Sylvia followed, though cautiously maintaining a distance of three to four feet. "Go away!" Elaine stormed at them. "I don't want either one of you within fifty feet of me." She softened her voice a tad to ask her mother for her charge card. "I'll meet you in an hour at Minelli's for lunch. And don't keep me waiting. It's not good for the baby!"

Vera took the lead, and Sylvia followed, angry at herself for the years she had spent lauding her niece's rather ordinary feats, while downplaying her own daughter's many real accomplishments. They got on the down escalator.

"Elaine hasn't been herself lately," Vera said.

"Yeah, that was some temper tantrum."

"I'd hardly call that a temper tantrum. You have to understand. Elaine's in a lot of pain. The baby's been pushing down on her bladder."

"Probably because of the big weight gain."

"She hasn't gained much weight. It's mostly water, and once she's had the baby and lost the water, things will be better between her and Paul."

Sylvia tried not to look too interested. Or pleased. "Elaine and Paul are having problems?"

"Did I say they're having problems? More like issues. He's just not as attentive as he used to be. He's getting to be more and more like Al."

"She probably took advantage of his good nature."

"I don't know why I even bother talking to you about relationships. You haven't been married to anyone for twenty years, and even *then . . .*"

Sylvia had never understood why a nice young man like Paul had married Elaine. The only explanation she could come up with was the same one she used when any attractive man liked any unattractive woman—the woman must be good in bed; not that she had a clue about what a woman did to make herself "good in bed," but one thing she did know . . . *she* was not good in bed. At first she blamed Morris for her failure, but after his death, when she realized that it was a relief not to have a man touch her, she acknowledged it was her problem. She did not like men. They had an acrid smell, like male dogs, which intensified when they were in heat. She would try to hold her breath when Morris got on top of her, but no man could come fast enough for her to survive on one mouthful of air.

"Did they pick a name for the baby yet?" Sylvia asked, as they reached the bottom of the escalator.

"Goisha ones, like Heather, Brittany, and Heidi. I suggested they name her for Mamma, but Elaine thinks Sophia is too old fashioned. I also suggested an 'F' for Daddy."

"Peh for Daddy!"

"His heart was in the right place. He was just a bad money manager who bought a home and other things he couldn't afford."

"And died leaving Mamma with hundreds of thousands of dollars in debt."

"Get over it already!"

"Easy enough for you to say. You weren't the one who had to give up a four-year college scholarship to the University of Chicago to help Mamma support the family—not that you or Clara ever thanked me!"

"I know you think you'd have become another Madame Cure-all, but the truth is you'd have ended up just like you did, like we all did, getting married, and having children. That's just the way it was back then."

"I was different."

"No you weren't." They got on the next up escalator. "Furthermore, you could've gone back to school later, after you married Morris."

"Later was too late."

"No, it wasn't."

"Yes, it was. It's not like a degree in English, where you keep on speaking and reading the language. In science things change. Competing with eighteen-year-olds, fresh out of school, minds un-cluttered by spouses and children, would have been suicidal. Some turns in life cannot be overturned."

Vera stepped off the escalator, and Sylvia followed. They entered The Sharper Image.

"What are you getting here?" Sylvia asked.

"Paul's birthday gift. What are you getting him?"

"I didn't know it was his birthday."

"Yes, you did. I invited you and Mary to his fortieth birthday party next Sunday."

"You didn't tell me about it."

"Yes, I did."

"No, you didn't!"

"Did."

"Didn't."

"Did."

"What did I answer?"

"What you always answer. Yes. What else do you have to do?"

Vera stalked off, leaving Sylvia alone—and wounded.

"May I help you?" a saleswoman asked.

"My sister is a liar," Sylvia vented, pointing in Vera's direction.

The saleswoman followed Sylvia's finger and nodded in agreement. "She looks like a liar."

Sylvia considered the woman standing beside her. The sales-woman smiled. She was in her mid-fifties, Sylvia guessed, a tall, handsome woman with steel blue eyes and light brown hair. "In fact, no one would ever know you're sisters."

"Actually, I'm not sure we are. I've always suspected that they switched babies on my parents when my mother was in the hospital." The saleswoman laughed, and Sylvia, blushed, pleased with herself. It wasn't often that she made someone laugh. There was, after all, nothing funny about her.

Vera looked up then and saw them staring at her. Her eyes narrowed and her lips tightened before she turned away.

"Your sister has a hard look, nothing like you." Sylvia blushed. "My name is Molly. Are you looking for something in particular?"

"A gift for my 40-year-old nephew. Actually, he's my nephew through marriage. He married my niece, a decision it now seems he's having second thoughts about."

Molly laughed again. "You are one funny lady. Well, let's see what we can find for your unhappy nephew."

Sylvia followed Molly around the store, taking in as much of the merchandise as she could. It was her first time in The Sharper Image, and she found it fascinating. Molly pointed to a small mechanical box.

"How about an electronic day keeper?" Molly asked, pointing to a small mechanical box.

"I don't think so. What's that?" she asked, pointing to an odd-shaped pot.

"A coffee pot."

She checked the price. $189. "You really think this pot makes a better cup of coffee than my $19.95 Mr. Coffee?"

"How about a shower radio?"

Sylvia examined the plastic radio hanging from a silver cord. "Why would any sane person put a radio in the shower? First of all, how much time did you spend there, and secondly, how can you hear anything with water pouring over your head?"

"Maybe an air purifier?" Sylvia shook her head. No. "A shoe deodorizer?" No. "Hair removal kit?" No.

Sylvia ran a finger across a display table. It was covered with dirt. She looked around the room. Most of the displays were in disarray. "Does the store have a manager?" she asked.

"Yeah, Rio. Now if your nephew is starting to lose hair, this laser comb guarantees to thicken hair in ninety days or your money back." Half of the laser combs were out of their boxes, Sylvia noted, which could lead to breakage, shrinkage, and theft. "How about a battery-operated revolving tie rack?" Molly pushed the button on the rack but nothing happened. "The batteries must be dead."

"Who are they?" Sylvia asked, pointing to the two young men leaning up against a wall near the checkout counter.

"Two of our salesmen."

"Why aren't they doing something, like helping customers or cleaning the shelves or replacing dead batteries?"

"They don't want to. And the manager is afraid of them."

"You're working."

"I like work, but you know what this generation is like. They all want something for nothing." She pointed to a radio-like box. "If he has trouble sleeping, he might like a Ultra Heart and Sound Soother, guaranteed to give eight hours of uninterrupted sleep by lowering your heart rate and relaxing your brain. There's six mode choices: ocean waves pounding against a rocky coastline, waters rushing down a rocky brook, birds chattering in a rain forest, etc., etc., etc. Costs less than $100, which makes it cheaper than sleeping pills and a lot healthier."

"I don't think so."

"Maybe a TruthSeeker. It operates on the same principle as a lie detector. You attach it to any digital phone and it interprets the voice patterns of the person at the other end, letting you know if the caller is telling the truth or lying."

Sylvia pictured Vera's lies racing up the tower, faster than the speed of light. "How much is it?"

"Two hundred dollars." Sylvia let out a low whistle. "Or an electric label maker. It makes professionally typeset labels for file folders, shelves, or anything else. You can print in three different type faces, three different sizes, and six different colors. A bargain at $39.95"

"I'll take one, but it's for me." Sylvia reached for a label maker and dust bunnies chased each other from one corner of the display table to another.

"Sylvia!" She looked up. Vera was signaling her. She was ready to leave.

"And the electronic tie rack for my nephew."

"I'll ring you out." Molly handed Sylvia her bag, along with her business card. "I moved to town a few months ago," she explained, "and I don't know many people. I was thinking maybe you'd like to get together sometime. Like have lunch. I really enjoyed talking to you."

Sylvia wondered if Molly was tetched in her head. No stranger had ever asked to have lunch with her before. "Why would you want to do that?" she asked.

Molly laughed again, a deep, rich laugh. "Have lunch with you?" Sylvia nodded. "Maybe because you make me laugh, and nothing much does." Sylvia put Molly's card in her purse. "My cell number is on it. That's the best way to reach me."

Sylvia hurried out of the store. Vera was waiting, impatiently.

"Your saleslady was very weird," she said.

"What was weird about her?"

"Didn't you think it was odd? How friendly she was getting with you, a perfect stranger? She can't be up to anything good." Sylvia didn't answer. "We better hurry. You know what Elaine's like if she's kept waiting."

Yes, she knew what Elaine was like, and she was a fool to be here. When was she going to learn that there was no free lunch—at least not with her sister and her niece. "I'm sorry. I can't have lunch with you."

"Why not?"

"I forgot something."

Sylvia returned to the Sharper Image. Molly was at the cash register.

"Yes, I will," Sylvia told her.

Molly grinned. "Yes, you will what?"

"Yes, I will call you. I promise I will. I don't laugh much either."

CHAPTER ELEVEN

Mary and Simon

"Love is such a funny thing, It's very like a lizard.
It twines itself round the heart and penetrates your gizzard."

Anonymous

MARY was on the staff elevator heading down to Dr. Hodas' office when the elevator stopped on the tenth floor and Dr. Simon, preeminent plastic surgeon got on. He and Mary nodded politely at each other.

She didn't know him personally, but she knew a lot about him. He was demanding, aloof, and sometimes abrasive. His temper, even among surgeons, was considered formidable. He was admired by most, resented by many, and disliked by a few. Those who didn't work with him sang his praises. The hospital administration loved him because he filled hundreds of hospital beds each year. His patients worshipped him because he transformed their lives, and the public adored him because he was part of a humanitarian team of surgeons doing pro bono work in Central and South America. Society editors chased him for interviews because he was considered one of Chicago's more eligible bachelors. Mothers and grandmothers pursued him, hoping to marry him off to an eligible daughter or granddaughter. Nurses and doctors, hoping to make his acquaintance, accosted him in parking lots, hospital cafeterias, and departmental offices. Personally, she couldn't understand why all the brouhaha over this average-looking man of average height and less than average deportment. She was not impressed, no matter how skillful a surgeon he was.

Simon pushed the button to the second floor. He didn't know Mary by name, but he had seen her around the hospital for years, and every time he did he wondered why she was still wearing her God-given nose. Noses like hers were fast becoming an anomaly on the American facial landscape—not that he was on a personal crusade to eliminate them. God forbid! The palms of his hands began to itch, and he rubbed them against his white jacket, imagining her on his operating table. Give him an hour or two, he thought, and she would exit a classic beauty.

Mary felt Simon's eyes on her—or, rather, on her nose. She turned away from him, pretending to take a sudden interest in the graffiti on the side wall. He was like a straight man confronted by a lesbian, she thought, responding to her rejection of cosmetic surgery as a rejection of him. Suck it up, she thought.

Not that she wasn't damned attractive just the way she was, Simon conceded. She had good bone structure, beautiful hair, fine skin, and from what he could tell, an incredible body. He stared at her breasts in profile and wondered if her tits were brown or rosy-tipped.

She caught him scrutinizing her breasts and turned even further into the side wall.

He realized he'd been caught and studied his shoes.

He must think I'm stupid, she thought. He's no more interested in his shoes than I am in elevator walls.

Most of the time he saw her, in the staff cafeteria, sitting with other nurses. She listened more than she spoke, and he couldn't remember seeing her laugh.

She frequently saw him in the staff cafeteria, eating lunch alone and determined to keep it that way. He'd shove any extra chairs to another table and hide himself behind a journal or newspaper.

The elevator stopped on seven. A pretty young nurse got on and smiled brightly at Simon.

"Hi, Dr. Simon. I'm Janet Fazio. I assisted you in surgery last week." He nodded at her. "Five, please," she said to Mary. Mary ignored her, and Fazio pushed the number five button. Seconds later the elevator stopped, and the door opened. "You can usually find me in the cafeteria around noontime," Fazio said, winking at Simon before she exited.

The door closed, and the elevator continued down the shaft.

BANG!

Simon and Mary looked at each other, quizzically.

"What do you think that was?" Simon asked.

"I don't know, but we just passed my floor."

"And now mine." Simon tried to sound amused.

The elevator headed down the shaft.

BANG!

The elevator reversed itself and returned up the shaft. Simon and Mary smiled apologetically at each other, as if they were somehow responsible. The elevator stopped, but the door didn't open. Simon pushed all the panel buttons. When nothing happened, he shoved a fist through the rubber door seams and looked out.

"We're between floors," he announced, letting the rubber edges snap closed again.

His fingers were surprisingly long and thin for a man of his height and build, Mary noted. And he took good care of them. His nails were buffed, cuticles trimmed, half-moons shining. She watched him fold one beautiful hand into a fist and pound it against the door.

"Fuck!" he said, kicking the elevator door. "Fuck! Fuck! Fuck!"

Seeing the worst in others always brought out the best in Mary.

"Fuck, fuck, fuck," she mocked, surprising him. Most people were intimidated by him and his temper. "Why don't you try the intercom instead of throwing a hissy fit?" She pointed to the steel grid below the button panel. Simon pushed it.

"Helloooooo," he coo'd sweetly, mocking Mary. When no one answered, he kicked the grid with his shoe, bending the soft metal. "This new system was touted to be the Mother of all security systems! Bullshit!"

"There may not be anyone at the other end to hear us."

She tapped her keys against the elevator door. Ping. Ping. Simon laughed at her.

"You really think someone's going to hear that pin-pinging through six inches of steel?"

Her eyes narrowed. What the good doctor knew about elevators probably wouldn't fill a thimble, she thought, but that wouldn't stop him from playing the numbers game with her. Men did that a lot, especially with women. "You have a better idea?" she asked.

They glared at each other.

"I was on my way to release a patient," Simon said, in a tone reeking with self-importance.

It was a Mexican stand-off, medical style.

"And I was on my way to consult with Dr. Hodas about one of his oncology patients."

The elevator was on the move again, this time down the shaft . . . until it came to a sudden, screeching stop. Mary slipped to the floor in a dead faint.

It could've been worse, Simon thought, feasting on the sight of Mary's cleavage as she lay quietly at his feet. She could've been a screamer, and there was nothing worse than a screamer, except maybe a whiner. He knelt beside her, and rubbed her hands.

"You all right?" he asked. She opened her eyes. "You OK?"

She yanked her hands away from him.

"Of course! Why wouldn't I be?"

"You fainted."

"I did not."

"OK, you didn't faint. Where's your cell phone?" he asked.

"Where's *my* cell phone? Where's *your* cell phone?"

She had starch in her underpants, he thought, and he liked her style, which was diametrically opposite to his ex-wife Jane's. Jane came on purring like a kitten and ended up clawing and chewing live flesh. But he could be wrong about this one, too. He often was. His mother liked to tell him that he was the worst judge of human nature in the history of the world, especially when it came to women, and his mother was almost always right. She, on the other hand, was probably the fastest and best judge of character in the Midwest. "How do you do it?" he once asked her. "It's easy. I don't have a penis," his then seventy-five year old mother answered. "The thing about them is that when they're up, the brain is down." Then there was no hope for him, he concluded; at least, not until every last bit of testosterone had been drained from his body.

The elevator started up the shaft at an accelerated speed. Simon joined Mary on the floor.

"What's that?" he asked, pointing to the stone around her neck.

"A lodestone." She could hardly breathe he was so close. "It's my good luck piece," she added, laughing at herself.

"Listen, we may be here for awhile so why don't we introduce ourselves? I'm Simon."

"*Dr.* Simon, I know. What's your first name?"

"Simon is my first *and* last name."

"Isn't there an initial D before the Simon?"

"I don't use the D except on legal stuff. My friends call me Simon."

"How bad can it be?" she pursued. "Dudley Doolittle? Donald Duck?"

"You don't give up, do you? OK, D is for David."

"David is a beautiful name."

"My life experiences as David were anything but beautiful."

"My life experiences as Mary *Mazol* have been anything but lucky, but I didn't change my name."

His curiosity was piqued. "What's unlucky about your life?" he asked.

"What was unhappy about yours?"

"Do you always do that? Answer a question with a question?"

The elevator lights flickered . . . and died, leaving them in darkness . . . and silence.

***

His parents were unremarkable enough, Simon thought, except for the fact that they looked alike and that his parents' parents looked alike. Both parents and all four grandparents had long, narrow faces and pointy chins. His mother's and father's siblings all had similar face and body types and married people who resembled them.

Predictably, they produced offspring who, almost without exception, resembled each other. The "almost" exceptions included himself and his Aunt Dorothy. He frequently overheard one or another of his relatives saying to another, "Where do you think he came from? He doesn't look anything like the family." And, then, in a whisper, "Do you think he was adopted?"

He had been a short, pudgy child with a fat lunar face and wide-angled ears. They had his ears pinned back when he was twelve. At family reunions, which took place once a year—usually at Passover—his cousins were always mistaken for each other, but he was mistaken for no one. He was odd child out, and because of that, they bullied and teased him. They made him the butt of their jokes and pranks, and called him hurtful names like Chubby Tubby, Roly Poly, and Jumbo Dumbo. And because many of his tormenters were also named David (in memory of the same grandfather), he grew to hate the name. His mother tried to console him by spouting inane clichés like "sticks and stones may break your bones," but he knew better. Words *can* break you—break your heart and break your spirit.

The children in public school weren't any kinder, but because there was a greater diversity of body types in school and there were many others like him, he was not singled out. The other fatties, though, were thicker skinned than he, willing to hang onto the fringes of the beautiful people in order to catch any crumbs of kindness that might come their way. He believed that no potential amount of goodwill would be great enough to compensate for the guaranteed razzings he would suffer. His strategy of preference was to make himself as scarce as possible, hoping he wouldn't be noticed.

The worst part of that period, he thought, was how he had treated his parents. First, he accused them of adopting him. When his father took off his shoes and socks and showed him that they both had two webbed toes on each foot, he then insisted they had performed satanic rites during his conception. And when they flatly refused to discuss his conception and their copulation, he threw his first temper tantrum. It so terrified them that he changed his coping strategy. He no longer tried to make himself invisible at school. Now he fought off his enemies with rage—deliberate, controlled rage. They thought he was crazy and kept their distance.

* * *

Her world changed in a day. It had started out like any other day—except that she had gotten a late start in the morning, too late to pick up her precious "collectibles," which were strewn across her bedroom floor. She hurried home after school, anxious to pack up her bottle caps, marbles, mood rings, buttons, wind-up toys, and keys because it was Wednesday, and every Wednesday afternoon the Alley Hunters met to trade their treasures. Her newest and most prized possession was an IBM Selectric ball which she had found the day before in the back of an office supply store. There was no telling what she could get for it, she had thought, rushing into her room, but it was gone. All of it.

"I've told you over and over again not to leave your stuff on the floor," Sylvia said. "I can't vacuum over them, and I'm tired of picking up after you. I've thrown it out. All of it." Mary started out of the house. "Don't waste your time looking for it. The garbage man was here hours ago, and it's all gone."

Years of hunting and trading . . . gone.

Mary attacked Sylvia, both fists flying, pummeling her on her head and kicking her in her stomach, and Sylvia, smaller and weaker, did the only thing she could do to protect herself. She pushed her . . . and pushed her hard. She fell backwards into the full length mirror, which broke on impact. She fell onto shards of glass. Blood gushed from her arms and legs, and she thought she was dying. If she was, she decided, she wasn't going to her grave with her secret.

"Daddy has a friend, and her name is Aunt Estelle, and she's nicer and prettier than you."

Sylvia didn't believe her, not until she took the photo from its hiding place and showed it to her. And that night—to get away from the sound of her mother screaming at her father—she pulled her blanket and pillow into the far left end of her closet and felt the end wall move. Minutes later, with flashlight in hand, she discovered that beyond that fake wall lay a large, unfinished space the size of a room.

In the morning, a man she didn't know was in the living room with her mother and aunt. He motioned for her to come closer.

"Your father died last night," he said.

There is nothing more unlucky, she thought, than to lose the parent who is warm and loving and be left with the cold, angry one. Mazol was not a lucky name. .

* * *

"When we get out of here," Simon said, wrapping an arm around Mary's shoulder, "what are you going to do differently?"

"Take the stairs."

He laughed. "Do you have any regrets in life?" he asked.

"That's all I have."

"I regret not spending more time with my mother. I will in the future, when we get out of here."

"I promise to spend *less* with mine," Mary rejoined.

Simon promised himself he would take Gert to the Lyric fundraiser. So what if he hated large social gatherings? It wasn't her fault that he'd married Jane; in fact, if he'd listened to her, he wouldn't have. Then he wouldn't have been dragged to dinners, balls, benefits, auctions, cotillions, banquets, exhibitions, and fundraisers in support of dozens of causes Jane didn't believe in because Jane's only cause, in the end, was Jane. For two long, miserable years he had been subjected to people who'd kiss and hug him one day and not remember his name the next; people Jane expected him to fawn over, the way she did.

He tried for a time, but he'd made a very bad lackey. He became sullen and quarrelsome. She called him gauche and boorish and no fun at all and punished him by turning her exquisite back on him when they got into bed. "Bad dog. Bad dog," she breathed, sleeping next to him. By the third year he was more than tired and edgy. He had become ferocious at work, not that he'd ever been easy.

"I don't know what's going on in your personal life," the hospital CFO said to him behind closed doors, "but you can't go on like this.

Your reputation can only carry you so far. I'm getting a lot of complaints, and many on the staff refuse to work with you. You're risking too much for whatever."

That was when he took off his collar and refused to trot alongside Jane to any more gatherings of Chicago's finest. She continued to party, of course, but without him—just as he knew and hoped she would. He said and did nothing, having decided to give her all the time and space she needed to find his replacement because a classy lady like Jane wouldn't trade down. She'd gone from realtor's wife to dentist's wife to plastic surgeon's wife, and she'd hold onto his silver balls right up until the time she found a pair of gold ones to caress and pamper with her expert hands. Sure, he could have handled it differently, he thought. Most men would have, but he wanted her to think it was her idea. That approach, he reasoned, might expedite the process and cost him less, emotionally and financially. And he had been right. It took Jane fifteen months to find her new ball carrier, a Duke.

"I'm just asking for what's fair," she announced. He wondered what was fair for lying on your back for two years and doing the one and only thing you did well. Her lawyer told his lawyer. "Fifty percent of everything." "Postpone, postpone, postpone," he told his attorney. "Not only didn't she add to my assets, she decreased them by at least a hundred thousand a year." Time was on his side, he figured. Jane wouldn't want to lose her Dukey to some younger and prettier woman. Three months later she agreed to a modest settlement, and they were divorced.

The elevator lights flickered . . . and died. Simon pulled Mary closer.

She felt warm and protected, the way she had in the crook of her father's arm, and later, after his death, inside his camel's hair coat that had hung for a time in the hall closet. She would thrust her arms into the coat's long arms and breathe in the scent of his after-shave cologne. That coat became her refuge. Every day after school she would wrap herself inside the coat's great arms and pour her heart out to him.

"She had a locksmith remove all the locks from the doors, including my bedroom door," she cried. "She says I can't be trusted." He suggested she pay the locksmith out of her babysitting money and replace her bedroom lock. She followed his advice, but two days later her bedroom lock was gone again. "She'll always have more money than me. I can't afford this war."

The next day her father's coat was gone, and in the hallway sat three cardboard boxes marked "Salvation Army." She found his coat in the second box and hid it in the unfinished room at the end of her closet.

* * *

A motor whirred. The lights came on, and the elevator suddenly sprang into motion. A voice blasted through the intercom.

"We're bringing you up now."

Mary and Simon jumped to their feet. When the door opened, they were standing on opposite sides of the elevator, looking like two children caught with their hands in the cookie jar. Security personnel, police, hospital staff, reporters, and spectators cheered as they exited.

First there was a power failure, someone explained, and then the back-up power tripped. While the newsmen gathered around Simon, Mary hurried towards the visitors elevators. She did not want him to think he had any obligation towards her. What they shared was simply the fear of dying together at the bottom of the elevator shaft.

"Hey! Wait up!" Simon was running after her. "Where are you going?"

She stopped walking. "To Dr. Hodas' office. I'm an hour late."

"I didn't get a chance to ask you." They stood nose to nose. "How about dinner next week?" She pictured Simon at Sylvia's dining room table and wondered if this one could survive a dinner at Sylvia's.

"It isn't necessary."

"Of course, it isn't, but I want to see you again. I want to know why you're unlucky." He waited. "And don't you want to know why I changed my name?"

"My house is difficult to find."

"Then we'll meet somewhere. You tell me."

"Call me at my office."

"And by the way," Simon said, touching her good luck piece. "Lodestones, you know, attract metal, and elevators are made of metal, and not that I'm superstitious or anything, but maybe you should get rid of this thing."

CHAPTER TWELVE

Irene and Mel

"Change: To shift one's position and be bruised in a new place."

Washington Irving

IRENE was in no hurry to get home. What lay ahead was the same as what lay behind: she would make dinner, they would eat; they would sit together on the couch and watch TV; they would go to bed. There might even be some predictable lovemaking, after which Mel would quickly fall sleep and the snoring would start.

She boarded the bus, scoped the passengers, and took the empty seat next to an elderly African American woman.

"Do you think people can change?" Irene asked her traveling companion.

"What kind of people? Men people or women people?"

"Men people."

"Sure, but not for the better."

"You don't think they can be re-educated?"

"Maybe. Maybe not. Give me a-for- example."

"How about something as simple as lowering the toilet seat?"

The woman laughed at her. "Honey, that's not simple. That's as complicated as it gets 'cause that's political. You know, it's all about who's on top." The bus stopped, and the wise, old woman got off.

Even if Mel learned to lower the toilet seat today, Irene thought, he would come up with some absolutely new and nasty habit tomorrow. Yesterday was another first. He'd left a teabag in the sink, and it had taken her five minutes scrubbing with Ajax to remove the stain.

73

Passengers boarded. The ghost of her mother came towards her and took the now empty seat by the window.

"We have to talk," her mother's apparition said.

"Beat it."

"Nice way to talk to your mother, but strangers you take advice from." Irene twiddled her thumbs. "You need to remember that Mel is a lovely man with many wonderful qualities. He has money in the bank. He's generous, and he loves you." She wondered if her mother's ghost was able to watch her fornicate. "You think marriage should be all fun and games, but it isn't. You have to work at it. If Phil were living today, you'd be complaining about this or that thing he did; instead, you've made him into some kind of saint. If you look for trouble, you'll find it. Consider your infantile hostility towards Mel's boxer shorts. Your father wore boxer shorts, and I think we had a very good marriage."

The bus stopped and an elderly couple boarded. They carefully helped each other up the aisle.

"Are you OK, Eleanor?" the man asked.

"Yes, yes, John, just fine."

"That kind of love and devotion doesn't just happen overnight," her mother continued, nodding at the old couple. "You need to make an emotional commitment and soon, or one day you may not have anyone to help *you* on the bus." She softened her tone. "Growing old with someone is one of life's most beautiful experiences."

Her mother's mantras had changed with the seasons. In high school it was "One of life's most beautiful human experiences is sex between a *married* man and woman." To ensure obedience, a warning followed. "Remember, if you do "it" before you're married, he won't respect you, and men don't marry women they don't respect." So she and her contemporaries didn't do "it," but they did everything else, things far more sophisticated and imaginative than the simple "it." They did finger-fucking and hand jobs, and a technique she thought she'd invented. Years later she learned it was called a Dry Hustle. She hadn't invented it at all.

"Did you hear one word I said?"

"Yes, and you're wrong. The most beautiful human experience is having the skills and credentials needed to get an interesting, creative, and well-paying job so you can give your children what they need growing up and protect yourself in your old age."

She got up to leave.

"Where are you going? This isn't your stop."

"I know, and don't follow me!"

* * *

The voices of *Two and a Half Men* greeted Irene as she opened the door.

"That you, Hon?" Mel called. "I'm in here!"

Of course he was in *there*, she thought. Where else would he be? She went into the living room. Mel patted the cushion next to him, never taking his eyes off the TV. He was wearing his silk paisley print robe.

"Have a nice day?" she asked. He didn't answer. He hadn't heard. She picked up the drink can sitting on the wood table and railed inwardly at the white ring. "Is the program almost over?"

He looked at his watch. "Another ten minutes."

He reached for her hand, which she reluctantly gave him. "Let's go out for dinner. There are things I want to talk about."

"Tonight?" he whined. "Hey, how about tomorrow night instead? There's a comedy special on after this that I want to see."

There would be no tomorrow nights, she thought, if she left it up to Mel. "No! Tonight!" She had his attention.

"I promise, honest to God, Renie, tomorrow night we'll meet after work, which makes more sense than coming home first and then going out again." That's what men did, she thought. Labeled *their* ideas "sensible," implying that women's ideas were not. "I promise tomorrow night. Honest."

She gave up, went into the kitchen, and made an omelet mixed with too much cheese and cooked in too much butter. She called Mel in to eat. He sat opposite her, dressed in his funereal robe.

"Do me a favor, Mel, and change into your street clothes."

"Something wrong with my robe?"

"I'm tired of looking at you in it."

"But I'm comfortable, Honey. Hell, you can wear whatever you want to dinner, and I wouldn't mind."

She stood, unbuttoned her blouse and threw it on a chair. Then she unzipped her slacks and dropped them to the floor. Dressed in only her Lily of France underwire bra and matching black underpants, she cut into her omelet.

"You really going to eat dressed—rather, undressed—like that?" he asked, staring at her cleavage.

"Do what I do. Try not to look."

A cherry tomato fell in her crotch. She carefully picked it up and set it at the edge of her dinner plate.

"I have an idea," Mel said, winking at her. "Why don't we eat dinner later and head to the bedroom now?"

"I'm not interested."

He pouted. "Why not?"

"Because you look like an old man in a long-term care facility, and women my age don't do it with old men." He tightened his hold on his fork. "Mel, we have to talk about your habits. They're making me crazy."

"Yeah, yeah, I know, and I'm working on it."

"You might be more successful if you worked on one problem at a time, starting with lowering the toilet seat."

Mel took a stab at his omelet. "I don't think these eggs are cooked."

"And before you lower the toilet seat, you might also check the bowl rim for pubic hairs."

"You must've put a pound of cheese and butter in it." He pushed his plate away. "This one meal alone could block a major artery."

They sat in silence, carried their silence into the living room, and later to bed with them. Mel turned on the small bedroom TV.

"Do me a favor and scratch my back, ok?" She backed up into him. He scratched blindly. "No! Not there. Where the bra hooks come together." He rubbed. "That's too high and you're not scratching. You're rubbing." He lowered his hand. "I don't get it. Before you moved in, you knew exactly where to scratch. Now you don't."

"I'm sorry, Renie. I guess I'm too tired to concentrate." He turned off the TV. "Sleep tight, Hon. Love ya."

Irene retrieved Mr. Fingers, her plastic backscratcher, from under her bed. She had almost thrown it out when Mel moved in, thinking she'd never need it again.

"Mel?" She shook him. "Mel, this isn't turning out the way I thought it would." The snoring began. "Mel! Shut the hell up!" She shoved him, hard in the shoulder. He woke up.

"You OK, Renie?" She stared at him, mystified. "Why are you looking at me like that?" She was looking at him "like that" because, suddenly, the Mel laying next to her in bed didn't look anything like the Mel she had dated. *That* Mel was younger and thinner and had more hair on his head than this Mel. "Night, Renie. Love ya."

When she was dating the *other* Mel, she thought she was lonely and suggested he move in, but now what she wanted was to live alone again.

CHAPTER THIRTEEN

Rochelle, Barbara, and Mark

"Divorce is the psychological equivalent of a triple coronary by-pass. After such a monumental assault on the heart, it takes years to amend all the habits and attitudes that led up to it."

Mary K Blakely

ROCHELLE had invited Barbara for dinner. Richard was out of town.

"On business," he said.

They sat in the kitchen, drinking a 1990 Merlot and feasting on homemade chopped liver, smeared on party rye.

"I don't know why you put up with it all." Barbara said, eyeing the children's books and toys strewn across the kitchen.

"Same reason you put up with Richard's fiascos. I don't want to be dumped."

"That was never a possibility," Barbara answered. "At least, not until now."

"You could be wrong, you know, and worrying for nothing. Maybe you should take Sylvia's advice and hire a detective."

"I'm not wrong. I didn't tell you. I haven't told anyone yet, but I went to the bank and checked for myself."

"And?"

"This one isn't going away. She's wearing a Buccarelli initial pin, like mine but with the initial *R*. *R* is for Rhonda. She said her boyfriend had it commissioned for her, and you know Richard. His commitment to anything and anyone can be measured by the size of his economic investment."

"I'm so sorry. What are you going to do?"

"I don't know."

"Remember, you can't catch bees with vinegar. Use honey. Put that great body of yours to use." Yes, there was always that, Barbara thought, but then Rochelle wasn't the one who would have to sleep with Richard. She was. "You ready to eat?" Rochelle opened the refrigerator. "I made a fabulous shrimp pasta salad. From *Bon Appetit*." She searched the shelves, opened and closed bins, moved jars and containers before slamming closed the refrigerator door. "Sonofabitch!"

"What's wrong?"

"It's gone."

"What's gone?"

"Our dinner!"

"It can't be gone."

Rochelle opened the refrigerator door open again—wide. "Do *you* see it? A medium-sized yellow ceramic bowl?"

Barbara got up and eye-balled the shelves. "No. So where could it be?"

"One of them took it."

"One of whom?"

"One of my daughters."

"Why would they steal your dinner?"

Rochelle suddenly turned protective.

"I didn't say steal. I said took."

"OK, why would one of them take it?"

"Whoever must have needed it."

"Who needs food in Chicago?" Rochelle didn't answer. "How many times have we told you to change the locks and throw away the keys?"

"Get your purse. We're going out for dinner. My treat."

The front door opened and closed. Heavy footsteps tromped through the foyer and into the kitchen. Mark patted his ex-wife's butt, grabbed a bottle of Sam Adams from the refrigerator, and sat down at the kitchen table.

"Hi babe. Hi Barbara. How's everything?"

"We were just leaving," Barbara said.

"Hey, don't let me stop you." He shook Rochelle's house key at them. "I can let myself out. Rochelle, I just wanted to tell you about this guy I sold a two million dollar house today. He was in my office, signing papers, and noticed your painting. You know, the one on the wall behind my desk. He said he wanted to buy it from me. Offered me $2,000."

"You're not going to sell it to him!"

"No, of course not, but when he heard I knew the artist, he said he'd like to commission you to do some work for him. That's when I explained that you're not painting anymore; that you now run a day care for your grandchildren."

"Who is he?" Barbara asked.

"Who's who?"

"This big money guy who wants to commission Rochelle."

"B.J. Moss. He owns Moss Plastics."

It was nothing more than a coincidence, Rochelle thought, but Madame Savansky had said to look for someone with the initials B.J. B.J. will be your guide. Follow him. "What's his phone number?" she asked, trying to hide her excitement.

"You really want it?" Rochelle nodded, and Mark looked pleased. He handed her B.J.'s business card. "He also has a new office building with lots of blank walls just begging to be covered." He got up from the table. "Got to go now. Nice seeing you all."

They listened to the front door close and the dead-bolt turn in the lock.

"So Mark not only has a key to your house, but you're stocking his favorite beer." Rochelle put the dirty dishes in the dishwasher. "Is that what you call 'taking back your life?' You're still everyone's doormat."

"Come on, let's go."

Barbara started to follow, but a tapping noise stopped her.

"What's that?" she asked.

The butterfly was beating its wings against the glass door that separated the kitchen from the dinette.

"Nothing. Nothing at all." But it was odd, she thought, how it reminded her of her children when they were toddlers; how they would scream bloody murder when she and Mark were going out for the evening. In the early years, Mark would take the sitter home, and they would stay together, but later, he went without her.

CHAPTER FOURTEEN

Mahjongg at Barbara's

*"Everyone that flatters thee
Is no friend in misery.
Words are easy, like the wind,
Faithful friends are hard to find."*

Richard Barnfield

"Ten dot," Barbara said, throwing out a tile.

"Big mistake." Irene grabbed the tile and set her winning hand on top of the rack. "You all owe me 25 cents except for Barbara, who owes me fifty." They paid up and mixed tiles for the next game. "I've been meaning to tell you, Sylvia. You may be right about Bambi. She just might be after my job."

Being right made Sylvia look almost pretty.

"You think?"

"I think."

"I found her going through my personal files the other day, and a short time later I saw her leave the building with the CFO, a married man, old enough to be her father. They looked very comfortable with each other."

"What are you going to do about it?" Sylvia asked.

"Nothing. Like I said, you *might* be right. Going through my files doesn't necessarily constitute trying to take my job."

"Well, when you decide that she is, I hope you'll be as clever as Olive."

"Who's Olive?"

"Heather's boss on *Days of Our Lives*. Olive manipulated her Bambi into negotiating an early retirement package for her."

"How'd she do it?"

"Easy. She told Heather that she wanted to quit her job, but that she couldn't afford to; at least, not until her pension kicked in. Next thing you know she was offered a generous early retirement package."

Now there was an idea, Irene thought. If Bambi *were* having an affair with Charles and she did want her job, he was certainly the right person to make it happen. *And* if she could retire two years early and on her own merits, she would feel stronger, less compromised when airing her grievances with Mel.

"For someone who rarely leaves home, you certainly show a lot of street smarts," Barbara remarked.

"That's because in the workplace and at the country clubs and in your volunteer organizations you get a prettified and politically correct view of the world, while what I get on TV is the real thing. I see all the nasty, cowardly, disgusting, conniving, murdering, lying, shameful things that one human being can do to another."

Barbara's phone rang. She read the caller I.D.

"Speaking of all the nasty, cowardly, and disgusting things one person can do to another . . . Richard's on the phone." She took the call. "Hello. Yes, the girls are still here." She listened, impressed with how glibly he told his lies and how convincingly she pretended to believe them. This game they'd been playing for years operated on two unspoken and synergetic principles: "If you look the other way, I won't leave you," and "I'll look the other way if you promise not to leave." For twenty-five years only the left shoe had fallen. Now the right shoe was hanging over her head, waiting to drop. "Yes, OK," was all she said before hanging up. "Richard says his new law clerk is an idiot and forgot to prepare some important legal briefs for court tomorrow. He's going to have to take care of it himself tonight, and depending on what time he finishes, he may sleep downtown." She paused and added sarcastically, "So he won't disturb me," he said.

Sylvia touched her arm. "I'm so sorry."

"We're all sorry," Irene added, quickly.

"He's been taking greater and greater risks. It's almost as though he doesn't care if he gets caught. Maybe that's it. Maybe he wants me to catch him."

"Rochelle said you've seen her," Irene said.

"Yes. She's older than the others. And much more expensive."

"How old?" Sylvia asked.

"Early forties. Why?"

"By the time a person is forty, she should have a history, like Lucy on *Till the End of Time*. You absolutely must hire a P.I and get the dirt on her. There's this retired cop advertising on TV. Call 1-800-GET-HELP and ask for J.W. He looks OK, for a man."

"Look, I know you mean well, but if I hire a detective, chances are Richard will find out that I know, and once he does, there's no turning back. That's what I've spent twenty-five years hoping to avoid. No, no detective. Period. End of conversation."

They mixed the tiles and built their walls.

"I have news for you," Rochelle said, quietly. "Good news. I've been commissioned to do a painting."

"You called the B.J. guy?" Barbara asked.

"Yes. We met, and he paid me 50% up front. I get the other 50% upon delivery and satisfaction." They applauded her. "Funny thing about it is that a few days earlier I was at Madame Savansky's for a reading, and she told me to be on the lookout for someone with the initials B.J. His name is B.J. Moss."

"It's just a coincidence," Irene said. "Don't be reading more into this than exists."

Barbara's phone rang again. She noted the number and took the call.

"Hi, Joan. You sound upset." She listened for some minutes. "I'll tell them. They're here now." She hung up the phone. "That was Joan. Judy Potash died this afternoon. It happened just like— she snapped her fingers—like that. They were at Bistro 110, having lunch ..."

"Don't tell me she choked to death!" Sylvia cut in.

"No, she didn't steal your thunder. She died of a heart attack."

They were conspicuously silent for several seconds. People are always silent for several seconds after just hearing that someone has passed on. Sylvia was the first to speak.

"Very untimely."

"It's always untimely for the deceased," Barbara commented.

"I feel terrible," Irene confessed. "There was Judy doing something profound and permanent like dying while I was at Lord and Taylor's looking for a new face cream to plump up my wrinkles. It makes me feel petty and vacuous when something like that happens."

"You *are* petty and vacuous," Sylvia agreed.

"That's ridiculous," Rochelle defended. "Even if Irene had been giving blood or one of her kidneys, it wouldn't have saved Judy. Her time was up, poor thing."

Sylvia thought otherwise. "She was no poor thing. She was one of the lucky ones, dying quickly and painlessly and in a public place so her body didn't have to rot, the way my mother's did!"

Barbara suggested they take three minutes for a silent prayer, in memory of Judy, not that any of them knew anything about praying, silent or otherwise. Four heads awkwardly bent.

SYLVIA

Dear Judy: Please forgive me for not liking you, but let's be honest. You didn't like me either. You liked everyone else in the group but not me.

Sylvia stopped herself.

No, no, no. I'm being unkind. It's one thing to think unkindly about the living, but never the dead. I should be more charitable.

Dear Judy: I'm happy for you that your death was fast and painless, and I hope your family's grief will be minimal.

She stopped herself again.

Wrong. Survivors' grief shouldn't be minimal. It should be over the top painful because suffering is an expression of loss, and the greater the suffering, the greater the loss.

Dear Judy: If no one grieves at your passing, then what difference did you make during your time on earth? Who will grieve for me? Mary might, but only later, when she gets bored with her newly-won freedom. Vera won't grieve. She'll do exactly what she always does when some friend or acquaintance of hers dies. She'll send a $15 check to her Temple because that's the minimum amount you can send and still get your name printed in the monthly newsletter. Clara won't grieve; in fact she probably wont' come to my funeral . . . unless there's a good play showing at the time.

Dear Judy: Trust me. You were one of the lucky ones, dying in a public forum, surrounded by friends. Amen.

Sylvia looked up. The others were still with bent necks. She dropped her head again.

IRENE

Dear Judy: May your family find comfort in many loving and happy memories of you. Amen.

Irene looked up. The others were still praying. She dropped her head again.

Dear Judy. I always liked you, even though we didn't see much of each other after graduation—just at big events like weddings or reunions. I think that's because we didn't have much in common, except for being young together, and that's only good for about ten minutes. Anyway, the truth is I wasn't all that surprised to hear you were dead because the last time I saw you, you looked so bad I almost didn't recognize you. Not until you said, "Irene, hi. It's Judy."

Irene looked up again. The others still had their heads down. She dropped her head.

Judy, did you have a death scene of choice? For the longest time I thought I'd like to die with a man on top of me, but after menopause, I gave that up. Now I think the idyllic death would be lying in bed on my stomach, my back bare, and my husband or lover scratching that spot where the bra hooks come together and dig into your skin. You may not have noticed, but the older you get the deeper the bra hooks bite into your flesh, and the longer it takes for the skin to go back to normal after you've taken your bra off. Anyway, in my idyllic death scene my lover scratches my back on that spot . . . and scratches . . . and scratches . . . until I fade . . . off into a deep and permanent sleep.

She looked up. The others were still praying. She dropped her head again.

Of course, there's no guarantee I'll get my death wish, no matter whom I'm living with, but the longer I live with Mel, the more certain I am that it won't happen with him. The girls tell me I don't know how to compromise, but they're wrong. I do. I compromised with Phil. He hated the structure of a nine- to- five job and taking orders from anyone so he worked for himself and not all that hard, but I never pressured him, even though his income was minimal and undependable. He was happy, and I was happy with him . . . until he was murdered by that drunken driver, which I'm sure was not his idea of an ideal death. Anyway, I think I'm realistic which is why I'm saying that there's a limit to what each of us can live with, and I may have reached my limit with Mel. Amen.

Irene opened her eyes. The others were still praying. Enough already, she thought, clearing her throat, loudly.

BARBARA

Dear Judy. I'm sorry you're dead. I wish I could say or do something to bring you back, but we both know that's impossible. You died better than most, though, surrounded by friends and eating a good meal—not a great meal, mind you, but an OK one. Personally, I've always found the food at Bistro 110 to be quite pedestrian. I wouldn't give it more than two stars though I suppose you could've been caught dead in worse places.

As I was saying, in my opinion you lived a good life and died a respectable death, with your marriage intact and a grieving husband left behind, which is not how it would happen to me if I died today. Richard wouldn't shed a tear. He'd make a quick appearance at my funeral, then hurry home to his slut, who will have already moved into my house, and before my body is cold in the grave will be swinging my new Arnold Palmer golf clubs, traveling on Baedecker Tours with my friends, and putting her name next to Richard's on the patron's page for the Chicago Symphony.

I don't mean to minimize your very real corporeal death, but there are other kinds of deaths, deaths that I think are more painful than a body being snuffed out. For example, the death of a marriage. Our marriage has been dead for years, not that Richard is totally to blame. You see, I've never had much of a sexual appetite—probably because I've never had an orgasm, at least not one attributable to Richard, and, by the way, according to a leading New York dermatologist, one orgasm gives you the same cosmetic benefits as a $300- an- ounce face cream, which is why she recommends having an orgasm three times a week for a beautiful, healthy skin—even if you have to DIY, which is, of course, the only way I get one. Not that I think sex is solely about orgasm. I view it more as a social event, *a form of communication between a husband and wife, who, otherwise, might not be communicating at all.*

But even a dead marriage is better than a divorce because divorce is a death knell socially. Oh, there would be a splattering of invitations for a time, mostly motivated by curiosity and guilt rather than loyalty and friendship, but even these would stop after a while. I imagine I'd be treated in much the same way I've treated others—excluded from private dinner parties because it would make some other woman's table uneven.

Divorce is also an economic killer; not that Richard's the kind of man to leave me begging on a street corner. He's honorable and can be trusted to divide our assets equally because he knows that I'm 50% of the reason he enjoys a successful law practice today and 100% of the reason we have two successful children. God knows he never spent any time with them; at least, not quality time. So even though there would be a fair division of assets, we'd both have to give up certain amenities we've become used to since there'd be half the assets for each of us. Not that I want another 5,000 square foot house because I don't. It's creepy when I'm here by myself at night. Sometimes I hear nails scraping across windows, floorboards creaking and voices floating up through the shower drain and heat registers. If we divorce, I will move into a downtown condo and not just any condo, but a luxury condo, and not just any luxury condo, but one wedged between two other luxury condos, shoulder to shoulder, top to bottom, sandwiched in so tightly together that no noises can squeeze in.

By the way, I can't believe you're being buried at Woodlawn. Nobody, simply nobody, is buried there anymore. The Arbors is now the in-place---no pun intended. I'll be at your funeral, Judy; unless, of course, it's on a Wednesday at 1:00 because Wednesdays at one I have a standing hair appointment with Fuad.

ROCHELLE

Dear Judy: I've always enjoyed talking to you, even though we didn't see much of each other these last few years. I would say, "Let's have lunch together," and you would answer, "Yeah, give me a call," but I never did, and we never did, and now we never will because you're dead.

Rochelle thought back . . . .

Now that I think about it, I don't think I heard from you again after the party a few years back at the Levys. That was when I found you and Mark out back in their garden, head to head in what he later explained was a discussion about where to buy opals because he wanted to buy me one for my birthday and you seemed to be an authority on the subject.

And then forward . . .

By the way, I never did get that opal—not that I wanted or needed one—but that wasn't the only time I saw the two of you very chummy. There was that Halloween party at your house some years back, when you and Mark both disappeared for—for too long.

Rochelle was heading down a path she probably shouldn't take.

Dear Judy. I'm not going to let the fact that you and Mark were probably fucking each other during our marriage get in the way of my final thoughts of you. I sincerely hope you got what you wanted in life—even if that included my husband—because there's nothing worse in life than dying with regrets. I know because that's how my mother died—with a liturgy of regrets she repeated over and over again as she lay dying in her hospital bed. Who knows? Maybe it was all those regrets that gave her the cancer. Maybe that's why she made me promise not to die like her, with regrets. "Get out from under your children," she told me. "Do something for yourself! Now! Before it's too late." I promised I would. "Then maybe all this dying has been for something," she said.

"Hey, Rochelle, come back to us!" She looked up, confused. "We're done praying."

"Does anyone read the obituaries?" Sylvia asked.

"I do," Rochelle admitted. "I'm always looking for the ones who got away." They didn't understand. "Let's say four of the five surviving children live in the same town with the deceased parent, like Arcola, Illinois, and the fifth lives in San Diego. That's the one who got away, the one who had the courage to chase a dream. They're my heroes."

"I read them to see how old they were when they died," Sylvia admitted. "Did you know that fewer people die in their seventies than in their sixties and even fewer die in their eighties and nineties? So if you can get past seventy, you might live another ten to twenty years."

"So according to you, if you make it past ninety, then you're a good bet to live to 120?" Irene asked. "Is that what you're saying? If you are, that's the most cockeyed bit of thinking I've ever heard. Fewer older people die because there are fewer older people left alive. Most are already dead."

"I find epitaphs fascinating," Barbara said. "For a while I was collecting them. My favorite is: 'I told you I was sick.'"

"The problem with epitaphs," Sylvia added, "is that someone else writes them for us. We should be writing our own; after all, who knows us better than we do?"

"Now you're talking!" Irene commended. "Let's do it. Let's write our own. Right now!" They agreed. Barbara passed out paper and pencils. "Raise your hands when you're ready."

Sylvia went first. "I told you I'd choke to death."

Rochelle followed. "I died with no regrets."

Barbara cleared her throat. "I have a poem. Ready?

"His grief was so great
For his departed Venus,
He beat himself up
And cut off his penis."

"That's no epitaph," Sylvia said. "That's a death wish."

"And I've got a limerick." Irene read:

"When our dear friend Irene was ill,
She asked that this wish be fulfilled:
To have her back scratched
Where the bra hooks attach,
Then she'd go silently under the hill."

CHAPTER FIFTEEN

Irene and Bambi

*"One often passes from love to ambition but rarely returns
from ambition to love."*

La Rochefoucauld

Bambi had been included in a top-level meeting of the Advertising Department. And it didn't comfort Irene to hear the vice president explain her presence with a string of clichés: "We need to bring in fresh blood sooner rather than later; new brooms sweep clean; and let's make hay while the sun shines." She wanted to point out that his last platitude was non-parallel to the first two, but decided it might be better to keep her mouth shut. Her position, after all, was somewhat precarious. Bambi had friends in high places.

Bambi, for her part, avoided all eye contact with her. She leaned far back in her chair, using the Vice President's shoulder as a blocking agent, and said nothing until she was called upon to present "her original proposal for a back-to-school ad campaign." It was all she could do not to scream out that this was not an original idea, and it was certainly not Bambi's. It was hers, one she had proposed ten years earlier that had been vetoed. The meeting ended and Bambi lingered behind. Irene returned to her office and when she saw Bambi enter her cubicle, she called her.

"Let's talk," she said. "In my office."

Bambi dragged herself in.

"I didn't know I'd be invited to the meeting," she began. "No one was more surprised than me."

"Than I," Irene corrected, "but there's no need to apologize. We do need to bring in new blood sooner rather than later; that is, if we want to keep the organization fresh." She motioned for Bambi to sit down and pulled up a chair close to her. "The truth is," she started, then paused, lowered her voice, and started again. "The truth is …but I don't want you repeat this to anyone." Bambi's doe-like eyes opened wide and innocent. "I would love to retire. I've been doing this job for almost twenty-five years, and I'm tired. If my pension gave me today what it will two years from now, I'd retire tomorrow."

"Is it *that* much of a difference?' Bambi asked.

"Not really, especially when you consider that no one in my family lives past 72, but it's enough to make the difference between squeezing out an existence and having a few extra dollars at the end of each month to enjoy life a bit." Bambi looked very sympathetic. "Of course," Irene repeated, "you do understand this is just between you and me, right?"

"Of course," Bambi answered, reassuringly.

Irene watched her scamper back to her cubicle, get on her cell phone, and minutes later, leave the office. She's on her way to see Charles, she thought, pleased with herself. She called Mel.

"Sorry, Renie, but I'm in the middle of something here. I'll call you back."

"Let's have dinner out tonight. I have something to tell you."

"Why don't we talk about whatever when we get home? Got to go now. Love ya, Renie."

CHAPTER SIXTEEN

Barbara, Richard, and Rhonda

"Prayer gives a man the opportunity of getting to know a gentleman
he hardly ever meets. I do not mean his maker, but himself."

William Inge, *dean of St. Paul's Cathedral*

"YOU'RE not getting up?" Richard asked, standing over Barbara as she lay in bed, the blanket pulled over her head. "I'm starving." She would be starving, too, she thought, if she'd been out half the night, screwing. "Barbara?" She lay motionless, like Rochelle had after Mark left her. She might still be there if her two demanding daughters hadn't forcibly pulled her out of bed. Not out of concern for their mother, of course, but for themselves. Their nannies had quit. "Barbara? I'd like breakfast. I want you to get up."

She forced herself to leave the comfort and security of her bed, stand, and walk to the bathroom. She closed her eyes, brushed her teeth, washed her face, and dragged herself downstairs to make her fucking husband his fucking breakfast. She glanced at him, and it gave her satisfaction to see that he looked even worse than she felt. His eyes resembled raw egg whites, pale and weepy, and his skin hung from his jowls like gray silly putty. He looked at least eighty, and she almost felt sorry for Rhonda, who had to be truly desperate to let this old man mount her or however they did it. It was one thing to marry a young man pumped up with testosterone and a body to go with it and watch him turn to pork and beans, but quite another to take him on in his senescence.

"What in the Hell are you looking at?" Richard growled, laying a piece of omelet on a half bagel. The sound of his labored breathing played like a concerto. He might be on the verge of a heart attack, she thought, hopefully, and the status of a widow was higher than that of a divorcee. It could easily happen on his way to work, she imagined, considering the intense morning traffic, and the number of crazies on the road. "I brought down my gray suit," he said, pointing to where he had laid it over a kitchen chair. "It needs to be dry cleaned."

"It was just cleaned."

"Someone on the Cleveland flight spilled something on it." She eyed the gray suit suspiciously. "What's your schedule today?" he asked, trying to sound friendly.

"I have an appointment with my personal trainer, lunch at the Club, and a meeting at three."

"Did you remember to invite Phyllis to the dinner party?"

"I tried to reach her, but she wasn't home," she lied. "I left her a message." Richard grunted. "What time do you have to be in court?" She could see that the question had caught him off guard. He'd forgotten that he told her he had to work late the night before, preparing court briefs.

"In an hour," he lied. "Do we have any plans for tonight? I should be home early."

"Nothing."

"Why don't you see if the Wolkows can join us for dinner? We haven't seen them for a long time." He didn't even like the Wolkows, she thought, but they were usually available, and he did not want to be alone with her. He got up from the table and clumsily touched her shoulder. "See you tonight," he said.

She listened to the garage door open and close and imagined Richard backing out of the driveway, turning down Elm and onto 294. On 294—if she had her way—he would cut off a driver high on drugs. The pothead, furious with Richard, would pull along side, honk, and when Richard looked up, would give him the finger. Richard, not to be outdone, would return the finger. That's when the pothead would take a gun from his glove compartment and shoot Richard in the head, killing him instantly. Being the widow of a man shot to death on the interstate was far more interesting and respectable than being a divorcée, a woman dumped by her husband for a trophy wife, she decided.

She went through the pockets of Richard's suit jacket. She found a few coins in one pocket and a folded piece of paper in the other. She opened it, read it, and reached for the phone.

"Rochelle?" There was mind-numbing screaming in the background. "Can you hear me?"

"Barely. Emily! I'm on the phone. Be quiet! Barbara, you OK?"

"No. I just found the charge receipt for Richard's hotel room in Cleveland."

"And?"

"He stayed at the Four Seasons to the tune of $450."

"For one night?"

"For one night, and this from the guy who likes to say you can't get any bigger bang for your buck in a $400 hotel room than you can in one for $150."

"I guess that depends on who you're banging—or is it *whom?*" They had a short laugh. Very short. "What are you going to do?"

"I don't know."

"Remember, honey before vinegar. You can use the vinegar later, if you have to."

* * *

For the first twenty years of their marriage, Barbara and Richard had met downtown, once a month, for lunch. For some unknown reason the tradition had ended years earlier, and obviously neither one of them felt it needed to be reinstated. But now . . . maybe Rochelle was right, Barbara thought, about using honey before the vinegar. She called Richard's office to check his noontime schedule. His secretary said he had no lunch plans on the calendar. "Then I think I'll take him to lunch," she said, "but please don't tell him. I want it to be a surprise."

She exited the downtown parking garage feeling confident and upbeat. She'd had a body massage and a facial in the morning and was wearing a stunning new suit that had won her a few appreciative glances on her way to Richard's office. But when she got there, he was gone.

"I'm sorry," his secretary said. "He's already left for lunch, and you told me not to tell him you were coming."

"It's not your fault. Did he say where he was going?"

"No, but he's got a one o'clock appointment so he wouldn't have gone very far."

Barbara walked the block to Murphy's Pub, a favorite of Richard's. She pushed to the head of the line and made a fast sweep of the restaurant. She saw him—at a table towards the back of the room—with Rhonda, their arms and hands entwined like snakes, she thought. They were laughing. She couldn't remember the last time she and Richard had laughed together. She wasn't sure they ever had . . .maybe in the company of others, but just the two of them? Alone?

Richard and Rhonda kissed, and she felt her breakfast backing up on her. She hurried to the bathroom and locked herself inside one of the stalls. She swallowed and swallowed hard, trying to keep down the rising vomit. The bathroom door opened. High heels clicked against the tile floor. Donald Pliner shoes stopped at her door, the same style she had considered buying at Niemann Marcus but hadn't. Too pricey, even on sale, she thought. The wearer of the Donald Pliner shoes pulled on her door.

"Taken," she said.

"Sorry."

The door to the stall on her right opened, closed, and locked. The Donald Pliner woman set a $400 Coach bag down on the bathroom floor, a floor undoubtedly laced with urine drippings and feces, she thought. Vomit threatened to rise again. She swallowed and concentrated on the sounds and sights in the stall next to her: zipping, followed by pants legs dropping to the floor; the sound of urine, softly splashing, which meant that the woman was sitting on the toilet seat, not standing. If she had been standing and peeing, falling urine would have produced a louder splash, she deducted. Furthermore, she was probably sitting on an unprotected toilet seat. Murphy's did not provide toilet seat covers, and she hadn't heard toilet paper coming off the roll. Yes, there was an outside chance that the woman had placed a Kleenex from her pants pocket or purse on the seat, but that seemed highly unlikely. Someone who would put her purse on a public bathroom floor was not the kind of person who would be concerned about sitting on a dirty toilet seat!

The urine flow stopped. Toilet paper turned on the roll. The woman stood, pulled up her pants, and zipped them. Now would she flush with her shoe, use paper on the handle, or flush with her bare hand? The door unlocked, and the woman walked towards the sinks.

The door unlocked and the woman walked toward the sinks . . . without bothering to flush!

Barbara peered through the gap between the door and sidewall and watched. Rhonda Berger—without first washing her hands—licked her fingertips, smoothed her eyebrows, licked her fingertips again and ran them through her hair. Rhonda then added cheek gloss and lipstick, and without protecting her hands from the bacteria on the door handle, let herself out.

Before leaving the restaurant, Barbara took one last look at the loving couple. Richard was sucking on Rhonda's urine-tipped fingers.

She dialed 1-800-GET-HELP.

"Get Help!" a gravelly voice answered.

"J.W., please."

"This is J.W."

"I have a job for you."

CHAPTER SEVENTEEN

Mary and the Mugger

*"If Cleopatra's nose had been shorter, the face of the world
would have changed."*

Pascal

B Y the time Mary left the El at Damen Avenue, it was dark.
Somewhere between Hoyne and Concord Streets, a man jumped
out of a building recess and grabbed her purse strap. She held fast,
and a tug of war was on. He pulled. She pulled back.

"I have a gun," he warned. "Let go or else." She didn't believe him,
not until he hit her on her nose with the gun butt. She fell to the
ground, unconscious. He took her purse and yanked her lucky lodestone off her neck before disappearing down the street. An elderly
couple found her.

"My goodness, John" Eleanor said. "She's covered with blood.
We have to help her." Mary was coming to. The old man took her
right arm, the old woman her left, but they were too frail to lift her.

"I'm fine," Mary said. "I can do this alone."

"You're not fine. Is she John?"

"Certainly not."

The three struggled against each other until Mary was upright.

"You live near here?" Eleanor asked.

"Just around the corner."

"We'll walk you there," John said.

They walked together, slowly, Mary carrying the weight of
Eleanor and John.

"It could've been us," Eleanor said, pushing a mothball scented handkerchief at Mary, who had been using her sleeve to mop up the flow of blood from her nose. "And it would've been us if I hadn't ordered dessert. Weren't we lucky?"

"It's all in the timing," John agreed. "I keep telling the police they need to add foot cops to the neighborhood, but no one listens to me. Not anymore. They used to when I was somebody."

"Let's not forget to tell Floyd next time we're there how two pieces of tiramisu saved our lives. Three minutes earlier, and it would've been us. Do you think he could use this for an ad?"

"My wife is crazy about tiramisu," John explained.

"And *you* didn't even *want d*essert," she accused.

Mary stopped. "This is where I live. I can manage from here. Thanks for your help."

"We'll wait," Eleanor insisted. "To make sure you get in all right."

Mary climbed the stairs, reached for her purse, which she didn't have, and rang the bell. After some minutes, Sylvia flung open the door and pulled Mary into her arms, sincerely distraught.

"My God! What happened to you?"

"It could've been worse," Eleanor yelled up at Sylvia. "It could've been us. We would never have survived."

"Who are they?" Sylvia asked.

"They found me and helped me home."

The couple continued to stand on the sidewalk, looking up at them.

"Do you think they want money?" Sylvia asked.

"Don't worry about the handkerchief," Eleanor yelled, just before Sylvia closed the door.

"What happened?"

"I was mugged on the way home." Mary examined herself in the hall mirror. "I think my nose is broken. I may need surgery."

Sylvia immediately thought of Morris' favorite quotation—"If Cleopatra's nose had been shorter, the face of the world would be different"—and her concern for Mary evaporated. She didn't want her world to be different. It wasn't the life she would have chosen for herself, but it had been hers for too many years now to change it into something else. "It's just banged up a bit. A little ice, and it'll be as good as new."

"It was never good; not even when it was new." Sylvia followed Mary into the kitchen. "Weren't you in the middle of something?" Mary asked, hoping to get rid of her mother. "A TV program?" She took a white towel out of a kitchen drawer, recently labeled in 20-point Lucinda Bright typeface.

"No! Not a white one! I'll never get the blood out!"

Mary exchanged the white towel for an orange one, filled it with ice, and laid it gently against her nose while Sylvia continued to hover.

"I'm sure it's broken," Mary repeated, her smile hidden behind the kitchen towel.

Scissors or knives, it didn't matter, Sylvia thought. Plastic surgeons were like hair stylists. Once they had Mary on the operating table, they'd never be satisfied with just resetting her nose. They'd cut . . . and style . . . until they created something very different, different enough to attract a different kind of man, a man who wasn't a wuss, a man worth her dying for. "You're always so impatient. Give it a day or two."

"My God!" Mary shouted. "My credit cards! And my keys! The mugger has the keys to the house and our address!"

After she cancelled her credit cards, she called Tony the locksmith. An hour later, the locks had been changed. "He'll probably show up here later tonight. That's what they do, but once he sees you've changed the locks, he'll be gone—fast, too fast for you to have time to call the police," Tony warned them.

* * **

Some people, when they can't sleep, count sheep jumping over fences. When Sylvia couldn't sleep, she would line up her betrayers and march them in front of her, one by one, and review a lifetime of perceived injustices. First in line came her father, a man whose lack of business sense robbed her of a college education and the life of a scientist. Next came her two sisters, wearing caps and gowns, their college degrees and college-educated husbands in hand, all of it stained with blood— hers. Fourth in line came Morris, who had betrayed her with another woman and humiliated her before the world. Last but not least came Mary, who may not have understood the full significance of "Aunt Estelle" but was, nevertheless, an accomplice to her father's betrayal.

"Who's that woman?" Sylvia had asked at Morris' funeral. The unknown woman, her face hidden under a large floppy hat, wept loudly, louder than anyone else, louder than Morris' brother and certainly louder than Sylvia.

"That's Aunt Estelle," Mary said.

They tried to stop her, but she moved too fast, and using her copy of the *Newly Revised Union Prayer Book*, she beat "Aunt Estelle" repeatedly on her head. Aunt Estelle fled the Temple, and when the Rabbi said, "May he rest in peace," she prayed: "May he rot in Hell."

Sylvia looked at her watch. It was barely three in the morning. If she had bought the Ultra Heart and Sound Soother, she might be sleeping now, she thought. So what if it cost $100? Even if she only lived for another six months that came out to sixty cents a day, which was a cheap price to pay for a good night's sleep, and if it didn't work, she had up to sixty days to return it with a full money-back guarantee. That was what was great about America, she thought. Yes, of course, it went without saying that the right to vote and the right to free speech and the right to practice your own religion were also great, but the right to return a purchase and get 100% refund was up there with all those other rights.

She heard a noise at the front of the house and got out of bed. Mary was already in the hall.

"Did you hear something?" she asked.

"Shh!"

It was the sound of metal scraping against metal. Mary stealthily walked towards the foyer. Sylvia followed, a half dozen steps behind. Through the lace door curtain, they could see a figure bending toward the door, trying to unlock it. After some minutes, the figure disappeared.

"Tony was right," Sylvia whispered. "He's gone."

Sylvia made a move towards the phone, but Mary stopped her, digging her nails into Sylvia's fleshy upper arm. Nail Therapy, she called it.

"Don't move! I hear him at the back of the house."

Mary walked stealthily towards the kitchen. The light from the back of the neighbor's house illuminated the shadow of a man at the back door. When the key didn't work, he disappeared.

"Let's call the police," Sylvia said.

"Shuh!"

The upper rung of the double-hung kitchen window dropped, and a leg came over the top. When the second leg appeared, Mary rushed into the kitchen, grabbed an eight inch knife from the counter butcher block and plunged it deep into the man's calf. He screamed and fell backwards to the ground below—but not before Mary spotted the lodestone around his neck.

Simon was right about that, she thought. This supposed good luck piece was downright lethal. Fortunately, it wasn't hers anymore!

"Now we can call the police," she said, picking up the phone.

CHAPTER EIGHTEEN

Mary and Simon

"Love is a season pass on the shuttle between heaven and hell."

Donald Dickerson

MARY was hanging up her jacket in the front closet when she heard Sylvia approach. She moved quickly to the hall mirror and examined her nose.

"Quit putchking with it!" Sylvia said. "It's almost back to normal." Mary gently pushed up the tip of her nose, "trying it on," so to speak, for Sylvia's benefit. "Peh! You'd drown in the first rain with a nose like that. Dinner's ready."

Sylvia headed towards the kitchen and Mary followed.

"I'll keep you company while you eat, but I've got a dinner date."

"Now you tell me? After I made your favorite? A pot roast."

"I told you I was going out," she lied. "You must've forgotten."

"Who's your date with?"

"A doctor I met in the elevator."

"Does the doctor have a name?"

"Simon."

"Simon what?"

"Simon Simon."

"Like in 'The Donald'?"

"Something like that."

"That's ridiculous."

"I agree."

"Has he seen you?" Sylvia asked. "I mean since the mugging?" She cut into the brisket. Mary's silence was Sylvia's answer. "Maybe you should postpone the date until you're 100%."

"A minute ago you said it's almost back to *normal*. Now it's so bad I should cancel a date?"

"What's normal between you and me isn't the same as what's normal between you and some doctor on your first date." Mary's anxiety level rose. "Besides, what's one more week in the lives of the young?" Sylvia could see Mary was wavering. It wouldn't take much more, she thought. "And he'll be much more anxious to see you if you put him off for a week. Or two. That's what Chelsea did on *Guiding Light*, and it worked like a charm for her. They got engaged." Sylvia wrinkled her brow. "What's that funny sound?"

"I don't hear anything."

Sylvia closed her eyes. "Ah hah! It's air, struggling to get through your swollen nasal passages. Hardly the best background music for a dinner date."

Mary left the kitchen, and in the privacy of her bedroom called Simon on her cell. She explained that she'd been mugged earlier in the week and had to cancel their date.

"Did you go to work?" he asked. She admitted she had. "Then you're well enough to keep our date."

"No, I can't," she insisted.

"Can't or won't?" Before she could answer, he'd hung up.

Sylvia stood in the doorway.

"Sounds like he didn't even bother to give you a rain check. Not a man worth giving even an hour of your time. Let's eat."

Mary sat in the kitchen with Sylvia, half listening to her description of Elaine at Macy's and the saleswoman at The Sharper Image who wanted to have lunch with her sometime.

"What were you doing there?" she asked.

"Buying Paul a gift for his fortieth birthday. They're giving him a party next week, and we're invited."

"I'm not going."

"Of course you are. It's family, and there's so few of us left." Mary stabbed holes in the now cold piece of brisket on her plate. "Elaine looks dreadful," she added. Mary smiled. "And she and Paul are having problems."

Mary's face lit up. "Really?"

"Vera said Paul ignores her. It might be fun to see it close-up."

"Might be."

The doorbell rang. Mary went to answer it. Simon stood on the porch, trying to see in through the lace curtain.

"Who is it?" Sylvia called from the kitchen.

Mary opened the door. "What are you doing here?"

"Keeping our date. I'm not taking no for an answer." He stared at her nose and grimaced.

"Who's he?" Sylvia asked, joining them in the foyer.

Simon reached for Sylvia's hand. "I'm Simon, and you must be Mrs. Mazol."

Sylvia did not like the look or the smell of Simon. He was older and more substantial than the others, she thought. Getting rid of him, she guessed, would not be easy. "I thought you cancelled your date," she said to Mary.

"She did, but I'm keeping it." Simon answered.

"Mary's already eaten," Sylvia rebutted.

"I haven't touched a thing," Mary corrected.

"But *I'm* still eating, and I don't eat alone."

"I'll be more than happy to keep you company while Mary changes her clothes. Eating alone is no fun."

"It's not a matter of fun," Sylvia answered. "It's a matter of life and death."

* * *

Simon sat across from Mary at the Wicker Park Café and positioned his wine glass to block his view of Mary's probably broken nose. As she moved, so moved his glass.

"I plunged the knife into his leg and felt the blade tear through fabric, then skin, and finally muscle."

Remembering the thrill of the kill had cast an attractive glow around her, Simon thought. "Obviously, the experience hasn't upset you too much."

"Upset? On the contrary, it was an incredible sensation. I had to go down to the police station later to identify him. And guess what?"

"I can't."

"He was wearing my good luck piece around his neck."

"The *nose*stone?" Mary froze. "I'm sorry," Simon said.

"OK, let's talk about it."

"OK, have you seen someone?" She shook her head, no. "It might be broken, you know."

"Find me a surgeon who'll reset the bone without making cosmetic changes, and I'll consider it."

Simon scratched his palms against the table edge. He was itching to get Mary on the operating table and into bed, he thought, though not necessarily in that order.

"Most surgeons would respect your wishes, but it's not what I would recommend."

"Things like noses shouldn't matter."

"They shouldn't, but they do. If they didn't, I wouldn't be as popular as I am."

"What I mean is that noses don't matter to *my* kind of people; people who see below the surface."

"Most people can't see beyond the tips of their own noses, let alone yours. Anyway, it's not about you. It's about the others, the illusions people have about themselves. When they look at you, they want to see their fantasies looking back at them."

"I'm not here on earth to fulfill a stranger's fantasy."

"What about your own?"

"My fantasies are my own business."

He held up his hands in defense. "Fair enough! I shouldn't be pushing my agenda on you, but what about breathing? Most people like to breathe, and you sound like an asthmatic whale."

The waiter brought their dinners, and Simon wondered how Mary would describe her chicken Kiev. Jane and her phony gourmand friends had made every meal an epicurean competition. They would identify—or pretend they could identify—the herbs and spices in whatever they were eating and go on to describe the dish as subtle or denatured, complex or tangy. One of their favorite lines was "This reminds me of .." which would lead them to a personal story about some other dish—always of superior quality, always eaten in some exotic place, and always in the company of someone rich or famous or both. Jane's friends had apparently never eaten in a dive, a diner, or a dump.

At the beginning of their marriage he thought there was something wrong with his gastric memory and taste buds since he had never experienced food in the same exquisite way that Jane and her friends did. After almost fifty years of eating, he could remember only two dinners: one on a Nile boat tour the first night of Passover, surrounded by German-speaking tourists, and another in a restaurant in Marrakech, when a fifty foot snake wrapped itself around his leg, and the owner refused to collect his viper until he paid him off. Even then he couldn't remember what he ate; only the events. His father, the most uncomplicated and beautiful man in the world, had the right idea. He ended every meal saying, "*That* was the best meal I've ever had." His philosophy was that the best meal is the one you're currently eating.

Mary snapped her fingers at Simon.

"Yoo hoo. You there?" she asked.

"Yes, sorry. How's your dinner?"

"Excellent. I'm glad we came here."

"That's it? Excellent?"

"Excellent isn't good enough?"

One night at Charlie Trotter's, the foodies had argued for ten minutes about an unidentifiable spice in the bouillabaisse. Someone said it was sumac. Someone else said it was Hyssop from Peloponnesia. When he tired of their nonsense, he marched into the kitchen. "What's the mystery spice in the Bouillabaisse?" he asked the chef. "Curry." He returned to the table. "Curry," he told them. Jane didn't talk to him for days.

"You promised to tell me when and why you dropped the name David," Mary said.

"First, more wine." He refilled their glasses. "It was my bar mitzvah. The Torah had been returned to the ark and it was time to give my speech, which had been written weeks in advance and approved by the rabbi. My notes were on the lectern, and for the first time that morning I was relaxed enough to look up and into the faces of the congregants. I saw my parents and grandparents, looking very proud. Even my sister seemed impressed, and she hadn't talked to me for years. Then I saw my aunts and uncles, and their children, including all of my cousins named David. These Davids had made my child-hood a living hell—because I was short and chubby, and they were lean and mean. I decided then and there not to give my planned speech, the one approved by the rabbi. I had something more impor-tant to say to those gathered—about a parent's responsibility towards other people's children as well as their own, a kind of *It takes a Village* treatise, only decades before Hillary."

Mary laughed, and Simon felt pleased with himself.

"When I tore up my notes, I saw my parents slump forward in their pew. That didn't stop me. 'Because I am a man today,' I began, 'I'm making my first adult decision. I'm changing my name from David to . . .' I stopped. I didn't know what name to take. I hadn't thought that far ahead, but the congregants were waiting. The first name that came into my mind was my last name. 'My first name is now Simon,' I announced, so don't call me David anymore. If you do, I won't answer you.'

"I had them in the palm of my hands, so I continued. 'Do you want to know why I hate the name David? Because of the three Davids sitting in front of me today.' I pointed at them, and in a voice reminiscent of Charlton Heston at Mt. Sinai, I told those gathered that when I was a child, these Davids had bullied me because I didn't look like them, and they all looked like each other. 'Who's to blame?' I yelled from my pulpit. 'Their parents, that's who,' I said, answering my own question. 'They knew what was happening, and they didn't stop them.'

"That's when my aunts and uncles with their sons named David and their other children got up to leave. I had to talk and talk fast. 'The scars I've suffered will never go away. That's why in addition to changing my name, I am liquidating all my gifts not already in cash and sending everything to the Tennenbaum Home for Abused Children in Jerusalem.'

"That brought a round of laughter and applause. Encouraged, I continued. 'I want to thank everyone who helped me get through my bar mitzvah. My parents, who have always loved me and tried to understand me, though I know it wasn't easy.' My father actually blushed, and my mother reached for a handkerchief. 'I also want to thank my sister who's been kinder to me than she realizes by basically just ignoring me most of my life. I'd also like to thank my tutor, Benjamin Glass, but I can't because he missed half our scheduled lessons on account of he couldn't get out of bed, and when he did show up, he was usually stoned out of his mind.' Benjamin fled the scene. 'And, lastly, I want to thank the rabbi, whom I have no feelings about one way or the other.' Then I thanked them all for coming and invited them to lunch."

"You made this up," Mary accused. "You couldn't remember it the way you do, something that happened thirty or more years ago."

"It was taped, and no one thought to turn off the recorder. For the next few years on the anniversary of my bar mitzvah, I would play it back, thrilling to it like any powerless pubescent would." Simon refilled their wine glasses. "Now it's your turn. I want to know why your life has been unlucky."

"Because I never had what you had at thirteen . . . the courage to stand up to all the authority figures in my life and wave my thumb at them. You don't get that kind of courage unless you feel loved and supported, no matter what. That's why you were lucky, and I wasn't."

"That's it?"

"As Hillel said, 'All the rest is commentary.'"

"And you think you're going to find your good luck in a charm?"

"No. Collecting amulets is just something to do, like some people collect frogs. Or owls."

"David? David Simon! Is that you?" A beautiful and expensively dressed woman rested one French-manicured hand on Simon's shoulder. "It *is* you." She was exactly the kind of woman who made Mary feel fat and frumpy. "You don't remember me, do you!" Whoever she was, Simon thought, she and Jane were cut from the same cloth, and he wasn't going down that road again. "Laura. Laura Friedman." A light flickered and he smiled up at her, not because he was interested but because she remembered him. Being remembered was still important to him. He had been invisible for too many years. "But I forgive you. It's been a very long time."

He thought back to the day they had met. She was twenty years old, wearing beaded moccasins and a short Indian suede dress that clung to her full body. Her hair was twisted into one long, thick braid, pierced through with a feather, and strapped to her calf was a knife. Every finger of both hands was decorated with a silver ring, all bought, she later told him, at the local Salvation Army. That Laura was real and more interesting than this cardboard model hovering over him now.

"Laura, I'm sorry. I didn't recognize you." He started to get up, but she pushed him back down.

"No need to get up. Someone is waiting for me at another table." She pointed to the far side of the room.

"Laura, I'd like you to meet a friend of mine. Mary Mazol." Laura barely looked at Mary, having already eliminated her as a serious contender. She removed a business card from her purse and dropped it on the table. It fell halfway between Mary's butter dish and Simon's water glass.

"Here's my new address and phone number. I just moved back to Chicago after twenty years in Cleveland. It would be nice to get together and catch up on old times." She laughed. "Like the first time you effed." She turned to Mary. "Nice to meet you, Miss *Schnozel,*" she said, before walking away.

"She did that on purpose!" Mary said, red with anger.

"Probably."

"Was she the one, the first woman you effed?"

Simon swallowed his smile. It wasn't often that two beautiful women fought over him. "No, she wasn't." Girls like Laura hadn't been interested in boys like him. Not back then anyway. He took Mary's hands in his and kissed them. "So here's the deal. I don't want to hear about your first time or any subsequent time for that matter, and I'm not going to tell you about mine. OK?" He signaled the waiter for the check. "I'd like you to come back to my apartment with me."

"I can't."

"Can't or won't?" She didn't answer. "Why not?"

"My mother would know."

"Know what? That her thirty-something year old daughter effs?" He handed the waiter his charge card. "What's your real reason?" Simon's old insecurities rose to the surface. "You don't like me."

"I like you."

"You don't like me enough."

"I like you enough."

"Maybe you think I'm too old for you."

"How old are you?"

"Forty-eight."

The waiter returned with the charge slip. While he signed it, he saw Mary slip Laura's business card into her purse. He felt thinner.

"Come home with me," he repeated. "Please. I want to make love to you, and I'm not going to ask a third time."

"You won't have to. The answer is yes."

CHAPTER NINETEEN

Sylvia and Mary

"The jealous are troublesome to others, but a torment to themselves."
William Penn

"I'LL only be a minute," Mary said, her hand still clinging to the door handle.

"I'll be here," Simon promised. "Take your time."

It had been the kind of night that made insecure men like Simon feel confident and indifferent women like Mary possessive. He turned off the car engine and watched her walk seductively up the walk. How many years ago was it that Laura had come to his house to pick him up? More than twenty-five. His mother had arranged it with Laura's mother because his mother was tired of seeing him at home every night. But why had Laura and her mother gone along with it, he'd wondered, as he got into the shiny red BMW parked at the curb.

"Why? Because I get this car two nights a week for the rest of the summer," Laura explained.

"OK, that's why *you* did it, but why your mother?"

"My parents are upset with my grades, and they don't like the pot-smoking, bad-smelling, foul-mouthed, unemployed people I'm hanging out with," she explained. "They were hoping you'd be a good influence on me; after all, you're going to medical school, and anyone who can do that can obviously deal with . . ." She'd made a face. ". . . can deal with structure."

"Structure is bad?" he'd asked.

"It's the worst! Structure kills spontaneity and creativity so don't tell anyone at the party tonight that you're in medical school 'cause if people find out, it would ruin my reputation." She spit, then, into the summer night.

"But everything good in life requires some kind of structure," he argued.

"Fucking doesn't. Fucking is spontaneous so I'm going to fuck my way through life."

He tried to sound cool. "Can I volunteer myself for tonight's spontaneity?" he asked, but she must have seen virgin written all over him.

"You need someone with patience," she said, letting him down, easy. "I'll introduce you to Julia. She works in Customer Service at Neiman Marcus. Anyone who can do that for three years has more patience than Moses."

"Job," he'd corrected.

"What-ever!"

After he and Julia had finished their joints, she waved at him to follow her into the bedroom. In retrospect, he thought he had performed admirably, crediting his know-how to the dozens of porno flicks he'd watched at the fraternity house over the years. His favorites had been *Debbie Does Dallas*, *Long John and his Ding Dong*, the *Candy Strippers*, and the *Raunchy Real Estate Lady*.

It has been a simple matter of putting theory into practice. What he hadn't anticipated, though, was the prose and poetry he would discharge in the throes of passion: that when he sucked on Julia's breasts, he'd gush Donne couplets . . . and that lines from *Lady Chatterley's Lover* would flow when he spread her legs . . . or that when he mounted her, he would ride to the beat of Kipling's *Gunga Din*.

Later, when he asked if he could see her again, she'd said yes, but on one condition. He could never, not ever, say one word to her when they were doing it. She heard enough words every day to last a normal person a year, and those, at least, made sense, while his were total gibberish.

But then one evening in late July when he went to Julia's apartment, she was gone. "Moved to San Francisco," her roommate said. "They drove off to California this morning in a red BMW convertible to join a commune. Can you imagine? A BMW at a commune?" "They?" "She and Laura." There'd been no good-byes. No letter, no note, not even a stinking phone call, he remembered. He was convinced that by the time Julia crossed the Mississippi, she had forgotten his name, though it was possible she never knew it.

* * *

Sylvia was knocking on Mary's bedroom door when Mary entered the house. She came down the hallway quietly, and tapped Sylvia on the shoulder. Sylvia screamed.

"What's wrong with you? It's only me."

"I thought you were in your room. You're always in your room at 7:00 in the morning." Mary entered her bedroom, and Sylvia followed, close on her heels. "You were with that old man all night, weren't you? I can smell him on you." Mary took off her clothes, and Sylvia inspected her body for teeth marks, whip welts, and chain weals, all visible signs of S & M as portrayed on daytime TV. But Mary's body was unmarked; it was, in fact, glowing with good health.

Mary took a fresh uniform from her closet. "Would you mind leaving?" she asked.

"A stranger sees you butt naked, but your mother . . ."

"Buck naked."

". . . but your mother, the person who brought you into this world is asked to leave?" Sylvia followed Mary into the bathroom. "You could've called, at least." Mary turned on the water faucet and brushed her gums until they bled. "What if I had decided to eat something solid last night, thinking you were in your room, and it had gotten stuck in my throat? I might have choked to death." She followed Mary back to her bedroom. "God only knows what that old man thinks of you now—going to bed with him on your first date. He's probably sitting in some coffee shop telling his friends about the pushover he had."

"No, he's not. He's sitting in his car in front of the house, waiting for me, Sylvia."

"*Sylvia?* Since when do you call your mother Sylvia? What happened to 'Mother'?"

"I haven't called you 'Mother' since I was thirteen."

"That's ridiculous."

"What's ridiculous is that you never noticed. I'll see you tonight."

"But my breakfast!"

"Suck it up!"

After Simon's car pulled away from the curb, Sylvia called Irene. Irene was at a meeting. Barbara's number was busy, and Rochelle couldn't talk. Emily had just thrown a bowlful of sugar on the floor. In desperation, she dialed Vera.

"I can't talk now," Vera said. "I'm on a very *important* call. I'm putting you on hold. I'll get back to you in a minute or two."

"But *this* is important. *I'm* important."

Sylvia paced the short distance her phone cord would allow. While her friends had graduated from decorator to princess to cordless to cell and to other things she didn't understand, she was still anchored to her canary yellow wall phone. She couldn't put people on hold, she thought, and she couldn't tell who was calling until she answered the phone. Maybe it was time for a change.

"Vera!" she shouted into the mouthpiece. "That's not a minute or two!" She jiggled the receiver, disconnecting herself. She redialed.

"Hello," Vera said.

"It's Sylvia."

"I thought I put you on hold."

"You did, but we were cut off."

"I'm putting you back on hold. If we get disconnected again, *I'll* call *you* back. Don't call me."

"I may not be here when you call."

"Where would you go?"

Sylvia hung up and retrieved Molly's business card from her purse. "It's Sylvia," she said. "The woman who makes you laugh."

Molly laughed. "Nice hearing from you. How's everything?"

"Not so good. Could you meet me for lunch?"

"Sure, but I only get a half hour so how's about we meet at the store and eat in the food court?"

"Sure. By the way, what kind of service do you need for a cordless phone?"

CHAPTER TWENTY

Sylvia and Molly

"Happiness is a woman."

Frederich W. Nietzsche

WHEN Sylvia arrived at The Sharper Image, Molly was working with a customer. She signaled Sylvia. Ten minutes. Sylvia headed to the display of TruthSeekers. All the units were out of their boxes. She repacked them and was arranging them in an attractive display when Rio, the store manager, stepped onto the floor.

It was true, he thought, that he rarely left his office, but was it possible he didn't know who was on staff? He approached Sylvia.

"Excuse me, do you work here?" he asked.

"If I worked here, this place wouldn't look like this."

"I take it you don't think much of the management."

"What management? The inventory is a mess. The displays are dirty, and most of the employees think all they have to do for a paycheck is show up."

She wasn't wrong, he thought, but then he hadn't asked for this job. His parents had used their connections to get it for him when he dropped out of the MBA program, but one good thing had come of it. He still didn't know what he wanted to do, but he sure as hell knew what he didn't want and that was to manage people.

"When there are no customers, staff should be cleaning, replenishing inventory, and reorganizing merchandise. There's no excuse for down-time in retail."

That was a great line, he thought. It must've come from the turn of the last century. No one talked or thought like that anymore.

"I have to go now," Sylvia said. "My friend is waiting for me. If you still need help in a half hour, ask for Molly. She's the only one doing any work around here."

Sylvia and Molly took the down escalator.

"I saw you talking to Rio," Molly said.

"Who's Rio?"

"The store manager. What did he want with you?"

"I didn't know he was the manager. He acted like he was a customer."

They bought their lunches, and Sylvia led the way to a table next to a wall. She removed a laminated Heimlich poster from her bag, unrolled it, and taped it to the wall.

"What's that, Syl?"

Sylvia blushed. No one had ever called her "Syl" before, and for a very good reason. "Syl" conjured up images of sylph-like creatures like Audrey Hepburn and Mia Farrow, women she had nothing in common with. "These are instructions for the Heimlich maneuver. I told you, didn't I, that I have this swallowing disorder?" Molly nodded. "Most people think I'm crazy, but the truth is, I never know when it's going to happen."

"It's wise to err on the side of caution," Molly said. "Caution is the oldest child of wisdom." She glanced at the instructions "Is it hard to do?"

"No, easy."

"Can you show me how?"

"Sure." They got up. "First, you stand behind me and wrap your arms tight under my arms." She felt Molly's warm and competent arms around her and sighed. "Now press your thumbs into my rib cage and pull hard towards my belly button. You do that three times."

"Like this?" Molly asked, whispering in Sylvia's ear, tickling her ear drum. "One, two, three," Molly counted, squeezing Sylvia against her.

"That's all there is to it," Sylvia murmured, her face flushed with pleasure. "What kind of perfume is that you're wearing? It's very nice."

CHAPTER TWENTY-ONE

Rochelle and Amy

*"Grown-ups never understand anything for themselves, and it is
tiresome for children to be always and forever explaining things to them."*

Saint-Exupéry

THE Butterfly flew back and forth over Rochelle's head as she lay
in bed half-awake.

"All right, all right," she said, opening her eyes. "And, I don't have
to tell you, do I, that this is the first day of my sixty-third year?" She
got out of bed. "And I'm making you a promise, here and now, that it's
also going to be the first day of a new life, one that's about me. I will
not die with regrets." She headed to the bathroom. "And in honor of
my birthday, I am going to linger this morning over a cup of coffee,
read the entire art section of the *New York Times*, make a seven-layer
rum torte for dessert tonight, and finish B.J. Moss' painting." She
washed, brushed her teeth, and added a bit of makeup before starting
downstairs, dressed in only her shorty pajamas. The Butterfly flew
ahead of her.

"The children will remember me in their fashion. Adam will be
the first to call. 'Happy *bird*-day,' he'll say, like he did when he was
a toddler. Then he'll tell me that he'd hoped to have dinner with me
tonight, but that this or that important thing came up at the last
minute. Then Bette or Amy will call, suggesting an alternate date to
celebrate my birthday, a time when 'the four of us can all get together.'
If they pick a date I've already made plans for, they'll expect me to
cancel whatever because they don't think that what I do adds up
to much of anything.

"And whatever gifts they buy me—not that I need or want any-thing—will come with an apology about how impossible it is to buy for me because I already have one of everything. Mark calls it a cop-out. I should tell them what Irene tells her children when they ask what she'd like. 'I'd like you to be inconvenienced,' but they never are, she says."

The Butterfly was back, flying now up the stairs.

"Hey, Butterfly, where are you going? You don't want fresh sugar water?"

A man was in the kitchen, standing in front of the stove, his back toward Rochelle, dressed in only his BVDs. Rochelle grabbed a kitchen chair and rammed the legs into his back, leaving four angry-red pockmarks in his flesh. He spun around, a mix of surprise and pain on his face. She came at him again. This time he yanked the chair from her and held it in front of himself for protection.

"Hey, it's OK. I'm a friend of Adam's. We were fraternity brothers together at Illinois, and like he told me it was OK to sleep here last night. Like he said he was going to call and tell you." Her face said it all. "Like maybe you were already sleeping when he called? He gave me the key to the house and told me which bedroom to take."

His eyes dropped from her face to her lightly clad body, and she saw the boner rise in his underpants.

"Get out of here!" she ordered. "Right now!"

"Hey, like I can see how you'd be upset and all, and I don't blame you for that, but like I've got this muy im-por-tan-té interview this morning for a muy im-por-tan-té job with a muy im-por-tan-té ad agency, and if I don't get my brecky, I'm not going to make a good impression."

They were insane, she thought, this whole generation of self-absorbed adult children, and she and all her generation were respon-sible. "I said, I want you out of here. Now!"

The uninvited guest turned off the gas under his eggs.

"But my eggs are ready and soz the jav-ah. You should taste my coffee. I have this special little trick that makes it incredible." He stared at her breasts. Rochelle crossed her arms in front of her chest. "I can remember the first time I saw you. It was my sophomore year of college, and you and your husband were at the frat house. You looked like a movie star. You're still terrific looking, you know?"

He made a move towards her.

"If you don't get out of here right now, I'm calling 9-1-1."

"Hey, where's your sense of humor? Like if this happened to *my* mom, she'd be real cool about it. Maybe even laughing."

Rochelle picked up the phone, and her uninvited guest began moving towards the open doorway. He grazed her body as he passed. She dialed Homes and Gardens Realty and got a recording, asking her to leave a message.

"Call Rochelle Fox at 232-4456. I want to put my house on the market."

"I'm moving," she promised the Butterfly, who had returned to the kitchen. "I'm going to buy a place in the South Loop, near the Art Institute, and go back to school full time. Yes, I am, and nothing and no one is going to stop me!"

She heard Adam's friend coming down the stairs and hurried to the foyer closet for a coat.

"Hey, I'm really sorry about what happened," he said, as Rochelle opened the front door. "And like I know how upset Adam's going to be when he hears about it." He was wearing a pair of khaki pants, a light blue Oxford button-down shirt, and a lightweight sports jacket. She guessed that his dirty underwear and toiletries were in the leather briefcase he was carrying. "So, like thanks for the hospitality even if it's not exactly hospitality since you didn't know I was here," he joked. The Butterfly swooped into the foyer and landed on Rochelle's shoulder. "I've never seen an indoor butterfly before," he said. She opened the door wider and motioned for him to leave. "Say, maybe you can help me. I'm a little nervous about this interview, and I was wondering if you think I look all right."

"The key," she said, shaking a fist at him. "Where's the key?"

"Like I told Adam I'd give it to him at lunch today."

So Adam had time to meet his old fraternity brother for lunch but not his mother on her birthday, she thought. "You either give me that key right now or I'll call the police and have them detain you on your way downtown." He handed her the key.

"And, by the way, that's a very creative valet you have upstairs."

"I don't have a valet."

"In the bedroom I slept in. The easel."

When he turned to leave, she saw the streaks of black and red paint on the back of his khaki jacket. Days of work on B.J.'s painting had been destroyed.

* * *

An hour later Rochelle was still in her kitchen, reading the morning paper and drinking coffee doused with Bailey's Irish cream when she heard the front door open and close. She listened to a pair of clunky shoes strike the quarry tile on their way to the kitchen.

"That's Amy," she said to the Butterfly. "Maybe you should stay out of sight while she's here. She won't understand. No one would, and why should they? I don't understand." The Butterfly flew into the sunroom.

"Happy birthday, Mom, and many, many more." Amy threw her arms around Rochelle. "Don't get up." She set a large box wrapped in Bloomingdale's signature gift wrap on the floor. "I've got time for *one* cup of coffee before teaching." She took a photo mug of herself from a kitchen cabinet and smiled at the image. "This is a really good picture of me, don't you think?" She poured herself coffee and took a sip. "What did you put in it? It tastes different."

"A friend of Adam's made it. I found him in the kitchen this morning, dressed in nothing but his BVDs, making himself breakfast. I didn't know he was in the house. Adam didn't bother to tell me." Amy stared dreamily out the kitchen window. "*I said*, I didn't know he was here. Adam invited him without telling me."

"Doesn't it give you goose bumps knowing that *your* children *and* mine—that's two generations—have played in this yard?"

"What gave *me* goose bumps was coming downstairs this morning and finding a stranger in my kitchen, dressed in nothing but his BVDs and making himself breakfast."

"Who was he?"

"A friend of Adam's. He didn't give me his name."

"It's amazing, Mom. I look out this window, and it's like nothing's changed in twenty-five years."

"I've changed," she answered. "I'm twenty-five years older."

Amy laughed. "You never change, Mom. You're always the same." Of course she'd changed, she thought, but her children didn't want to see it. It was more convenient for them to pretend she was their age. That made her more useful. "How does it feel to be sixty?"

"Sixty-*three*," she corrected, knowing Amy hadn't heard her. She was far away, probably thinking about some research paper she was writing or planned to write. It must be nice, she thought wistfully, to be a grown-up, to dress up and go to conferences and meetings and talk with other grown-ups about grown-up things. Her daughter was enjoying her life, while she was still quarantined to the kiddy pool, like last summer when they barred her from the adult area. And while her contemporaries read and lounged and talked adult talk to each other, she had been forced into the company of thirty- and forty-year-old mothers and their toddlers, obliged to listen to the same conversations she had heard thirty years earlier—about the recipes, the rotten in-laws, and the pediatricians. She had not progressed in life. She was stuck in a time warp, she thought.

"To the best mom in the world," Amy said, lifting her coffee cup in tribute. "You're that rare kind of mother and grandmother who creates stability and continuity in this increasingly rootless society. Continuity is critical to a child's emotional growth and psychological well-being, but that's a dying phenomenon. You have given your grandchildren deep and lasting roots. They think of you as another parent. There's no one like you, and Adam, Bette, and I always say how lucky we are to have you." Familiar, comfortable guilt washed over her. "Thanks for everything you've done. You're the very best!"

If Mark were here, he would be waving a red flag at her. "A boomerang is on its way. You better duck!" He had been right about that, too. Three or more compliments in a row from one of their children were generally followed by some major request. She wondered what it would be this time. Amy controlled her world by walking in through the back door and taking you by surprise. Bette was more direct. She pushed herself in through the front door, blitzkrieg style, and Adam? Well, he came in quietly through a side door, oiling his way with finesse, charm, and good looks.

"You're the mother of all mothers, an anchor in life's storm, a nurturing root in a floating, transient, and rootless society." It was Amy's first year of teaching, and she was quite taken with herself. "The nuclear family," she continued, speaking slowly and deliberately since she did not believe her mother had the acuity to grasp abstract concepts, "is *still* the nuclear family, but it's a different kind of nuclear today. It's not the nucleus that holds a family together but the nuclear that blows a family apart, like in an *explosion.*" Amy paused, reflected, and smiled, obviously pleased with this developing metaphor. She would flag it for future development, Rochelle guessed. "You and you alone have provided stability in our lives." That was a not-so-subtle attack on their father. "So here's to you, Mom; a better mother doesn't exist." Amy raised her coffee mug in her direction and paused again to study her own image. "Do you think I should let my hair grow long again, or do you think short hair makes me look more professional?"

"Yes."

"That's what I think. So what was I talking about? Oh, yes, about the stability you've given your children and grandchildren. You know what most of my friends' parents did when they left home? Sold their homes and moved into condos, or, worse yet, relocated to other cities."

"The first or second time?" She could see that Amy was annoyed with her for having interrupted her heavyweight thoughts with light-weight banter.

"The first or second time *what?*" Amy asked.

"The first or second time the children left home." Amy didn't get it. "Surely you've noticed. Children don't leave home just once anymore. They graduate from college. They leave home, and they come back. Sometimes they come back more than once. Some of my friends' children have returned three times. One of the women at the Club said she and her husband were selling their home and moving to Arizona so their children *couldn't* come home again." Amy should have found her sociological observations of interest, she thought.

"Muh-uh-ther! That's not the point." It was amazing, she thought, how children could stretch a two-syllable word like "mother" into three and sometimes four syllables. "The point *is* that parents have removed themselves from the nuclear family and disrupted the natural flow of family life as we have known it for hundreds of years. They've pulled up roots and resettled in such la-la lands as Santa Fe and Sedona and Scottsdale." She smiled at the unintended alliteration. "Santa Fe, Sedona, and Scottsdale," she repeated, pleased with herself. "And San Diego, Sarasota, and . . ." She grasped for a third "s" to complete the trilogy.

"How about Styx?" Rochelle asked.

"Where did *you* hear about Styx?"

"Did I have to hear about it somewhere?" Betty had an MBA, Amy a doctorate, and Adam a law degree, and all she had, she realized, was sixty-three years of living and an unfinished BFA. She had no credibility with them.

"But thank God for you," Amy continued. "You've stayed. You haven't fled to the South or Southwest, and *my* children, unlike my contemporaries, know their grand*mother*." Another attack on Mark, she thought. Amy gazed beyond the $5,000 playground equipment to the landscaping. "We don't have mature trees in our backyards, just grass and flower beds." She made it sound as though there had been a conspiracy to keep mature trees and established landscaping out of the hands of thirty- and forty-year olds. No one forced them to buy new homes in exurbia, with 6,000 square feet, four bedrooms, five baths, Jacuzzis, no landscaping, and mortgages so high it took two paychecks to stay afloat. "Our roots are here, Mom, metaphorically speaking, of course. Metaphorical means . . ."

"I know what it means," she snapped.

"By the time *our* trees and shrubs have matured, our children will be in college."

Amy's face lit up like a pinball machine. Ideas were again bouncing from one contact point to another. "Another idea for a paper?" she asked.

"How *do* you do that?" Amy lifted the gift box off the floor and handed it to her. "Happy birthday to the greatest Mom in the world. I hope you like your gift, though you have no idea how hard it is buying for someone who already has one of everything."

"I'm sure I'll like it, whatever it is," she answered, pulling off the ribbon and paper. "They always do such a beautiful job of wrapping at Bloomingdale's." Inside the box was a ceramic flower vase, inlaid with variegated stones and dozens of sinister-looking marble eyes, a kind of modern Medusa. She turned the vase slowly, stalling for time, until she could think of something nice to say without sounding too insincere. "Words fail me," was the best she could muster, followed by: "You shouldn't have."

"I'm so glad you like it." Rochelle nodded and forced a smile. "I was sure you would. As soon as I saw it, I said to myself, Mom's gonna love this. She knows good art when she sees it." It was insulting, she thought, to be regarded as totally guileless, especially when you knew how insincere you sounded. The Butterfly returned to the kitchen and alit on the edge of the monster vase. "That's unfucking unbelievable," Amy shouted. "An indoor butterfly!"

"Watch your language!"

"Not *fucking,* Mom. *Un*-fucking. *Un* negates the fucking. How long has he been here?"

"It's a she."

"How do you know?"

"Her nose," she answered, facilely. "The female's nose is always longer than the male's." She waited for Amy to challenge her patently ridiculous lecture on the physiology of butterflies, but she didn't.

Amy checked her watch. "Sorry, Mom, but I've got to go or be late for class." They walked to the foyer together. "Stay as sweet as you are," Amy said, patting the small of her back.

She watched Amy back down the drive, thinking that something was missing. But what was it? Then the car stopped, and Amy got out. Yes, that was it. Amy had forgotten to throw the Boomerang, and if she didn't duck and fast, she would be hit on the head.

"I almost forgot," Amy said, joining her on the steps. "Steve's got this conference in San Francisco next month, and we thought it would be fun to go back there together *sans* Emily—that means 'without'—for just a couple of days. Actually, it'd be a bit more than two days, with travel time going and coming, and another day or two after the meetings. Steve said I should have asked you earlier, in case you had plans." Amy winked at her, implying that the idea that her mother might have plans was nothing but a big joke. "So, what do you think?" She could tell Amy she was selling the house and wouldn't be here; that by next month she'd be living in a condo, downtown Chicago, but she didn't. She didn't say anything. "Then it's settled. I knew we could count on you. By the way, that's the same week I have to work at the cooperative, which is perfect because you're so much better at that artsy fartsy stuff than I am. But we can talk about that later." She hesitated. "And I almost forgot. We're trying to find a date when we can all get together and celebrate your birthday. Bette's supposed to call you later today. Have a great day, Mom!"

* * *

She had just finished baking the seven-layer-rum torte—the only cake in the world worthy of two hours in the kitchen—when the doorbell rang. She looked through the sidelight. A tall, young man stood on the porch. When he saw her, he pressed a business card against the glass. "Ed Drago. Better Homes and Gardens Realty." The minivan parked in the driveway was emblazoned with the company's logo. She opened the door.

"Rochelle Fox?" he asked, extending his hand. "Ed Drago." Before she could invite him in, he was in the foyer . . . the dining room . . . the kitchen . . . and the living room, his eyes sucking up everything in sight, like twin plungers. He started up the stairs.

"No!" she shouted. He stopped. "Don't go up there. I've changed my mind. I'm not selling."

"Do you live here alone?" Ed Drago asked, coming back down the stairs, a look of morbid concern written on his face. Her mother's oncologist had worn that same epression when he'd told her they'd done everything they could. "The market's down now, you know, but I think I can get you—just maybe—about $700,000, though that might be pushing it." She was not impressed with what Ed thought he could get for her. She knew of two other homes in the neighborhood, smaller than hers and not as well maintained, that had recently sold for $800,000. He looked at his watch. "I think there's still time to get your house listed by the end of the day." He waved the contract at her, and she opened the front door. Very wide. She was getting good at this, she thought, struggling not to smile.

"I'd like you to leave now," she said.

"I'm sorry, Rochelle, but is there a problem?"

"Yes. First of all, I don't like strangers calling me by my first name. Secondly, I told you. I'm not selling. Not now. I need more time to think about it." It was self-defeating, she knew, to let Amy's speech about roots and continuity affect her, but what if disappearing into downtown Chicago did damage her grandchildren's psyches?

The phone rang.

"I'm sorry, Mr. Drago. I'm very busy."

"You'll call me as soon as you decide, yes?"

"Yes, of course," she lied, closing the door.

The answering machine kicked in, and she listened to Bette's message: "Mom? I know you're there. Pick up the phone." Bette thought she was always at home; that she had no place to go and nothing to do. Bette believed that when she and Amy asked her to baby sit, they were doing her a favor; otherwise, what would she do with her time? "Hey, Mom, I'm too busy here at work to stay on the phone any longer. I'll call you later. Don't call me. And happy 65th birthday!"

The phone rang again. She read the caller I.D. It was Adam.

"Hi, Mom. Sorry to miss you." Unlike Bette, Adam believed she had a life, though not a very interesting one, and if she didn't answer the phone, she must be out of the house. "I just wanted to say happy . . ." He paused. "*Bird*-day. Get that? Happy *Bird*-day." Another pause. "Still not home, Mom? Hope you're there later when they deliver your birthday present. I'm sure you're gonna love it, even thought it's next-to-impossible to buy something for someone who has everything. As for tonight, I was kind of hoping to be able to take you out for dinner, but now I can't make it so how about one night next week with Bette and Amy? Give me a call at the office when you get in. Oh, and by the way, about Dennis. Mistakes happen. I don't know how I let this one get by me. Too busy, I guess, but still it was unforgivable. It'll never happen again, I promise, although Dennis said it was really funny, like something out of a Woody Allen movie. Got to go now, Mom."

CHAPTER TWENTY-TWO

Mahjongg at Rochelle's

*"The road to wisdom? Well, it's plain and simple to express,
To err ... and err ... and err again, but less and less and less."*

Pier Hein

ROCHELLE stared at her mahjongg tiles and reviewed the first day of her sixty-third year. Although it had started out badly, she had, on her own initiative, made it come out right. A magnificent seven-layer rum torte sat in the refrigerator waiting to be shared with her three best friends, and despite the fact Adam's friend had destroyed her painting, she was well on her way to finishing its replacement, a finer piece, in her opinion, than the original. The children had called back, anxious to set up a day to celebrate her birthday—not that they knew how old she was. Amy thought she was 60. Bette wished her a happy 65th, and Adam, well, she guessed that he didn't have a clue.

"Rochelle, your turn," Barbara said.

"Give me a minute."

"Got any jokes?" Sylvia asked Irene.

"Yeah. I've got a new Abie and Sarah." She cleared her throat. "Abie and Sara are living on a very limited budget, and this one particular month, they have a shortfall. Sara says to Abie. 'There's no food in the refrigerator and no money in the bank. I have no choice but to sell my body on the streets.' Abie answers, 'That's ridiculous, Sara. You're eighty years old. Nobody's going to want your body.' But she doesn't listen to him and leaves their apartment. She returns home four hours later, looking like something the cat dragged in. 'How'd you do?' Abie asks. 'I made twenty-five dollars and twenty-five cents,' she answers. 'Who gave you the twenty-five cents?' he asks. She answers, '*Everyone* gave me twenty-five cents.'"

"That's not funny," Sylvia said.

"It certainly isn't," Rochelle agreed. "You can be sure that while the parents are starving to death in Florida, the children are vacationing at Club Med in Puerto Vallarta."

"You said *what?*" Irene asked. "I don't believe I heard right."

"I said . . ."

"We heard what you said. We're just stunned to hear it coming from you, the great defender of the children. What's going on?" Barbara asked.

"What's going on is that this morning I found a stranger in my kitchen, wearing nothing but his BVDs, making himself breakfast. It seems Adam had given him the key to the house and told him he could sleep there—without telling me."

"Telling?" Irene interrupted. "Whatever happened to ask?"

"I threw him out," Rochelle bragged.

"And took away the key?"

"And took away the key."

"And changed the locks?"

"No, not that yet."

"It's a work still in progress," Sylvia commented, "When you're ready for the full Monty, call Tony at 1-800-New-Lock. He'll be here within the hour."

"Remember that," Barbara advised. "It turns out that Sylvia's advice is quite good." They waited. This was a story that was going somewhere, they thought. "I called her television detective this week, and he's going to do a background check on Rhonda."

"And not a minute too soon," Sylvia said, "considering what just happened to Lucy on *Till the End of Time.*"

"The one with the philandering husband?"

"One and the same. Her husband moved their life savings to an offshore bank somewhere in the Caribbean—Grand Bahama Island, I think—without telling her. The account's in his name only. Lacy may end up living out her days in her son's garage."

"Are you suggesting that Richard would do that to *me*?" The three of them studied their mahjongg cards. "Richard is not that kind of man."

Irene thought otherwise. "Any man who would cheat on his wife for twenty-five years is *exactly* that kind of man; furthermore—she turned to Sylvia—you were right about Bambi. She *is* after my job so I did exactly what the soap opera character did. I took her into my confidence and told her I wanted to retire early and what it would take. She was practically drooling. As soon as she left my office, I saw her make a phone call. I'm guessing it was to the CFO, so keep your fingers crossed."

"If it doesn't work out, you still have Mel," Sylvia said. "Married to him you could retire early."

Irene shook her head. "No, I don't think so. The relationship is doomed. He goes from sloth to slop. I don't know how one person can find so many new and different ways to terrorize me."

"But he's seems so good-natured."

"Of course he's good-natured. Who wouldn't be with free maid and laundry service and never having to do anything except what you want to do?"

Sylvia handed Irene a small package.

"What's this?"

"A little something I picked up for you to give Mel." Irene took off the wrapping and stared at the blister pack. "It's called Snore-X," Sylvia explained. "Guaranteed to stop someone's snoring or double your money back, in this case mine. I saw it advertised on TV and decided to get it for you."

"That was really nice of you, but, trust me, you've wasted your money. Mel won't wear it. He thinks I'm making it up—that he snores. He says his wife never complained."

"Do you have a tape recorder?" Barbara asked. "Tape him and make him listen to it."

Irene's cell phone rang.

"It's Nancy," she said, taking the call. "I won't be long . . .. Hi, Nancy."

"Mom. I've got a problem."

"I can't talk now. We're in the middle of a mahjongg game. Can I call you back when the game is over?"

"But it's about Susan."

"I said I'll call you back."

"Susan chose a $500 maid of honor dress for me and a $250 dress for Maya. We can't afford that, but even if we could Benjamin says he'd never agree to spend that kind of money on such foolishness. But you know Susan. If I don't buy them, she'll never speak to me again, but Benjamin says if I do, he's not going to the wedding and neither is Maya."

"Why are you telling *me* all this? Tell Susan."

Nancy started to cry. "I tried to tell her, but . . ."

"Honey, I promise to call you back in just a few minutes."

"It's your fault, you know, that I'm afraid of her!"

"How do you figure that?"

"Maybe if you hadn't started dating so soon after Daddy died."

"Soon? It was two years. What's more, you were in high school and dating yourself," she snapped back. "Nancy, I'm hanging up now. This conversation is over, and my best advice to you is to listen to your husband." Irene turned off her phone. "Next time around I'm going to give birth to other people's children, and other people can give birth to mine. Then other people will be blamed for my children's disappointments, and I'll be able to have an amicable relationship with them."

"But then other people's children will be angry at you," Sylvia reasoned.

"What the F do I care what other people's children think of me?"

They laughed until the tears came.

"Have you noticed," Barbara asked, "that when we call them they're too busy to talk, but when they call us, we're expected to drop everything and talk to them?"

They nodded their heads. Yes, they were aware of it.

"That's because *their* time is more valuable than ours," Irene explained, "which is why they're always doing something when they're on the phone with us, like washing dishes or ironing clothes or putting groceries away—so they don't completely waste their time."

"Evie usually keyboards when she's on the phone with me, and Daniel calls when he's out walking the dog," Barbara confessed.

"Where did we go wrong?" Rochelle asked.

"It was inevitable according to Christopher Lasch," Irene explained.

"Who's he?"

"A social critic and historian. Decades ago he predicted that the exploding technological age would lead to depersonalization of the human condition, create narcissistic personalities, a loss of individualism, and ultimately lead to the breakdown of the American family."

"The Women's Movement did its fair share, too," Sylvia added. "By the time women become professionals today, marry and have children, they're ten to fifteen years older than we were. For thirty-five to forty years they never had to think about anyone or anything but themselves."

"When Matt Damon's wife was pregnant with their first child he told the papers he was glad he was going to be a father because now he'd have to stop thinking about himself."

"Where'd you hear that?" Irene asked Barbara.

"I read it . . . probably in a doctor's office . . . or a checkout counter. Where else?"

"Christopher whatever was right. They're all narcissistic which is why there are literally thousands of memoirs on the market today. Everyone thinks his or her life is fascinating."

"Anthills are more interesting."

"They think they invented it all; that their children were the first children to be born. Remember how we were? We just spit them out. No fuss, no muss, no conversation."

"Fetuses are now posted on the Internet. Bette wanted me to send you photos of Jonathan in her womb, but I refused."

"Thanks for sparing us."

"Today's maternity clothes tell it all—t-shirts so tight you can see the unborn baby kicking. We tried to hide ourselves under yards of fabric."

"And then when they're *not* pregnant, what do they wear? Yards of foo-foo ruffled tops that make them look pregnant."

"And the exposed cleavage. Double A to double D. They don't care. Everyone's letting it all hang out."

"You forgot to mention the butt exposure.

"They put quasi-porn pictures of themselves on the web, tell a thousand of their closest friends the most intimate details of their lives, but run to the ACLU when a government agency wants to know what books they've withdrawn from the library."

"And the amount of stuff they have! Remember how we went off to college? We had one suitcase filled with a pathetic wardrobe, and if we were lucky, a typewriter, a radio, and a stereo. Today they have to hook a trailer to their personal car to bring their stuff up to school."

"It's our fault."

"They got too much, too soon."

"It couldn't be helped. There's too much out there, and everyone knows about it."

"What are our grandchildren going to be like?"

"I hate to think about it."

"Someone once said if you get a 50% return on your children, you're doing well."

"If Adam marries the right kind of woman, I'll get 33-1/3."

"Sylvia's got 100% but she doesn't know it."

"I know you all think Mary is a saint . . .." They nodded, vigorously. " . . .so what if I told you she recently spent the night with a man on their *first date*?"

"I'd say that if she'd moved out ten years ago like she should have, her mother wouldn't know her personal business."

"You're right," Sylvia answered. "I wouldn't know because I'd be long dead."

"Do you know who he is?" Irene asked. "The new man?"

"Some doctor with a double Biblical name."

Barbara was suddenly interested. "Simon? Could it have been Simon?"

"Yeah, that's it. Simon. Simon-Simon. Do you know him?"

"Mary had a date with David Simon?" Sylvia shrugged. "Sylvia, he's not only one of Chicago's finest plastic surgeons, but he was voted MEB this year."

"What's that?"

"Most Eligible Bachelor." Barbara clapped her hands. "This one, Sylvia, is no wuss. If he wants Mary, he'll get Mary, no matter what you serve him for dinner!"

Irene hummed the funeral march.

"You're all very cavalier with my life. Did you know that if you go for even two minutes without air you could become comatose and never regain total brain functioning? Think about it."

Rochelle leaned across the table and overturned the four racks.

"No more mahjongg tonight. Let's have dessert. I made a seven-layer rum torte."

"What's the occasion?"

"My birthday."

Rochelle left the living room, and they looked at each other guiltily. They had forgotten.

"She always remembers our birthdays."

"Because we remind each other a week ahead."

"She could have told us."

"That's so like Rochelle. She never makes demands."

"And look what it got her."

They heard the refrigerator door slam shut . . .and shut again. They heard cabinet doors banging. They heard Rochelle go down the basement stairs . . . and come up again. They heard a crash, but it wasn't until they heard her scream "Sons of Bitches!" that they ran into the kitchen. Rochelle stood in the middle of the floor, spinning like an angry top.

"It's gone! That torte was for me and my three best friends!"

"Who do you think took it?"

"Bette or Amy, that's who!"

They expected her to cry, but she didn't. Her anger had dried up her tears. Barbara brewed a pot of coffee.

"Now will you sell your house?"

The phone rang. Rochelle read the caller I.D. and turned on the speaker phone.

"Hello," she said, coldly.

"Mom, is that you?" It was Bette.

"Uh huh."

"You sound funny." Rochelle waited, silently. "I've been trying to get you all day," Bette lied. "Matt and I wanted to take you out for dinner tonight, but when I couldn't get hold of you . . .well, *we* were very disappointed." Bette was the victim. "Did you hear me?"

"Yes, you were very disappointed," Rochelle repeated, robotically.

"Did Amy or Adam get hold of you about dinner Thursday night? That's the first night the three of us can get together."

"I have tickets for a concert."

"I'm sure you can exchange them for another night . . . or give them away. Like I said, it's the only night the three of us are free."

"Can we talk later? The girls are here, and we're in the middle of a mahjongg game."

"Muh-uh-thur, this is very *important*. The girls can wait. Also, I'd like to bring Jonathan over tomorrow morning for a few hours. I have an important business meeting at ten, and the nursery school is closed for some kind of foolish holiday."

Three pairs of eyes, narrowed.

"No, tomorrow isn't good. I need the morning light for painting."

"Surely your grandson is more important than a painting. You can paint on Friday."

"Bette, did you take my torte?"

"What's that?"

"The seven-layer cake that was in the refrigerator."

"That was Amy."

"How do you know?"

"Steve invited his boss and his wife for dinner at the last minute, and she was in a bind. She probably took some other stuff, too. You can't survive on cake alone," she joked.

"That cake was for me and my friends."

"If you didn't want her to take it, you should've put a sign on it."

"Put signs on the food in *my* refrigerator? No, I don't think so. A better idea is to change the house locks."

"I wouldn't do that if I were you," Bette threatened. "That would be like locking your children and grandchildren out of your life." Bette's love, Rochelle was finally willing to admit to herself, was conditional, and the condition was to provide Bette with everything she needed, when she needed it, and when there was nothing more Bette needed from her, Bette would dump her. "I'll see you tomorrow morning at eight." Bette hung up.

Rochelle started to cry. Irene followed, imagining herself dying with an itchy back and no one to scratch it. Barbara added her tears to the flood, fearful she was on the verge of losing everything she had spent a lifetime building, and Sylvia tried to cry, but the tears wouldn't come. She hadn't cried in years, not since her mother's death, and she wasn't sure if she still knew how. The phone rang, and a booming male voice put an end to their pity party.

"Hi, Babe. I have a surprise for you, which I'm personally delivering tonight at eleven. So be up and ready for your birthday woo-woo."

"Woo-woo?" they repeated together, laughing.

"The road to wisdom is simple to express," Irene began. "To err . . .and err . . . and err again . . . but less and less and less."

"How do we get it—this thing called wisdom?" Rochelle asked.

"It comes with age," Sylvia answered.

"Sometimes age comes alone," Irene cynically added.

CHAPTER TWENTY-THREE

Irene and Mel

*"Words are really a mask. They rarely express the true meaning,
in fact, they tend to hide it."*

Herman Hesse, *M. Serrano*

M EL was asleep (and snoring) when Irene returned from the mahjongg game. She got into bed and smacked him hard in the shoulder. He woke up and smiled at her, lovingly.

"Hi Renie. Have a nice time tonight?"

"Uh huh. Say, Mel, I have a little surprise for you." She handed him the packaged Snore-X.

He was suddenly alert and hopeful. "New sex toy?" he asked, sitting up in bed. He opened the box and stared at Snorex, confused. "It looks kinda kinky," he said. "New age, I guess?" He fingered the pincher and grimaced. "Do you wear this or do I?"

"It goes on your lip, Mel. It's guaranteed to stop your snoring."

"It looks like some kind of Chinese torture."

"After the first few minutes, it says you won't feel a thing because your lip will be numb." Mel didn't move. "Come on, Mel. Give it a try. For me."

He removed Snore-X from the box, squeezed open the pincer, and clipped it to his lower lip. Seconds later, he removed it.

"Jeez, Irene, I can't wear this thing. It hurts like hell!"

"You didn't give it a chance," she answered, ignoring Mel's thickening lower lip. "Just try it for three minutes. Please. I'm sleep deprived."

Mel clipped it to his lip again.

"Ein nev cumlend," he said.

"What?"

"Ein nev cumlend."

"I still can't understand you."

He removed the Snore-X. "I *said*, Helen never complained."

"Helen must've been a saint."

"Maybe she was, but it doesn't matter. I'm not going to wear this thing and that's final!"

Three minutes later Mel was asleep, and the rumbling began. Irene retrieved her old tape recorder from her office and taped Mel snoring. After several minutes, she stopped the machine and rewound the tape.

"Mel?" She shook him hard. "Mel!"

"Now what?"

"I want you to hear this."

She pushed the play button, and they listened to what sounded like a dying hippo.

"What's that?"

"That's you. Snoring."

"Get outta here. That can't be me."

"That's you. I just taped it. Now what do you think?"

"I think you're right. Helen must've been a saint. Night, Renie. Love ya."

CHAPTER TWENTY-FOUR

Simon and Gert

*"If we open a quarrel between the past and the present,
we shall find that we have lost the future."*

Winston Churchill

W HEN Simon makes a promise, Simon keeps a promise, he told
himself; otherwise, a hundred wild horses pulling him naked
across the desert couldn't have gotten him to this fundraiser at the
Shedd tonight. He forced a finger under the tight collar of his tux-
edo shirt and wondered why money couldn't be sucked from people
dressed in jeans and tee shirts. He, for one, would have gladly paid
double not to wear a monkey suit.

He waved good-bye to the Finders and Mosses, old friends
of his parents whom he'd known since childhood. Nice people, all
of them, but they had nothing to say to each other after the first
twenty minutes of "do you remember when?" Yes, he remembered
when, but he preferred not to. "Do you remember when you were
a husky lad?" Husky was P.C., he thought. He'd been downright
fat! "Do you remember when you were pursuing our daughter
Diane?" How could he forget how brutally she'd rejected him? Of
course, now that Diane was divorced, and he had all the right credentials she found him very attractive, but where was she when he
needed her?

He looked at his watch. The crowd was thinning out, and he
hoped Gert would agree to leave.

"Ready to go, Mom?" he asked.

"I haven't seen Mildred or Vivian yet, and I promised not to leave until they had a chance to see you. Just relax, Simon. It's still early." Guilt washed over him. Why couldn't he just go with the flow? He knew how much she enjoyed showing him off. "I'm sure they'll be here in another minute or two. They're sitting with a group of widows. Widows and widowers stay up later than married couples," Gert said. He didn't ask why because he knew he could count on her to tell him. "That's because they suffer from sound deprivation. They're *alone* so much of the time." God almighty, he thought. She really knew how to turn the screws. She got to her feet.

"Be right back. Going to go take a leak."

Gert believed she had reached the Age of Entitlement, which meant she had the right to say whatever she wanted, whenever she wanted, and to whomever she wanted—"short of hurting anyone's feelings," she qualified. Her friends—even those who had rarely asserted themselves in earlier days—shared her philosophy; consequently, when he was with them, he felt like a pubescent again, terrified what one of them would say next.

He took off his tie, opened the top button of his shirt, and prayed he wasn't putting on weight. One could never get complacent. The Fat Boogey Man hid behind every door, hoping to get hold of him again: a sliver, a slice, a slab, and before you knew it, a slob. Occasionally the old dream returned. He was so fat that he had to roll from point to point. He didn't lose his baby fat until college. Half of his obesity problem was genetic. The other half was a working mother's guilt, which Gert overcame by stuffing the refrigerator and cabinets with cakes, cookies, and candy. The more he ate, the less guilty she felt, and by the time he was twelve, he was forty pounds overweight.

Despite his protests, they sent him to the Maccabi Sports Camp for Boys. He knew better, of course. Maccabi Sports Camp was a euphemism for a fat farm for Jewish kids. "You're not going to pen me in with hundreds of other piggy wiggies!" he screamed, but they wouldn't back down. He threatened to report them to the Department of Children and Family Services for child abuse, but they were not intimidated. "We're damned if we do, damned if we don't," his father said. "If we let you grow up fat, you're going to hate us, and if we force you to be thin, you're going to hate us—so we decided that we'd rather be hated by a thin son than a fat one."

And off to camp he went, returning eight weeks later ten pounds heavier. When Gert demanded a full refund, the camp charged that he had broken the contract by ferreting boxes of candy bars into his cabin and hiding them under his mattress. For proof, they sent her photos of candy wrappers, stuffed between a mattress and bedsprings. "Is it true?" she asked. "Did you take candy to camp with you?" He answered with a smile that spread from one candy-bloated cheek to the other. They never sent him to camp again.

Gert returned from the bathroom. He started to stand, but she waved him down.

"I hate it when you pretend to have manners, Simon. It doesn't become you." She sat and smoothed out her evening suit. "Guess who I ran into in the bathroom? Marilyn Zucker. I didn't know she liked opera. I've never seen her at any Lyric functions before. Simon, you're not listening."

"You ran into Marilyn Zucker in the bathroom. You didn't know she liked opera. You've never seen her at a Lyric function before," he repeated. "See, I *am* listening."

"Hmm. Anyway, something funny happened in the bathroom."

"Besides seeing Marilyn Zucker?"

"After I washed my hands, the assistant handed me a towel. I said thank you, and do you know what she said?"

"No."

"No problem." She waited for him to react. "Did you hear me?"

"She said 'no problem.'"

"Don't you get it?"

"No."

"The same thing happened this afternoon at lunch when I was with your Aunt Roz."

"She's not *my* Aunt Roz. She's *your* sister."

"You're so unforgiving, Simon."

"She didn't call *you* 'pudgy.'"

"As I was saying, I was at lunch with Roz, and I asked the waiter for the check. When he gave it to me, I said 'thank you,' and do you know what he said?"

"No problem."

"Exactly. So I said, 'What happened to you're welcome?'"

The waiter removed their dinner plates and set slices of strawberry cheesecake in front of them.

"Thank you," Gert said to the waiter.

"No problem," he answered.

She grabbed his arm. "Thank you," she repeated.

"No problem," he answered again.

"Have you ever heard of 'you're welcome'?" she asked.

The waiter looked puzzled, and Simon hid under his dinner napkin.

"That's what I said."

"No, I said thank you, and you said '*no problem.*'"

"That's what 'no problem' means."

"No, it doesn't. *No problem* means you're not having a problem. You're welcome is an acknowledgment that you have been thanked for doing something nice for someone. They are totally unrelated." The waiter didn't know what the old lady wanted, but management had made it very clear: short of letting patrons stick things in their orifices, they were expected to do whatever it took to make the guests happy. "I would love to hear you say 'you're welcome'."

"Sure. You're welcome," he said. "You're welcome," he repeated, walking away. "You're welcome," he said to one of the other waiters.

Simon dropped his head onto his chest.

"Simon?"

"I'm here, Mom." He was trying to behave. He didn't want to argue with her. He liked his mother; in fact, he loved her. *Some*times he even adored her.

"Did you know that I now have more dead friends and relatives than I have live ones? I made a count the other day. I don't know when the numbers turned on me." She plunged her fork into the strawberry cheesecake. "Nate Millett died last week. Remember him? Died at his dining room table, just sitting there, minding his own business, not bothering anyone, working the Sunday *New York Times* crossword puzzle. Fanny said she was in the kitchen when Nate yelled out, 'Hey, Fanny! What's a six-letter word for *mutter*, also starting with *m-u*? 'Mumble,' she'd answered, then heard a thud. She went into the dining room, and there he was, sprawled across the table, his pen still in his hand. He was something of a show-off, in my opinion, doing the *Times* crossword in ink." Gert took a deep breath. "And Bea Walker. Remember her? She used to be part of our bridge group until she moved to Scottsdale. Well, she died a couple of weeks ago."

"Do you need to be so morbid?"

"*I'm* morbid? Look at you! You look like you had a stroke. There's more life in Manny Sager than you, and he's been comatose for years." He didn't answer. "You'd think I was punishing you by getting you out of that dark, gloomy apartment of yours."

"I get out, Mom. Every day I get out. I make rounds. I operate. I see patients. I teach. I go home. I get an airing, I promise you."

"You know what I mean, Simon. You're always tense. Look at the way you're sitting. Your body language speaks for itself." Simon uncrossed his arms and made an outward effort to look relaxed.

"I haven't been sleeping well," he admitted. She looked alarmed, and he was sorry he had said anything. "Don't worry. It's nothing serious."

"Are you getting any?" Gert asked.

"Am I *what*?"

"Getting any?"

He laughed, insincerely. "God, just when I think you couldn't possibly get any ballsier, you prove me wrong. Since when do seventy-five year-old women ask their fifty year old sons if they're 'getting any'?"

"First of all, you're not fifty. Secondly, don't pretend I'm a virgin. I knew about sex long before you were born. Number three, you've probably been celibate since you dumped that awful woman you used to be married to. I forgot her name." She was reinventing history, and he loved her for it. "Don't deny it. You're still mooning over her like a love-sick cow. It's time to put it behind you." It was humbling, Simon thought, to be forty-eight years old, earn in the seven digits, have a reputation for being one tough hombre, and know that there is still that one person out there who can make you feel like a toothless toddler in a matter of seconds. "Anyone can make a mistake in judgment, dear. Even three." Three mistakes became acceptable earlier in the year when his sister divorced her third husband. "*That woman* was not worth . . ." Gert hesitated, wondering which part of Simon's body it was safe to mention. References to his ears, his torso, or his face still had a deleterious effect on him, although, in her opinion, he was a most attractive man. "That woman wasn't worth even *one* of your beautiful fingers. Not a pinky!" Fingers were an acceptable frame of reference. Simon was proud of his hands. "That woman was a gold-digging, social-climbing, intellectually limited Bimbo!" He tried not to smile. He did not want to encourage her, but the fury of a mother scorned is wondrous to behold.

"If you say so," he answered. "You ready to leave now?"

"Let's give it a few more minutes. By the way, do you remember Miriam's friend Shelly?" He nodded, yes, hoping Gert would not give him a long bio on Shelly Whatever, whom she obviously wanted him to meet. "Her husband died last year. He was only fifty-two years old and playing golf at the time. Miriam said that if he hadn't died just when he did, he might have broken par." Simon shuddered at the thought of going to bed with a woman whose dead husband's claim to fame was that he might have made par if he hadn't died prematurely. "Why don't you call her? She's such a . . .*nice* woman . . ." Simon grimaced. 'Nice woman' was a euphemism for a boring matron with a lot of money. "And . . ." He tried to look attentive. "She's never going to have to worry, if you know what I mean." He smiled. "Will you call her?"

"No."

"Why not?"

"Because I won't ever have to worry either."

"Of course you won't, but in case things didn't work out, you wouldn't have to be responsible for her four children." Simon raised his eyebrows. "The youngest is already in college." His heart was racing, a clear sign he was restraining himself for too many hours. "Forget it, Simon. Just forget it. It's only that I worry about you and have your best interests at heart, but I can see you're not receptive."

"Can you see? Can you really see?"

"*There* you are, Gert. We've been looking all over for you." They looked up. It was Vivian and Mildred. They kissed Gert and complimented Simon on how well he looked. Gert pointed to the two empty chairs. Vivian started the competition.

"Jennifer won the Pulstar Award for fourth-year architecture students." Jennifer was one of Vivian's grandchildren.

"Hannah was accepted to Harvard." Gert bragged. Hannah was Miriam's middle daughter. They nodded, happy for Gert, relatively speaking.

"Todd is engaged to a doctor from Cleveland who just finished her surgical residency." Todd was one of Mildred's grandchildren.

"Jewish?" Gert asked.

"Jewish, and her parents are both doctors."

Back and forth they went, briefing each other on the status of their grandchildren. Twenty-five years earlier they'd had the same conversations but with different names. Twenty-five years earlier it had been their children's milestones: Miriam was accepted to Brandeis; Miriam is marrying a Yale law graduate (that lasted ten years); Simon is graduating Magna Cum Laude; Simon's been accepted to Harvard Medical; Simon passed his Boards; Simon did a nose job on the president's daughter. Now it was their grandchildren who were center stage, and they rarely mentioned their children— except as points of reference: Miriam's daughter, Hannah; Celia's son Mark; Joel's son, Nat. It wasn't that they loved their own children any less. They loved them as passionately as ever, but they had become less interesting, in the same way that Gert and her generation had become less interesting to *her* parents after their children were born.

"I've started giving things away," Mildred announced.

"I'm duplicating all the family photos so the children won't kill each other after I'm gone," Vivian said.

"I'm taping names on the back of everything so there won't be any arguments," Gert said.

"I don't argue," Simon said, but no one heard him.

"Not that they want my things," Mildred admitted. "They don't. It's a different world."

"My children and grandchildren don't like my taste," Vivian confessed. "I was delighted to take *my* mother's things."

"They have Ikea. They don't need us."

Vivian tapped Simon on his arm. "Do you think I need to get my neck tightened again?" She stretched her leathery neck up and outward, articulating like a turtle.

"No."

"Why not?"

"Twice is enough."

"Three's a charm."

"I won't do it."

"You're not the only plastic surgeon in town."

"I'm the best."

Vivian pouted. "Look how loose the skin is."

"Leave the poor boy alone. One more time, and you won't be able to swallow," Mildred commented.

"If you weren't such a scaredy cat, you'd get *your* face lifted," Vivian told Mildred.

"If Simon had to make a living on people like me, he'd starve."

"Why is that?" he asked, suddenly interested.

"Why would any sane person want to put a fifty-year-old face on a seventy-five-year-old body? Think about it. You get up in the morning, hardly able to move, take a look at a face that should be out on the tennis court, and you spend the rest of the day depressed because your body can't live up to your face. There's a harmony now between how I look, how I feel, and what I can do. I prefer that."

Simon kissed Mildred on both cheeks. "I love you," he said.

"And you don't love me?" Vivian was wounded.

Gert laughed, watching her two friends fight over her very attractive son, who still didn't believe in himself.

"I love you, too, Vivian."

"But you didn't kiss me."

"My son doesn't kiss on ..." Gert stopped in midstream. "Look over there." They followed her finger. "Simon, isn't that the elitist

friend of that awful woman you were once married to and dumped?"
Simon looked up—and away. He hoped that Natalie hadn't seen him.
"I think she's seen you. She's heading our way. Now watch your manners, Simon," the mother of all political incorrectness warned.

Natalie swooped down on them, enveloping Simon in an aura of expensive perfume and designer clothes.

"Simon, dear! How wonderful to see you! Where *have* you been hiding?"

"My son doesn't hide," Gert snapped.

"Hello, Mrs. Simon. How *are* you?" Before Gert could answer, Natalie turned her attention back to Simon. "I hear you've become a virtual recluse."

"My son, unlike *some* people I know, doesn't need to have his comings and goings published in the *Tribune's* society page."

"Natalie, I don't know if you've met my mother's friends, Mildred and Vivian. Natalie."

They all nodded at one another.

"It's such good luck running into you, Simon. I was going to call you tomorrow. Honest." She looked at him for a reaction. "I can see you haven't heard." Simon felt his left eyelid twitch. "Jane left the Duke, the vi-yah, and Ital-yuh." The twitch became a full-fledged tic. He hoped Natalie couldn't see it.

"What do you call a Duchess who's lost her Duke?" Gert asked.

"A Ditchess," Vivian quipped. The three giggled.

"And she's on her way back to Chicago—as we speak." Simon felt conflicted between his hostility towards Jane and his pathological need to be remembered. "I thought it might be fun for the four of us to go out together. Like old times."

"Whose idea was that?" he asked.

"I know for a fact that Jane would *love* to see you."

So she *did* remember him. "I'd love to, Natalie except for one thing. I'm seeing someone."

"Is it serious?" Natalie asked.

"Very."

Gert waited until they were driving home to ask. "Are you really seeing someone, or were you just trying to get rid of that awful woman?"

"Both."

"How long have you known her? This woman you're seeing."

"Two weeks."

Gert restrained herself as much as Gert could. She exhaled a long, dramatic sigh.

"Take it slow and easy, Simon. You know what awful judgment you have when it comes to women."

After he took Gert home, he called Mary.

"She's not at home," Sylvia said. "Can I take a message?"

"Would you tell her Simon called?"

"Simon as in Simon Simon?"

"That's the one."

"This is Sylvia, Mary's mother. Could you come for dinner next Friday night?" He hesitated. "A fine home-cooked meal," she promised.

"Well, sure, why not?"

CHAPTER TWENTY-FIVE

Rochelle's Convenient Birthday Dinner

"Sisters are the crabgrass in the lawn of life."

Charles M. Schulz

A WEEK after her birthday, Rochelle was at Stoney's Restaurant with her daughters, still angry at herself for giving up her tickets to hear Perlman play Baruch. They would not have done the same for her.

"Adam's late," Amy said.

"He's always late," Bette complained. "He takes after Father."

"What's fifteen minutes more or less in a lifetime?" Rochelle asked.

"That's exactly the attitude that led to his laissez-faire attitude towards people and time," Bette lectured.

"Exactly," Amy agreed.

"There he is now."

Adam wasn't alone. With him was a pretty young woman, dark-haired and full-bodied, a change from his usual model-thin, blonde dates.

"He didn't tell us he was bringing someone," Bette complained.

"And we've got a table for four," Amy added.

"We can squeeze in," Rochelle said.

"Sorry we're late," Adam said. "And I know I should have told you Leah would be joining us, but I didn't know until the last minute if she could or not. So, everyone, meet Leah Kaufman/n." Rochelle wondered if Kaufman/n was spelled with one "n" or two. "Leah, my mother, Mrs. Fox, the birthday girl, and my sisters Bette and Amy."

"Nice to meet all of you," Leah said.

Rochelle extended her hand. "Please call me Rochelle."

Bette signaled the waiter to bring a fifth chair and place setting while Adam ordered a bottle of Chateau Neuf Pope.

"Only the best for the best Mom," he announced.

"It's not really my birthday today," Rochelle explained to Leah, "but it's the first night we could all get together."

"Muh-uh-ther, why can't you just pretend it's your birthday, like the rest of us are doing?" Bette asked.

The waiter brought the wine and while Adam approved it, his sisters rolled their eyeballs at each other.

"Happy Birthday to Mom," he said, raising his glass. They drank to Rochelle, and she drank to herself, and she continued drinking during the filial competition that followed.

She hated it—the way they measured their successes against each other's accomplishments. The sad part was that they were so busy patting themselves on the back, they rarely applauded each other.

"I was waiting until we all got together," Amy began, "to tell you that I was just elected to the Board of the American Professors of Sociology."

"And I just landed a new account for the office," Bette hurried to say, before anyone could congratulate Amy. "It's a giant corporation, a company we all know, but I'm not at liberty to disclose the name at this time. It's all very hush-hush."

"And you are now looking at a newly-elected vice-president at Charles Schwab," Adam announced.

Rochelle congratulated them all. She was proud of them. They were all smart, and ambitious, and successful. Now she would like to feel proud of herself.

"You have a remarkable family," Leah said to her.

"Thank you." She liked the way Leah looked at you when she spoke. "I don't think Adam said what kind of work you do."

"I'm in Litigation and Claims at Northwestern University Clinic. I've been there for two years, but I'm thinking it's time to get out."

"Why's that?"

"I'm totally disgusted with the operation. You expect a medical clinic to be a caring institution, to behave ethically; instead, you find that politics and money rule—even there. If they can get away with ignoring a legitimate complaint, they will. Like today, a patient had a serious bladder infection, and they didn't bother to tell her. She flew to Europe on business, became seriously ill there, and had to be hospitalized. She wants Northwestern to pay her expenses."

"Seems right," Adam said.

"Yes, since they knew she was sick and didn't tell her before she left," Bette agreed.

"My directives are to ignore the woman. Stall her and stall her until she finally gives up and disappears."

"Wouldn't she sue at that point?" Rochelle asked.

"It's too small an amount. A lawsuit would cost her more than she could recover. That's what the clinic is counting on."

"Did they apologize, at least?"

"An apology is an admission of wrongdoing, and this urologist Haeffer, well, he's well-known for screwing his patients, both literally and figuratively."

"Should you be naming names?" Bette asked.

"Oh, dear. Did I slip up and mention that that unethical fellow's name is Anthony Haeffer."

Rochelle decided she didn't care *how* Leah spelled Kaufman/n . . . one "n" or two she was a breath of fresh air.

The waiter brought their dinners. Amy complained about her fish. Bette said her vegetables were overcooked, and Adam reminded them that he had voted for Renaldo's.

"And I didn't get to vote," Rochelle complained to Leah, "even though it's my birthday we're celebrating."

"Muh-uh-ther! We wanted to surprise you."

"What kind of work do you do?" Leah asked Rochelle.

"Mother doesn't work," Bette answered. "She was a stay-at-home mom and now an occasional stay-at-home grandmother."

"Occa . . ." was as far as Rochelle got. Adam took over.

"I think Mom is perfectly capable of answering for herself." He waited for her to answer for herself, but she didn't.

"My mother *was* and *is* a homemaker," Leah said. "She says that in her next life she's coming back as a man because women work twice as hard as any man before he retires and three times as hard after."

"As a professor of sociology," the professor of sociology said, "I have to tell you that the world's not the same place it was in your mother's and my mother's day. Husbands of working women now do 50% of the workload. That's how it is in our house. Very egalitarian."

Rochelle wondered if Amy was going to define "egalitarian" for Leah.

"What I see in my married friends' homes is not 50-50," Leah answered. "They say it is. They may even think it is, but it isn't. Women are still doing more than their fair share."

Bette and Amy eyeballed each other.

"Where did you say you're from?" Bette asked.

Leah described a small town in western Pennsylvania, where her great grandparents had settled after emigrating from the Ukraine. "Most of the original families are gone. It was a one industry town, steel, and had nothing to offer the next generation."

"Leah has two sisters and two uncles who are twins," Adam added, "and her sister who lives in Santa Fe has twin daughters."

It hit Rochelle in the gut—twins! She refilled her wine glass.

"That's your second glass," Bette warned.

"Wrong. It's my third."

Leah excused herself from the table, and Bette and Amy followed. Rochelle watched the three of them walk away—her two slim-hipped daughters and a wider-hipped Leah, perfectly built, she thought, for carrying twins. If Adam married Leah before the end of the year, they could have their first set of twins by next year and a second set the year after that, and because she would feel guilty not giving to her children equally, she could still be babysitting and living in her 4,000 square foot house when she was sixty-eight.

"How do you like her?" Adam asked.

"Very much. She's lovely and obviously has two feet on the ground. By the way, is Kaufman/n spelled with one "n" or two?"

"I don't know. What difference does it make?"

"Probably none."

The three returned to the table, followed by a waiter carrying a two-tier birthday cake with candles blazing. Their waiter was joined by two other waiters, and Rochelle clenched her teeth. She could see where it was going.

"Tell them not to sing," she begged.

"They always sing here," Amy said. "They're known for it. That's why most people come."

"I don't want them to sing; furthermore, it's not my birthday. My birthday was two days ago!"

"*Pretend* it is," Bette answered.

The three waiters stood shoulder to shoulder. They sucked in their guts, and their mouths opened.

"No!" she screamed. If she couldn't lay claim to her own birthday, what hope was there for her, she thought. "No!" she repeated. The waiters closed their mouths. "If anyone's going to pretend, it's not going to be me. It's them! Let them *pretend* to sing!" Leah and Adam laughed, and she felt good—vindicated and encouraged. "I think at sixty-three, I've earned the right to decide if I want to be sung to or not, and I don't want to be sung to!"

"You've made your point," Bette criticized. "You don't have to shout!"

"Apparently I do."

"Make a wish and blow!" Amy ordered.

She blew.

"What did you wish for?" Leah asked.

"A 1500-square-foot condo in downtown Chicago."

"Sell *our* home?" Amy wailed, her voice climbing an octave.

"It's not *your* home. It's mine, and that's my wish."

"You couldn't possibly live anywhere else," Bette countered.

"Why's that?" Adam asked.

"Because Mom's always lived there."

"That's absolute babble," Adam answered. "Every day thousands of people move out of the homes they've lived in for forty years and into something different, usually smaller. It's called downsizing, in case you haven't heard."

They were talking about her like she wasn't there, Rochelle thought.

"But Mother's not like them. Her whole life has revolved around her home and family. Mother *is* her house. They're one and the same," the professor of sociology explained.

"That's ridiculous!" Rochelle snapped. "A house is where you live, not who you are!"

"What I mean, Mom, is that your home is your roots. If you give up those roots, you'll be giving up a major part of your identity and your history, which could rob you of your *raisin d'etre,* which means . . ."

"Don't you *dare* tell me what that means or what I want! I don't tell you what you want! I'm at a time of life when I want a smaller space, and I want it to be downtown."

"But the house is also about our children, your grandchildren," Bette pitched. "We bought our homes where we did so we could be close to you, and you could be close to them."

Adam tapped his wine glass. "I'm changing the subject," he said. "Leah and I have an announcement to make. We're engaged and planning a September wedding."

Rochelle hugged Leah, kissed her on both cheeks, and welcomed her into the family. "Adam couldn't have chosen a lovelier woman," she said, and she meant it, regardless of how Leah spelled Kaufman/n.

Bette and Amy kissed their brother and future sister-in-law and toasted them grandly, but on the car ride back to Evanston, they were more honest.

"Adam could do better," Bette said.

"A lot better," Amy concurred.

"And don't you think she's rather ordinary looking?"

"Actually plain. And how do you like those hips? They're going to spread like Oleo."

"Forget the hips. What about the mouth on her, especially when you consider this is the first time she's meeting her future in-laws."

"It can only get worse."

"She'll want to be center stage all the time."

"With roots in coal mining."

"Steel," Rochelle corrected from the back seat. "Yours are in *shmattas.*"

"Where's Pennsylvania anyway?"

Her daughters laughed loudly.

"Don't you think she's pushy, Mom?"

"I think she's wonderful, and she'll be a perfect wife for Adam."

Bette and Amy turned to stare at their mother. Even in the darkness, Rochelle could feel their eyes bearing down on her.

"You actually like her?" Amy asked.

"I do, and I think I'm going to love her."

CHAPTER TWENTY-SIX

Irene, Mel, and the Ultimatum

"When the writer becomes the center of his own attention, he has become a nudnick, and a nudnick who believes he is profound is even worse than just a plain nudnick."

Isaac Bashevis Singer

IRENE was in the elevator heading up to her office when the elevator stopped on two, and a former co-worker—now in contracts—got on.

"How you been?" Irene asked.

"Good, but not as good as you."

"What does that mean?"

"You haven't heard?" Irene shook her head, puzzled. "There's an early retirement package in the making—with your name on it." She winked at Irene. "It's an offer I wouldn't refuse."

"I haven't heard a thing."

"You should—any day now."

"Thanks for the information."

She could barely contain herself. She was getting out two years early, relieved of any economic constraints, and without Mel's help. Tonight there would be no excuses. She and Mel were going out for dinner, and when she listed all his shortcomings, she wouldn't hear that plaintive whine in her voice. She wouldn't ask; she'd *demand.* She went to her office to call him.

"Mel, I have something exciting news."

"I can't talk now. I'll call you back later."

"You don't have to. Just meet me at The Hong Kong tonight at seven. I made dinner reservations for us. Be there!"

"But *Two and a Half Men* is on tonight," he whined.

"I'm not asking. I'm telling."

* * *

She waited until Mel had finished his moo shoo pork before asking him if he remembered the time they'd impulsively taken the train to Cleveland for the day and gone to the Rock and Roll Museum. "Of course I remember. That was only a couple of months ago." "It was fun, wasn't it?" He agreed it was. "And remember the Saturday matinee we saw at the new Goodman? No plans. No tickets. We just walked in off the street and got two fabulous seats." This time Mel didn't answer. He could see where it was going. "We did a lot of different and interesting things when we were dating, Mel, but now . . ." He broke in.

"Listen, Renie. I know I fought you about eating dinner out tonight, but I'm glad you insisted. Sometimes I get a little lazy and need to be pushed." He took her hands in his and kissed the backs of them. Two months earlier—*before* he moved in—that gesture had pleased her, she thought, but now it made her skin itch. "What it all means is that I'm comfortable and happy just being at home with you. Just doing nothing with you is a pleasure, but if eating dinner out a couple of times a week is what you want, sure. Why not?"

"Mel, it isn't just about eating dinner out. It's the whole thing. The way we live together, which is very different from the way we lived *before* you moved in."

"How many times are we going to go around on this? We're grown-ups. We both know that that's not how people live on a regular diet. Life takes on a routine."

"It doesn't have to, and it shouldn't. I believe being busy and going to cultural and educational events keeps people mentally and physically healthy. When someone says, 'What's new, Irene?' I want to be able to tell them what's new. I can't now because nothing is new. I feel static, like life is passing me by."

Mel dropped his smile. "Then we have a problem because I don't like the new and different. It was only a short time ago that new and different things were coming at me from all directions. First my wife got cancer and after two years of treatment, she died. Then my son's wife left him for an old boyfriend she'd reconnected with at a high school reunion. Then my sister had to have her leg amputated up to her knee because of diabetes. That was about the same time the stock market plunged, and I lost 50% of my book assets in one month. So you can see why I don't share your enthusiasm for the new and different. I prefer a boring, predictable, ho-hum existence."

"That's not fair, and you know it. I don't mean new and different like in a Greek tragedy. You're hitting below the belt."

"I don't know what's come over you, Irene. You used to be so easy-going."

So that was how he was going to play it, she thought. She was the one with the problem. "You want to know what's come over me, Mel? It's you. *You've* come over me. You're boring and I'm bored!"

He looked surprised. "You think I'm boring?"

"Mel, it happens. It's called getting in a rut. It takes a concerted effort to avoid the ruts, which is why we . . ." She hesitated, groping for the right words. "Why we need to be creative . . . to find new and different paths to take." He gave her a dazzling smile. Apparently something she said had registered.

"OK, now I get it." He bobbed his head up and down. "And I'm with you 100%. After all, that's where we were headed anyway, though I tend to move more slowly than you. But that's OK. I'm glad you're pushing, especially when you consider the statistics. The average man my age dies at eighty-three, and the average woman your age at eighty-five. Take off five years for the thirty years I smoked, and I've got maybe thirteen good years left. You've got maybe twenty-two; that is, if you don't experience some kind of incapacitating, debilitating, or disabling illness or accident first. So, OK, when?"

"When what?" she asked, mystified.

"When do you want to get married? Isn't that what we're talking about?" Good God! They were more out of sync than she'd thought. She's thinking of ending their relationship, and he thinks she wants to marry him. "So set the date, quit your job, stay home, and write—or whatever you want to do—and in another three years, when I retire, we'll do some major traveling together. OK?"

"Mel, I'm sorry, but this isn't about getting married."

He smiled, paternally. "You're being coy," he accused.

"Me coy? I wouldn't know the first thing about being coy. I am the most un-coy person on God's green earth." The waiter left the bill.

"This is about boredom, my boredom, and your personal habits. They set my teeth on edge."

"What habits?"

"I've been telling you for weeks, but you don't listen. Like not rinsing out your drinking glasses, leaving dollops of toothpaste to harden in the bathroom sink, dropping used toothpicks on any flat surface, leaving pubic hairs on the shower soap and toilet bowl, dropping bloody dental floss on the bathroom floor. And your robe, Mel. Let's not forget your robe. That's all I ever see you in. And last but most of all is your snoring. It makes me nuts!"

"You know what, Irene? You're beginning to sound a lot like Helen! She could be obsessed with petty little things like this, too."

"*Petty?* Yes, I suppose it's petty, but then I live a petty life. It's not like I'm a foreign correspondent running between bunkers. If I were, I'm sure the petty little things in life wouldn't bother me, but petty is all I know; furthermore, I guarantee you that if *you* were the one cleaning up after *me*, you'd think long and hard before calling me petty!"

Mel looked ashamed. "Hey, I'm sorry, Renie. I had no idea these things were upsetting you so much. You know how I adore you. If I could, I'd give you the sun, the moon, and the stars."

"I don't want the sun, the moon, and the stars. All I want is to enjoy life before I'm wheeled off to some long-term-care facility. And if I can't have it *with* you, I'll have it without you."

"Is this an ultimatum?"

"Yes."

It was a minute-long stare-off, which Irene won, she thought.

"OK, if that's what you want, I promise to work on it, but remember, old habits die hard. You'll have to be patient with me."

She should have felt happier than she did. And she should have been pleased when he took her hand in his on the walk home. And she should have gotten that tingly feeling when he reached for her in bed—like she did *before* he moved in—but she didn't, and she prayed that things hadn't gone so far downhill that there was no way back. It wasn't that people couldn't change, she realized. They could. The problem was that by the time they did, you might not care anymore.

CHAPTER TWENTY-SEVEN

Barbara and J.W.

*"The art of closing your eyes to a situation
before someone closes them for you."*

Earl Wilson

MINUTES after Richard left for work, J.W., Private Eye, called. His report on Rhonda Berger was complete, he said, and if she liked, he could hand deliver it to her in a half hour. He would be in the neighborhood.

Barbara hurried to clean the kitchen and dress before J.W. arrived. She imagined a Dick Tracy-like character—barrel-chested, square-faced, and attractive—if a man-hater like Sylvia thought he looked "OK."

When she opened the door, her first thought was that his baby face and dimples was the best disguise a detective could ever wear. Her second thought was to invite him in.

"Would you like a cup of coffee?" she asked.

He looked at his watch. "Love it."

He followed her into the kitchen, and without waiting for any further directives, pulled out a kitchen chair, turned it around, and sat on it backwards, like a western hero mounting his stallion, Barbara thought. She poured them both coffee and joined him at the table.

"Briefly, you were right," he said, laying a manila envelope on the kitchen table. "She's got a long, dirty history, mostly in banks. She takes a job and ultimately gets involved with a senior bank officer or a customer with mega assets. When one wife found out that her seventy-something-year-old husband was having an affair with a thirty-eight-year-old bank clerk, she guessed that private bank records had been misused and threatened to tell the press. It cost the bank a quarter of a million to keep her quiet. Then, in Topeka, Rhonda had an affair with a bank officer, and when he tried to break it off with her, she said she'd tell his wife and the bank that if he didn't pay up, but no matter how much he paid, she kept coming back for more. Finally, he told on himself, just to get rid of her. In Cheyenne, it was more of the same."

"More coffee?"

"Yes, thanks. So you have to ask yourself why a smart and attractive woman like Rhonda, who could've made it up the ladder on her own merit, would decide to bang for bucks. That's got to be the worst job in the world."

J.W. had just described many of the married women she knew, Barbara thought, including herself. "Care for some coffee cake? I made it myself."

"Love some."

J.W. turned his chair around and moved in closer to the table.

"I did a bit of sleuthing myself," she said, hoping to impress him. "Things I'm sure you didn't find out." She could see he was amused but not convinced.

"Like what?"

She leaned across the table, closer to J.W. and lowered her voice. "Like Rhonda doesn't wash her hands after she pees and God knows what else."

He laughed and leaned closer to Barbara.

"You made that up. I mean, it's possible she doesn't, but how would you know?"

Barbara leaned in even closer to J.W. Their heads were almost touching.

"Last week, right before I called you, I saw them together at a restaurant. I went into the bathroom and was inside one of the stalls when she came in and took the stall next to me."

"How did you know it was her?"

"I didn't at first. Later, when she went to the sink, I saw her through the gap between the sidewall and the door."

"OK, continue."

"I could tell from the soft splash of her urine in the bowl that she was sitting on the toilet seat." He nodded, in agreement. "Unprotected."

"How do you know?"

She explained. He looked at her admiringly.

"Good job."

"The best is yet to come." Their foreheads were touching now. "She left the stall, stood in front of the sink, and licked her fingertips and ran them over her eyebrows without first washing her hands."

"Without washing her hands," J.W. repeated.

"Exactly. Then I left the bathroom, and when I looked back to where they were sitting, I saw Richard sucking on her urine-tipped fingers." J.W. laughed. He had a good laugh, she thought. "It's even funnier when you know what a hypochondriac Richard is. Germs are his personal boogeyman."

"Kudos to you for a goddamn beautiful piece of detective work." He looked at his watch. "Sorry, I gotta go." He got up from the table and stopped. "Say, I hate mixing business with what's been a real pleasure, but . . ."

"Oh, I'm sorry. Of course, I have to pay you."

She wrote J.W. a check, and the two walked to the front door.

"Here's a friendly piece of advice," he said, before leaving. "After you've read the full report, don't do anything for at least forty-eight hours. You'll need time to consider your options. The mistake most people make is telling everything they know, right away. Believe it or not, some marriages improve after jolts like this. The couple does some serious soul-searching, and they go back to the basics. I've seen it happen." He hesitated. "But if it doesn't work out . . ."

"If it doesn't, what?"

"If it doesn't, give me a call. You make a great cup of coffee."

* * *

Barbara did not take J.W.'s advice. After she read the report, she drove to the bank. Rhonda was at her window. Barbara tore off a deposit slip from her checkbook and wrote on the front of it, in large capital letters: STOP SEEING MY HUSBAND OR ELSE! I KNOW THINGS! She was certain this would scare off Rhonda; that she'd leave town quickly and quietly. She handed Rhonda the deposit slip. Rhonda read the warning and checked the pre-printed names on the slip before looking up.

"Move on, you old has-been," she hissed. "You're holding up the line." Barbara couldn't move. She was frozen in place. "Maybe you didn't hear me. You either leave right now, or I will have a security guard remove you forcibly." She should have listened to J.W., she thought. "I'm giving you to the count of three." Before she could move, a bank guard was at her side, his hand on her elbow.

"She's harmless," Rhonda said, "but she's holding up the line."

"This is a personal matter," Barbara argued.

"Personal matters are for *after* banking hours," the guard answered, gently guiding her towards the front door. She threw off his hand and left the bank, praying no one she knew had seen her. As soon as she closed her car door, she called Rochelle.

"I can't explain right now, but it's only a matter of minutes before Richard knows that I know. What do I do?"

"Use honey. And after that, use more honey. Vinegar is the court of last resort."

* * *

Barbara took a long, hot bath, dressed in a particularly flattering black jumpsuit, and waited. When Richard arrived, she was sitting on the living room couch, drinking a margarita. J.W.'s report lay on the cocktail table.

"Barbara," he said, melodramatically.

"Richard," she answered, mockingly.

He sat down on the opposite couch.

"Let's not beat around the bush. How long have you known?" She poured herself another drink. "I *said*, how long have you known?"

"From the beginning," she answered. She could see that her answer had confused him. He didn't know if she meant from the first of his affairs, beginning twenty-five years earlier or from the beginning of his latest affair with Rhonda. He would try to find out in some sneaky, underhanded, roundabout way, she thought, but he needn't bother trying. There was no reason to pretend anymore.

"You never said anything."

"They never lasted very long so I ignored them."

"Them?"

"Twenty-five years of them."

It took him several minutes to recover, but once he did, he moved ahead, quickly and gracefully.

"You were right to ignore them—the others. They were meaningless, but this one is different. I'm in love with Rhonda." She tossed the manila envelope at him. "What's this?"

"The private investigator's report on Rhonda." He eyed the envelope but didn't touch it.

"I'm very disappointed in you, Barbara," he began, and she started giggling.

"What's so funny?"

"The 'I'm very disappointed in you,'" she mocked. "You've overused it, Richard. It comes off like a comedy routine now; furthermore, don't you dare take the high road with me, you hypocrite!"

"Who's the detective you hired?"

"His name is J.W."

"Never heard of him. You've probably been flimflammed by a mail order detective who'll charge me an arm and a leg."

"What do you mean, 'charge *you*'? We're a married couple and have been for over forty years, in case you've forgotten. What's yours is mine." His eyes narrowed into ugly slits, which should have warned her. "As for the report, there are photos and court records. To summarize, your girlfriend blazed a trail of larceny between Omaha, Cheyenne, and Little Rock. Her M.O. is to stake out rich bank customers or executives, high roll them, and then move on. She's been named co-correspondent in three separate divorce cases. In Omaha she didn't go to jail because they were afraid a scandal would hurt the bank's standing in the community. Rhonda is what you could call a bank whore." Richard was on his feet, and Barbara guessed she had about thirty seconds to finish. "You didn't pick Rhonda. Rhonda picked you, and she picked you because she was impressed with our bank records. You were never anything more than a trick with deep pockets."

"I think it's time to separate," Richard said. So now that he was socially and economically successful, he figured he could just dump her. Well, he could think again. "I'll let you stay in the house, of course, and I'll take a place downtown near the office."

He'd *let* her stay in the house? Who in the hell did he think he was, she asked herself. She would decide for herself where she was going to live and when. Furthermore, she did not want a 5,000 square foot house that made creepy noises at night when she was there alone. It wasn't as though she'd be doing much entertaining. Once they were separated and divorced, the number of people who would continue calling her and that she'd want to see would be reduced by about 90%.

"I don't think so. First of all, you don't decide where I live. I decide for myself. Second, if we're separating, I intend to move downtown. You can live here."

"Don't be ridiculous. Someone needs to be here overseeing things, and obviously that can't be me since I have a law practice to run."

"Your whore can do it."

"This isn't like you, Barbara. You've always been so reasonable; besides, who knows?" His voice turned oily. "This separation may only be temporary. I could be going through a mid-life crisis."

"You're twenty years too old for a mid-life crisis. I repeat. I will not live in this house if we separate. Furthermore, I expect to live as well without you as I do with. Maybe even better."

Mr. Nice Guy evaporated.

"I'm going out," Richard announced, getting up.

"And one more thing—not in the detective's report. Rhonda doesn't wash her hands after she pees, and if she doesn't wash her hands after she pees, can we assume that she also doesn't wash them after she takes a dump?"

"*What* did you say?"

"I said . . ."

"Goddamn it, I *heard* what you said, and that's about the most vile and contemptuous thing I have ever heard one person say about another."

"Oh, puh-leeze. You represent the scum of the earth."

"Furthermore, how in the hell could you know anything about Rhonda's personal habits?"

She told him. "And after she left the bathroom and returned to your table, I saw you suck on her urine-coated fingers."

Richard was outraged.

"You must be desperate to make up a story like that!" he accused, "but it isn't going to help you; in fact, you're making it worse for yourself." She giggled. "I'll be back later tonight. Make up Daniel's room for me." He moved toward the open doorway, stopped, and turned. "As for the children . . ." His voice became solicitous. "There's no point to saying anything to them. Who knows? We may be able to work this out." He winked at her. Who exactly did he think he was, she asked herself. Paul Newman? "So for the time, let's just make it our little secret. OK?"

As soon as she heard the garage door close, she called her daughter, Eve. She could hear the keyboarding in the background.

"Eve, Honey, it's Mom. Are you busy?"

"Always busy. What's up?"

"I shouldn't be bothering you with this, but I have to talk to someone. Your father has a girlfriend, and we're separating."

The keyboarding stopped.

"What?"

"I said . . ."

"I heard what you said. Who is she?"

"A clerk at the bank."

"My father and a *clerk?* Absurd!"

"I hired a private detective. It's true."

"Have you seen a doctor?"

"A doctor? What for?"

"To check for STDs."

"What's that?"

"Jeez, Mom. This is the 21st century. STD, sexually transmitted diseases. If Daddy's been sleeping around, and his girlfriend's been sleeping around, God only knows what you could have; that is, if the two of you still do it." She could hardly breathe. "You could have herpes or AIDS even. You better get a blood test and as soon as possible. How old is she anyway?"

"Early forties."

"Then she's still of childbearing age, which means she might try to cement the economic part of her relationship with Daddy by getting pregnant with his child. That way, she'll be able to inherit a larger part of his estate when he dies."

A rush of vomit traveled up her windpipe. "I'm going to hang up now, Eve. I don't feel so good."

"Have you considered the possibility that a facelift might be helpful? Not that you don't look great for sixty-five, but . . ."

"Sixty-three," she interrupted.

"Whatever, but even a great-looking sixty-three year old can't compete with a bad looking forty-year old."

"I'm hanging up."

"Jealousy can do wonders to reinvigorate a marriage that's gone sour. Maybe you could have an affair and let Daddy find out about it; that is, if you know someone who'll do it with you."

"I said, I'm hanging up!"

"What if Hannah and I come to visit? There's nothing like the sound of toddler's feet running through the house to remind Daddy that he's already got a family and prior commitments."

"No. Absolutely not. Daddy and I will work this out ourselves. I'm really sorry I called you. And please, please, please, Eve, don't say anything to Daniel."

"Sure, I promise."

CHAPTER TWENTY-EIGHT

Sylvia, Mary, and Simon

"Courage is being scared to death but saddling up anyway."

John Wayne

MARY sat on the living room couch and watched a familiar drama unfold. There would be some variations on the theme, she knew, such as when the villain struck and how soon thereafter the would-be suitor would flee. Sylvia had made short shrift of Eric. He escaped before the entrée was served, an indication that she had found him boring and of little consequence. Only one dinner guest to date had made it to dessert, and she couldn't even remember his name now.

"These knishes are unbelievable," Simon said, sinking his teeth into a pastry stuffed with meat. "Best I've ever eaten. Where did you buy them?"

"I don't buy them," Sylvia answered, indignantly. "I make them. From scratch."

"I didn't know people made knishes. I thought you had to buy them at a deli." He turned to Mary. "You didn't tell me what a fabulous cook your mother is."

"You know how it is when you grow up with something," Sylvia answered. "You simply take it for granted."

"Food was never important to my parents, which is obvious to anyone who knew them. They both suffered from a peculiar disorder of only eating when they were hungry." Sylvia laughed, and Mary guessed that Simon would make it to dessert. "Do you ever watch the food channel, Mrs. Mazol?"

"Please call me Sylvia, and no, I'm not much of a spectator. I'm more of a doer." Mary thought *she* would choke. "Now if you'll excuse me, I'm going to check on dinner."

Sylvia left the room.

"You don't want to help her?" Simon asked.

"I'm not allowed in the kitchen unless I'm invited."

"You made that up."

"You think?"

Sylvia carried the beef Wellington into the dining room and called them in to eat. She exited, one more time, returning with a platter of caramelized carrots and oven-browned potatoes.

"A table set for a king," Simon swooned, wishing Jane and her phony friends could see this fine, honest meal. "Right out of the pages of *Bon Appetit.*"

"Would you like to do the blessing, Simon?" Sylvia asked, pointing to the pair of candlesticks sitting in front of him. "It doesn't have to be a woman."

"Sure, why not?"

Simon lit the candles. "*Baruch attay adonai elohanu melech chalom . . . asher kiddushanu b'mitzvah tov viztivaynu, la had lik ner, shel Shabbat.*"

Sylvia served. Simon ate.

"This is absolutely the best beef Wellington I have ever had. And the vegetables—perfect." He turned to Mary. "Do you cook like this, too?"

"Mary and a kitchen are like oil and water," Sylvia answered.

"You definitely missed your calling in life, Sylvia. You could have been a professional chef."

Simon had made his first mistake, Mary thought, and would end up paying for it.

"A *chef*? Peh! I should have been a scientist, and I would've if my father hadn't suddenly died and left us with a mountain of debts. As the oldest daughter, I was expected to go to work to help my mother support the family. I had to give up my four-year scholarship to the University of Chicago."

"I'm so sorry," Simon commiserated. "I know how it feels to give up a lifetime dream."

"You could've gone later," Mary said. "You could've gone after you married Papa. He would have been supportive."

"Later was too late."

"That's true for most of life's choices," Simon philosophized. "There's a season for everything and when the season passes, you have to move on or beat yourself to death with what might have been. I know. I wanted to be a lyricist."

"A *what?*" Sylvia asked.

"You know, write the words to music. The composer writes the music, and the lyricist writes the lyrics." Sylvia stared at him, uncomprehendingly. "Like Rogers did for Hammerstein. Lerner for Lowe." Sylvia blinked. It did not compute. "How about Rogers and Hart?" Simon felt like he was eighteen again and trying to explain himself to his parents. "In opera it's the librettist who writes the words."

"Are you saying you wanted to write *poetry* for a living?" Sylvia asked.

Simon heard shades of his father. "Does Simon really think he can make a living writing *doggerel?*" He'd fled to his room, slammed the door shut, and immediately looked up "doggerel" in Webster. Doggerel: trivial, poorly constructed verse. "Lyrics aren't exactly poetry. They're words written to fit the story line in music."

"Trust me, it was better to become a doctor," Sylvia counseled.

"And me a nurse?" Mary asked.

"You were both very lucky to go to college. It gave you choices."

"You think I had a choice?" Mary challenged. "You think indoctrinating a child opens them up to choices? You bought me Nancy Barton nurse books to read, nurse costumes for Halloween, and nurse games to play. What kind of free choice is that? I was programmed."

Simon tried to divert the war that had broken out across the dining room table.

"When I told my parents I was going to major in English and minor in music, my father went nuts. I can still hear him. 'How can someone who hasn't communicated with his family for five years, can't carry a tune, and can't write his way out of a pencil box think he's going to have a successful career in musical theater? You'll either major in pre-med or you're financially on your own.' My mother ministered with a lighter touch, suggesting I major in pre-med but take electives in the humanities. According to her, even doctors needed to sound literate at the country club." He had ended that discussion by racing upstairs to his bedroom and putting a fist through the flimsy drywall. Miriam, whose room was next to his, ran from the house with her girlfriend, sobbing that she was the only person she knew whose brother was so crazy she couldn't bring her friends home. "It wasn't that I didn't have any musical or literary talent, because I did," Simon continued, his tongue foolishly wagging. "In my freshman year I won first place in the national high school competition for the best sonnet written that year. It was based on the traditional Shakespearean structure of three ABAB stanzas, ending with a double A couplet." Sylvia and Mary were being drummed into submission. "Maybe you'd like to hear it. I'm sure I still remember it." Simon cleared his throat.

Despite the mocking laughter we received
When we revealed the love within our breasts,
'Tis she and I alone are not deceived
To think love flies to only older nests.
We cannot help them see the light of day
For aging eyes see only what they will
Although the sun emits her glaring ray
Along their darkened paths, they're blinded still.
In time we learn to cease our wagging tongues
And let Time lead us on his worn out path
While in our hearts the song of love is sung
For only us to hear and none to laugh.
But one day we shall rise on golden wing,
And none will laugh but only help us sing.

The silence that followed was punitive. What could he have been thinking, he asked himself. He'd hoped his sappy sonnet would lighten the mood, not darken it. Compared to the mood at this table, his parents' response had been jovial. "Amazing, isn't it, Sam?" Gert said to his father. "So many rhyming words. That can't be easy," and his father had answered, "Path and laugh don't rhyme, not *exactly* anyway. They're close, I'll give you that, but they're not *exactly* the same, like wing and sing." His mother covered up for his Philistine father by explaining that Sam was a numbers person. "Words were never his thing."

"I've never really understood poetry," Mary apologized.

"There's nothing to understand. Poetry's just words strung together, arranged to elicit an emotional response from the reader," Simon explained.

"Left to your own devices," Sylvia said to Mary, "you would've become a policeman or an FBI agent. That's where you were heading."

"So what? If that's what I wanted to be, it was my life to live, not yours. You confounded what should have been a natural process of self-discovery."

Simon covered his head with his dinner napkin, hoping to put an end to their bickering, but no one noticed.

"When you're young, you don't have the wisdom and foresight to know what's good for you. I saw your strengths, which is why I encouraged you to go into nursing," Sylvia said. "And I was right. You've been very successful."

Sylvia made this the final word on the subject by leaving the room. Mary plucked the napkin off of Simon's head. One look at his face told her that Sylvia could skip the choking routine tonight. Simon was as good as out the door. Sylvia returned with a 15"-high dessert küchen filled with raisins, nuts, and chocolate chips.

"Wow!" Simon said, happy for a way to change the subject. "That cake must be a foot high."

"Fifteen inches," Sylvia corrected. "This recipe won first place in a Chicago baking competition."

"*Hadassah* bake-off," Mary clarified. "*North Shore* Chicago. *1975.*"

"*Still,*" Simon said, feeling sorry for Sylvia. She had worked very hard putting this dinner together. "That's one beautiful cake."

Sylvia cut a large piece for Simon and smaller pieces for herself and Mary. Simon took one bite and a beatific smile crossed his face. He wolfed down the remainder, thinking as he did, a sliver, a slice, a slab, a slob. He would have to run an extra mile on Saturday.

"It's fabulous. What's in it?"

Sylvia listed all the ingredients, then explained that the most critical element in the making of a kuchen was in the kneading of the dough. "The wrist has to move a certain way," she explained, talking and eating, and swallowing bits and pieces of chocolate and nuts without chewing them thoroughly. A melted chocolate bit, glued to a piece of nut, stuck in her throat.

"Aaaggghhhhhh." Sylvia's eyes popeyed, and she clutched her throat.

Simon looked anxiously at Mary, who was counting tines on her fork.

"Mary! Your mother is choking."

"She's not choking. She's playacting. That's what she does when I bring a man home for dinner. Ignore her."

"Ignore her? She's choking to death! Do the Heimlich!"

"Aaaaaaggghhhhhhhhhhh," from Sylvia.

Mary did think that Sylvia's current performance was one of her best. This was the first time her mother had been able to make her eyeballs roll out of sight, leaving only the whites exposed. But, then, she reasoned, Sylvia was probably more motivated to eliminate Simon than any of the others. Desperate times call for desperate measures.

"Aaaaaaaaaaaaagggggggggggggggghhhhhhhhhhhh."

Simon was on his feet, jumping up and down.

"Do something! Do the Heimlich!"

"You *never* do the Heimlich on someone who's making sounds. You let nature take its course."

Sylvia flung her arms wildly about herself before collapsing across the dining room table.

"She's blue! For God's sake, do the Heimlich!"

"You do it. The others did."

"I don't know how," he admitted, crestfallen.

Reluctantly, Mary got to her feet, pulled Sylvia into an upright position, encircled her with both arms, and with the thumb of one fisted hand, hammered her ribcage: one, two, three quick upward thrusts, followed by three punches in her navel. A small hard object jettisoned from Sylvia's mouth and landed on the dining room table. Sylvia began to breathe again—labored and raspy. Mary loosened her grip . . . until she saw the runaway look on Simon's face. She grabbed Sylvia again, this time in a hammerlock, and pounded her furiously on her back and head . . . until Simon pulled her off.

"Are you crazy?" he asked Mary, helping Sylvia to the living room couch. "She was choking to death."

"She wasn't choking. It's all a game to scare you off."

"It's real. It's genetic," Sylvia answered, suddenly pumped up and full of air. "I inherited it from my mother, who inherited it from *her* mother, who inherited it from *her* mother. That's why I can't live alone."

Simon turned and fled.

"Chalk up another victory," Mary said.

"If you think I'm faking it, why haven't you moved out?"

Sylvia had never asked before, and Mary had never volunteered.

"Do you really want to know? Because I'm serving penance."

"Penance? Penance for what?"

"For killing Papa."

"You didn't kill your father. He died of a heart attack."

"But I gave him the heart attack. He died right after I told you about him and Aunt Estelle. If I hadn't, he might still be alive." If she told Mary the truth, if she absolved her of all guilt, Sylvia thought, it might result in her own death. "I killed him," Mary repeated.

"No, you didn't. His heart was very weak. He'd already had two heart attacks, and the doctors said it was only a matter of time."

Mary took her time answering.

"Then you don't think I owe you?"

"No," was all Sylvia meant to say, but she couldn't stop herself. "No more than any single daughter owes any widowed mother who has a choking disorder that will kill her if she lives alone."

Mary didn't need much time to think it over.

"I'm going to start looking for an apartment tomorrow."

"If you move out, and I die, my death will be on your hands."

"If I stay, your life will be on mine."

That's when they heard the front door close.

CHAPTER TWENTY-NINE

Sylvia at The Sharper Image

"Work keeps us from three great evils: boredom, vice, and want."

Voltaire

R OCHELLE didn't know how lucky she was, Sylvia thought, entering
the kitchen that next morning and finding the newspaper open to
"Apartments for Rent." Rochelle was lucky because she was the mother
of two self-absorbed and demanding daughters who in any given forty-
eight hour period would be at her house—either taking away something that didn't belong to them or dropping off something that did;
namely, their children. If Rochelle were to die at home, her body would
be quickly discovered, while hers, she thought, wouldn't be noticed for
weeks, not until the upstairs renters smelled her rotting flesh.

Mary would be leaving her soon, and she would be alone. Her
sisters didn't care if she lived or died, and her three best friends would
miss her but not for long. They had full lives of their own. There was
no one, she thought, no one except, maybe, Molly.

***

Molly was working with a customer when Sylvia arrived at The
Sharper Image. She quickly found what she wanted—the Sleep
Tight radio and TruthSeeker—and waited for Molly, who was help-
ing a customer.

"Can I take those for you?" one of the salesboys asked, reaching
for the boxes.

"No, I'm waiting for Molly."

"Molly is busy."

"I'm in no hurry. I can wait."

"We take our customers as they come, and you're mine."

"Maybe you didn't hear me. I said I'm waiting for Molly to ring these up for me." The salesboy lunged for the boxes, but Sylvia held on, tight. "I don't like your attitude. I'd like to speak to the manager," she said.

He laughed at her. "You think that'll do you any good? Be my guest." He pointed to the open doorway leading to the back of the store.

Rio was at his desk, studying a computer printout. He was in a *Catch-22* situation, he thought. He wanted to quit, but if he did now—with sales down 20%—it would stick on his record. On the other hand, the way things were going, it was only a matter of time before he was fired. Family connections carried you for only so long, and with Molly retiring in June, sales would plummet even further. She was also the only thing that kept the other salespeople on their feet.

Sylvia knocked on the open door.

"You busy?" she asked. Rio looked up and smiled. It was the strange woman who'd lectured him on poor store management. "We need to talk."

"Can I help you with something?"

"No, but I can help you. For your information, you have only one effective employee in the store, and that's Molly."

"Tell me something I don't already know."

"You're losing hundreds of dollars a week in sales."

He shook the printout at her. "Try thousands."

"You need to convert your browsers into buyers."

God, he loved it when she talked that way. It sent shivers up and down his spine. "Why don't you sit down?" he asked, pulling up a chair for her. "So tell me how to do it—'convert browsers into buyers'?"

She sat down next to Rio.

"You fire your staff and start over with people who don't think work is a dirty word." He looked at her blankly. "You know. Only hire people who have the Protestant work ethic."

"Get outta here! he said, laughing at her. "There's no such thing as the Protestant work ethic; at least, not anymore. That's something you read about in textbooks. It's a dead part of our economic history—like the Pony Express."

"Hey! We're not talking about finding speakers of Aramaic, just a few people who are willing to put in an honest day's work for an honest day's pay."

"God, I love it when you talk like that," he said. Sylvia stood. "Hey, where are you going?"

"I'm meeting Molly, for lunch."

"But you haven't told me how I find these people, people with a work ethic."

Her heart went out to Rio. He was an innocent babe in a sinister world, and he needed all the help he could get. "First off, you don't hire anyone under fifty. I'm not saying there aren't good people out there who are younger than fifty, but there's 90% more of them over fifty than under. I repeat. No one under fifty."

Rio's mind was racing. One of the reasons he had dropped out of his MBA program was that he was bored with the material and couldn't come up with a good idea for his master's thesis. Most research projects were too theoretical for his taste, but here was an idea. What if he studied two groups of workers on the floor, right here at The Sharper Image? One group would be between twenty and forty and the other group fifty and over.

Sylvia stopped. She wasn't sure Rio was listening.

"I repeat. No one under fifty."

He could do both a qualitative and quantitative analysis, he thought, and study the correlation between a list of pre-defined behaviors for each age group. He'd interview them as well as use a hidden camera to record their verbal and non-verbal behavior.

"Knock, knock," Sylvia said, trying to bring back Rio to her. "You still in there?"

The two populations would hate each other, he thought: the same way they hated Molly because she made them hustle or lose their commissions. Oh, God, it was so fucking exciting he thought he'd wet his pants. His findings would have wide commercial appeal. He could even write a short handbook, a manual for the wider business community. It was the kind of theoretical and applied study that could win him the coveted McDougal prize—best MBA thesis of the year. He'd call it *The Redux of the Protestant Work Ethic.* Who knew? Michael Moore might want to make a documentary of it. No! On second thought, he didn't want Michael Moore touching it. He'd turn it into something it wasn't, like *The Elderly Exploit the Young: Make Them Hustle for a Living.*

"Yoo hoo, Rio. I'm leaving!"

There would be other benefits for business, he thought; such as decreased payroll taxes because retired workers would only want to work part-time or risk losing their social security benefits.

Sylvia tapped Rio on the shoulder.

"Rio! I've got to go now. My friend is waiting. Yoohoo, Rio, are you in there?"

She even cared about being on time, he thought. Do not let her get away. "Sylvia, wait. I have to ask you something. Have you had a lot of retail experience?"

"Sure, from the other side of the counter. I've been a buyer for over fifty years."

If only she looked more like Lauren Bacall and less like an older Shelly Winters. "You want a job? I'd like to hire you."

"A *what*?"

"A job. I'd like to hire you part-time."

She was about to tell him no; that she wasn't good with people, when one of the salesboys stuck his head through the open doorway.

"Psst! Rio! Sorry I'm late. Got tied up in traffic, but I'm here now."

Rio looked at his watch. "You're over an hour late."

"Hey, you're lucky I'm here at all," he answered before disappearing.

Rio was living in a war zone and losing the battle, Sylvia thought. He needed all the help he could get. Even hers would be a plus, and there would be personal advantages. She would be out of the house, eating more meals in public, minimizing the possibility of choking at home. "What's the salary?" she asked.

"Seven an hour, to start, plus 10% commissions, which will increase as sales increase. There's a schedule in the staff room."

"Seven fifty an hour."

"Take the seven now because I promise you you'll be worth much more in the future. If I have my way, you're going to be the Dr. Ruth of Retail."

"$7.50," Sylvia repeated.

"O.K. $7.50. You start next Monday morning. Be here at 9:30. Doors open at ten."

"I have some purchases to make today. Do I get a discount?

You had to love her, Rio thought, nodding yes.

* * *

Molly and Sylvia carried their trays to a corner table in the food court.

"You won't believe what just happened," Sylvia said to Molly. "Rio offered me a job. I start Monday."

"You're probably my replacement."

"You're leaving?" Sylvia looked disappointed.

"In June. I got a full-time job teaching high school math. That's what I did back in Pennsylvania, you know. When my mother died, I decided to move here, to be closer to my brother and his family. I've been living with them since I got here, but now I'll be able to afford a place of my own." Sylvia taped the Heimlich poster to the wall. "You sounded really upset this morning. What's wrong?"

"My daughter is moving out."

"But your choking disorder—won't you be in danger?"

"I'll be OK. I can live on liquids. I've done that before, though only for a few days at a time. After that I get seasick."

Molly gently touched Sylvia's hand. "Have you thought about renting out your daughter's room?"

* * *

Sylvia had no problem connecting the TruthSeeker to her new phone, but when the instructions told her to initiate the "OGM," she was at a loss. Nothing on the phone was marked OGM, and OGM was not defined in the owner's manual. The only 800 number she could find was for something called "support." She readied her index finger for a rotary phone, laughed at herself, and punched in the 800 number.

"Support."

"Customer Service, please," she said.

"This is support."

"What's support?"

"You have a problem. You call. You tell me your problem. I solve it for you," Support answered impatiently.

"That's Customer Service."

"No, Madam. Support is not Customer Service. Customer Service answers questions about dishes and shoes. Support resolves *technical* problems."

"Technical schmecknical! I'm not impressed. You probably learned whatever you know in forty-five minutes."

"Up yours, lady," Support said.

"I want your name!"

"Puddin' tain, ask me again, and I'll tell you the same," Support answered before hanging up.

Sylvia called Barbara and Rochelle, but they didn't know what an OGM was. Their children had programmed their phones. She called The Sharper Image and asked for Rio.

"It's Sylvia," she said. "What's an OGM?"

"Out-going message. See you Monday."

She wrote out her message and hit the designated button.

If this call is for Mary, she doesn't live here anymore. If this call is for Sylvia, leave her a message. If she doesn't return your call in twelve hours, call the police because she may have choked to death. Have a nice day!

She turned on the TV, her new cordless phone in hand, and waited. Twenty minutes later the phone rang. Vera's number appeared on the caller ID. Sylvia hurried to the kitchen to watch the TruthSeeker do its work.

"Helloooooooo," Sylvia said.

"Hi."

"Who is this?"

"Who do you think it is? Your sister, Vera. You don't know my voice?"

The gelatinous liquid in the TruthSeeker lay quietly in Honest Green. "It's a bad connection. Speak louder."

"I called and called you this morning, but you didn't answer."

The liquid left Honest Green, surged past Ambiguous Yellow, and stopped at the very top of the cylinder in Liar's Red, and while Vera yammered on and on about day #255 in Elaine's pregnancy, Sylvia walked from room to room, testing the phone's reception.

"Did they name the baby yet?" she asked.

"It's a taboo subject." Sylvia stepped inside Mary's closet, the farthest point in the house from the phone base, and tripped over an extension cord. She followed the cord to the far left end of the closet where it disappeared behind a wall. She pushed the wall. It moved.

"You still there?" Vera asked.

"I can't talk now."

She turned off the phone, plugged the extension cord into the overhead outlet, and returned to the end of the closet. Only it wasn't the end of the closet, she discovered. Beyond that movable wall was an unfinished area the size of a small room, bisected by a staircase, which dead-ended at the second floor. It was space left over from when she and Morris converted their one-family home into two flats, she realized. She examined the room. It was furnished with a futon bed, two plastic night tables, a fan, two table lamps, one pole lamp, and two folding chairs. Morris' camel's hair coat was neatly folded and set at the end of the futon. Three watercolors and two framed photos of Morris hung from 2 × 4's and dangling on ribbons and strings from the underside of the staircase was Mary's collection of good luck pices, dozens of them.

Sylvia closed her eyes and prayed to God that when she opened them again, it would all be gone; that this spook house would be nothing but a bad dream. But it was still there. Now she would have to go back and reassemble everything she thought she knew be-cause nothing was what she had thought. For twenty years, when she thought she was knocking on Mary's bedroom door, she wasn't. It was an antechamber to her real home, this room at the end of a long narrow closet. And the barricade against the door wasn't there to keep her out of Marys' room. It was to stop her from learning the truth—that every night when she'd gone to bed thinking she was safe—because on the other side of the hall, in a room behind a closed but thin bedroom door, was her daughter, who would hear her if she started to choke—her life had been at risk. The renters upstairs were in closer earshot to her than Mary had been.

The first tears to fall—tears of self-pity—tasted rusty and bitter.

She examined the room again. The bed sheets, the bowls on the tables, the watercolors hanging from 2 × 4's, none of it was familiar. There was nothing, absolutely nothing, of her in this room.

More tears flowed, these less bitter, more salty.

"Forgive me," she cried. "I didn't know what I was doing. I was deathly afraid of dying. I'm so sorry."

Those next tears were sweeter to the taste.

"I promise to make it up to you. I promise I will, even if it's the last thing I do before I choke to death.

CHAPTER THIRTY

Barbara, Daniel, and Jennifer

"So he brews, so shall he drink."

Ben Jonson

Barbara thought Richard would break off with Rhonda when he heard about her criminal record, but she had been wrong. Then she expected him to move out, once he knew that she knew about the affair, but she had been wrong about that, too. For three nights running, he had gone out but come home to sleep . . . at the end of the hall, in Daniel's old bedroom. She interpreted his behavior to mean that separation and divorce were not a foregone conclusion so she went about her life, pretending that nothing had changed. She got up in the morning, made them breakfast, and suggested they meet friends for dinner, and every morning he told her he had plans for the evening and she shouldn't wait up for him. But this morning, unlike the others, Richard suggested they go out for dinner. She thought it was a good sign.

She was on her way upstairs to shower when the doorbell rang. It was her son and daughter-in-law. One look at the high glow on Jennifer's cheeks and the misery on Daniel's face told her why they were here. Eve had repeated their phone conversation, and Jennifer, the clinical psychologist, had come to save them.

"What brings the two city mice into the country?" she asked, opening the door.

"We just came by to visit," Jennifer answered. "We were in the neighborhood."

They followed her into the kitchen.

"Want some beer? Wine?" Daniel asked for a beer, Jennifer wine. Barbara and Jennifer sat at the kitchen table while Daniel stood awkwardly behind his wife, rolling his knuckles against the back of her chair.

"Daniel, please sit down," Jennifer said. "You're making me nervous." He sat, one leg crossed over the other, jiggling his free leg. "Good wine. Maybe we should get a case for our house, Daniel. What do you think?"

"I think I'm going to go watch the evening news," he answered, escaping into the family room. He turned up the volume on the TV, loud enough, Barbara guessed, to drown out the conversation in the kitchen.

"Anything new?" Jennifer asked.

"No. Nothing. How about you?"

"I had three new clients today. My practice is growing nicely."

"Pretty soon you'll have to turn them away."

"From your mouth to God's ear."

They sat in silence for some minutes, sipping their wine.

"OK, let's have it," Barbara said. "Why are you here?"

Jennifer didn't hesitate.

"Eve told us about you and Richard, and I thought—we thought—we could be of help. Sometimes talking to a professional is all it takes to set things right again."

"I know you mean well, but Richard and I will work this out for ourselves."

"If you don't want my input—being family and all—I can give you the names of colleagues."

"Jennifer, really, I appreciate your concern, but the answer is no. No help wanted."

"Eve said there's another woman."

"Eve has a big mouth."

"You have no idea how another woman can complicate the situation."

She started laughing. "I never thought of that."

"A good therapist might be able to get to the root of *your* problem in no time at all."

Her problem? Was Jennifer suggesting that *she* and she alone was the problem? "Daniel!" It was a voice she hadn't used in decades—the one of a mother reprimanding her misbehaving toddler. Daniel stood at attention in the doorway. He looked ready to take a well-deserved spanking. "Your father and I are having problems. I repeat. Your *father* and I are having problems. If we want to discuss them with you, we'll let you know. Until then, our problems are off-limits to you and Jennifer. Now I'd like you both to leave before your father gets home." Daniel touched Jennifer's shoulder, gently urging her to get up and leave with him. She threw off his hand. Seconds later they heard the garage door open. And close. "Whatever you do, don't tell him why you're here. It will only make matters worse."

Richard was not pleased to see his son and daughter-in-law, although he tried to cover it up with gusty hellos and quick hugs. "What a wonderful surprise," he said, leaning his briefcase against a wall. "Pinot?" he asked, looking at the wine bottle. "I'll have some, too. So what brings the two Gold Coasters out to the boring burbs?" When no one answered, he guessed. "Is there some kind of conspiracy going on?"

"We thought we could be of help," Jennifer foolishly answered.

"What kind of help do we need?"

"Resolving issues in your marriage. A forty-five year marriage is nothing to lightly throw away."

"Let's see if I've got this right. You and Daniel, ages 32 and 35 respectively, married for two years, are going to tell us how to save a forty year marriage?"

"I hope you're not going to pull that 'we're older than you so we know better than you' shit on us," Jennifer answered.

"You've got balls, Jennifer. Too bad they're not on my son!"

Barbara expected Daniel to turn and run. He was intimidated by authority figures, especially his father. She still didn't know how she could have made it come out differently. Hugged and comforted Daniel more? Or less? Or should she have confronted the father—in the presence of the son? One never knew the answers to such questions as this, though young professionals like Jennifer liked to tell you they did.

"Hey! You can't talk to my wife like that!" Daniel shouted at his father, suddenly coming to life.

"I can talk to anyone I want, any way I want in my house, and if you don't like it, you can get the hell out. Right now! Did you hear me?"

Barbara expected Daniel to turn and run; instead he confronted his father.

"Fifty percent of this house belongs to Mom. I didn't hear her asking us to leave. If she does, we will, but not until."

Barbara felt a sudden surge of affection for her daughter-in-law. Directly or indirectly, Jennifer had influenced Daniel for the better. He would never have stood up to his father two years ago.

"Barbara?" Richard was waiting for her to take his side. "Barbara?"

"Mom?"

"I'd like Daniel and Jennifer to stay. I haven't seen them in a while." Richard turned red with rage.

"I'm very disappointed in you, Barbara," he pronounced. When she didn't respond, he turned his wrath on Daniel. "And I'm very disappointed in you, too."

"Cut the 'I'm-very-disappointed-in-you' crap, Dad!" Daniel shot back. "The truth is *I'm* disappointed in *you* and have been most of my life, but so what? Life goes on anyway, despite our petty little disappointments."

"If you're all done," Richard answered, "I'm going upstairs to dress. I have a dinner date, and I'm late."

He made a grand exit.

"I'm sorry," Jennifer said. "I mean really sorry. We did make it worse."

"Don't feel too bad. It couldn't get any worse."

Jennifer threw herself into Barbara's arms and hugged her. Barbara was surprised at how soft and warm she felt. They pulled apart. Jennifer backed up, knocking over Richard's briefcase.

"I don't remember seeing Richard with a briefcase before," she noted.

"He hasn't brought one home from the office in years." Barbara paused. "So why now?" She opened the briefcase and withdrew a large manila envelope. It took her several minutes to realize that she was reading a legal document detailing the terms of their separation, a document apparently drawn up by none other than Richard himself. She read on.

What was it she had said to Sylvia? That Richard wasn't the kind of man to screw her financially? She was a major idiot, she now realized. According to these papers, she was to live in the house until it was sold and pay all its expenses out of a monthly stipend 30% less than the current household check. Not only would she not be able to maintain her current life style—the club, the luncheons, and other entertainment—she would be in debt at the end of each month.

That's when it hit her—that she didn't know what assets they had or where they were. She knew about the few accounts at the local bank and that was it. Where were the partnerships, the mutual funds, the IRAs, the 401k, and all the other ABCs? Richard had been sending all financial statements to his office for decades, and for forty years she had blindly signed whatever legal documents he'd handed her, never reading them.

"And get a load of these," Jennifer said, handing her a packet of travel brochures. "You and Richard planning a trip to Grand Bahama Island?"

Didn't Sylvia say that Grand Bahama Island was famous for illegal offshore accounts, a haven for hiding assets from the government—and stupid, trusting wives? She prayed to God it wasn't too late. She dialed 1-800-GET-HELP. J.W. answered.

"It's Barbara."

"I've been thinking about you," he said.

She told him what she wanted.

"You need to get hold of his office keys. Then call me, any time, night or day, and I'll take it from there."

CHAPTER THIRTY-ONE

Richard and Rhonda

"Knowledge of what is possible is the beginning of happiness."

George Santayanna

Richard left home angry and frustrated. He'd planned to have Barbara sign the separation papers, but the appearance of his son and daughter-in-law had screwed that up. Well, if not tonight, then tomorrow, he thought.

He stopped at a grocery store and bought everything Rhonda would need to make a cioppino and salad for dinner. In the two months they had been seeing each other, they had never shared a home-cooked meal. Whenever he suggested she cook for them, she had seductively protested. "I do my best cooking lying down," and he'd feel himself harden. Later they would go out to eat. Who gave a royal fuck about food anyway, he asked himself. He'd spent forty years with a culinary wizard who could whip up a dinner for ten in sixty minutes but had an iceberg between her legs. Furthermore, he was beyond the dinner party phase of life. If he needed to invite people, he'd take them to the country club or hire a caterer. With Rhonda it would be "minimalist," all the way, and he was looking forward to it. Still, a short repertoire of simple meals wasn't too much to ask.

She came to the door wearing a stunning jungle-green summer pants suit, small diamonds in her ears, and four-inch heels. She looked good enough to eat, he thought, feeling his prick stiffen.

"What's with the bags of groceries?" she asked.

"We're eating in tonight." He set the bags on the kitchen counter.

"Without telling me?"

"I thought you'd be pleased. A quiet evening at home together."

"But you know I don't cook."

"You don't have to be Julia Child to make a simple but appetizing dinner. Tonight you're going to make a fish stew. I bought everything you'll need." Rhonda looked sick. "Don't worry. It's intuitive. Trust me."

"But I'm all dressed and ready to go out," she wailed.

"Change into a pair of tight jeans and a tighter t-shirt. If God had it to do all over again, I'm sure that's how he'd dress Eve." She didn't move. "Go ahead. I'm waiting."

When she returned a few minutes later, wearing jeans and a tee, he had everything lined up on the kitchen counter, waiting for her.

"Here's what you do. Chop up an onion. Mix it with the tomato sauce, then add water and seasoning and let it simmer for ten minutes. Add the shrimp. While it's simmering, boil some water and drop in the linguini. When it's ready, rinse it, put it in a bowl, and pour the sauce over the linguini. That's it! What could be easier? And while you're doing that, I'm going to watch the news."

He turned his back on her like a matador in a bullring, confident of his prey's next move, and headed for the living room couch. He took off his shoes, put his feet up on the cocktail table, and turned on the TV. Rhonda, meanwhile, was frenetic. She couldn't find her can opener—actually, she wasn't sure she had one—but what she did find at the back of her refrigerator was a half-empty jar of Paul Newman's Own Spaghetti Sauce. She scooped off most of the mold and poured the sauce into a pot. When it was simmering, she added the shrimps and scallops.

"Hey, Rhonda!" Richard yelled. "How about fixing me a Manhattan?" Son-of-a-bitch, she thought. Fix it yourself. I'm trying to make you dinner, and you want me to play the barmaid to boot? "Hey, Rhonda, did you hear me? Can you fix me a Manhattan?"

She dropped the quartered onion into the moldy sauce, put on the oven timer, and left the kitchen. A few minutes later, the timer buzzed. And buzzed. And buzzed.

"Rhonda? You in the kitchen? The timer's buzzing."

When she didn't answer, Richard went into the kitchen and turned off the timer. He checked the pot on the stove and noted that the tomato sauce had a green cast. He sniffed it. It had an odd, unpleasant smell, he thought. That's when he noticed that the can of tomato sauce hadn't been opened. He looked in the garbage and found the jar of Paul Newman's Own, the cap covered with mold.

"Rhonda?"

He went down the hall. He could hear her in the bathroom. He stood outside the door and listened to Rhonda peeing. He heard the toilet paper roll spin. He heard the toilet flush, and he was still waiting for the sound of sink water when the bathroom door opened. They stood face to face.

"What are you doing here?" Rhonda asked.

"The timer went off. I wasn't sure what had to come off the stove."

She pushed past him, and he followed, close on her heels. Maybe she intended to wash her hands in the kitchen sink, he thought. And waited. Rhonda peeled a clove of garlic and rubbed it around the inside of a wooden salad bowl.

"This is an old family secret," she explained. "I learned it from my grandmother. It gives the salad a subtle garlic flavor. Clever, no?"

"From where?" he asked, waves of nausea sweeping over him.

"From where what?"

"Your grandmother. Your family. Where were they from?"

"Omaha. You pick the oddest times to ask the weirdest questions. I suppose that comes from being a lawyer."

Barbara *had* said Omaha, he thought, watching Rhonda toss the salad greens with urine-tipped fingers. A strong smoky odor filled the kitchen. He checked the second pot. The water had boiled out, and the fresh linguini, unwatched and unstirred, had stuck to the bottom of the pot. He looked at Rhonda. It wasn't a pretty sight. Beads of sweat were dripping off her face and into the moldy fish stew.

"Rhonda, I don't know what's wrong, but suddenly I feel sick. I think I'm coming down with something."

She reached for him, but he jumped back.

"No! Don't touch me. I don't want you to catch it—whatever it is. I'm going home."

"Why go home? Stay here and let me take care of you." But his hand was already on the door knob. "I have this old family egg recipe guaranteed to make a sick man well. Let me fix it for you."

He wondered what time of day she took a dump. "No, no. I don't want you to bother. I've got everything I need at home—Sudafed, Tylenol with codeine, and juices. I'll call you in the morning."

"But . . ."

She tried to kiss him good-bye, but he was already out of reach, and when she blew him a kiss, he held his breath.

* * *

Barbara was in bed when she heard Richard come in. She looked at the clock-radio. It wasn't even ten. Something must have happened, she reasoned. She heard him come up the stairs, but instead of continuing down the hall to Daniel's room, he stopped outside their bedroom door. The door opened.

"Barbara?" She pretended to be asleep. "Barbara, you up?" She heard him disrobe and go into the bathroom. He was in the shower for at least twenty minutes. When the bathroom door opened again, waves of steam poured into the bedroom. He had sanitized himself, Barbara guessed. Rhonda must have made a scatological mistake. Richard got into bed. She lay there, silent and motionless, waiting for his breath to deepen. When she was sure he was sleeping, she left the bed, quietly removed his keys from his pants pocket, and hurried downstairs to call J.W.

"I have his keys," she whispered.

"Put them outside, under the doormat. I'll be by in twenty minutes. I'll copy them and return the originals to you in less than an hour. Stay awake."

She did better than stay awake. She sat on the front steps and waited. J.W parked down the street. She watched him walk towards her.

"Moonlight suits you," he said, taking her in his arms.

CHAPTER THIRTY-TWO

Paul's Fortieth Birthday

"All progress has resulted from people who took unpopular positions."

Adlai Stevenson

O<small>F</small> the seven people sitting around Vera and Al's dining room table, four of them wished they were somewhere else. Mary liked Paul well enough, but she had just signed a lease on an apartment and was anxious to start packing. Paul's mother, Cynthia, was angry—angry at Vera but angrier at herself for having agreed to celebrate Paul's fortieth birthday party at his in-laws. Sylvia wished she were at home with Mary. There were things she needed to say. The fourth unhappy dinner guest was Paul himself. He didn't want to be here. He didn't want the marriage, and he certainly hadn't wanted this baby.

Vera's husband, Al, tapped the side of his wine glass.

"Forty is a wonderful time of life," he began, speaking directly to his son-in-law. "Everything is ahead of you. You have a wonderful wife, a baby on the way, and you're gainfully employed. What more could a man ask for?" He lifted his glass. "To Paul, may he live a long, happy life—with my daughter, of course." Paul blushed.

"L'chaim."

He might have had a long and happy life with Elaine, he thought, if only he hadn't changed. He didn't know why or when it happened but it did, and there was no turning back. Up until recently he was happy to have someone else make all non-professional decisions for him, leaving him to concentrate on his teaching and research. The nuances of social niceties confused him, which explained, of course, what drew him to Elaine from the beginning. She had made everything unambiguous. She told him when they were not going to see anyone else, when they would get engaged, when they would get married, and when they would have this baby. She had made him feel secure. Now he understood that he could just as easily married anyone else, if that someone else had told him to. What had the therapist said? "All that was necessary was for that other person's enthusiasm to be greater than your own indifference."

"Cynthia," Al said. "Would you like to say a few words?"

His mother raised her glass. "To my dear son, Paul, the best son a mother could have. May you live to be 120, and next year the party's at my house!"

"Mary?"

"The best to you, Paul," she said, simply. "And many more to come."

"I'd like to say something," Sylvia volunteered. "Thanks to Paul for enriching our gene pool."

"Touché," Cynthia added.

"Paul? Would you like to add a few words before we eat?" Al asked.

At his last session with the therapist, Dr. Diamond had neatly summed it up: "You're a perfectionist, my boy, and perfectionists don't like to make mistakes. So what did you do? You let other people make mistakes for you. My boy, it's time you started making your own. It's not so bad; in fact, you may learn to like it."

"Paul?" Elaine elbowed him in his side. "Daddy wants to know if you'd like to add a few words." He wondered if it was proper to lift the glass to himself. "Say something!" Elaine hissed in his ear, making it itch. He scratched the ear canal with his pinky. "Don't do that!" He stopped scratching. "You have to thank everyone for coming."

He stood, holding his wine glass on high. "Thank you all for coming, and a special thanks to my in-laws for putting on this lovely party for me."

"Next year at my place," Cynthia repeated, loud and clear.

Meat and vegetables were passed. They began eating.

"I'm decorating the baby's room," Elaine announced. "Thank God we didn't listen to Mom and wait until after the baby was born—all that superstitious poppycock."

"Which department do you work in at Northwestern?" Cynthia asked Mary, who was sitting to her right.

"Internal Medicine."

"Maybe you know my friend who works there. Madeline Fuchs?"

"As I started to say before I was interrupted," Elaine interrupted, "I've started decorating the baby's room with a simply adorable theme." No one asked. "That's the fashion now, you know—decorate with themes." Still no one asked. "I chose dolls. I found this adorable border wallpaper and matching fabric of Storybook dolls. I'm going to have a dressmaker make curtains, and I've started collecting the dolls. You all remember Storybook dolls?

"*Nancy Ann* Storybook dolls?" Sylvia asked. Elaine nodded. "Of course, Mary collected them for years. She has dozens of them."

Elaine's eyes narrowed, and Mary tensed. If Elaine thought she was getting her dolls, she could think again. She had very few good memories of her childhood, and 90% of them were of her and her father going to the toy store together on Saturday mornings to buy her dolls. Ironically, it was because of Elaine that she had started collecting them.

"There's something wrong wtih little girls who prefer cops and robbers and baseball to playing with dolls," Vera had told Sylvia. And because Vera had a college degree and her mother didn't, Sylvia deferred to Vera—on this and many other things. Not that Sylvia wanted to take her shopping for these dolls. She delegated that to her father.

Up and down the aisles they went at Dolls for You. She hated them all. "It doesn't matter which one," her father urged. "Just pick one, any one, so we can go home. You never have to play with it. You can even throw it out later, when no one is looking." In the end, she chose a Storybook doll. "They're not good for anything," the saleswoman warned. "You can't play with them. They're more for decorating."

"That's exactly what I want." They studied the rows of six-inch high dolls, dressed in costumes from around the world. "You can have any one of them," her father said, "except for Miss Austria, Miss Germany, or Miss Poland. There'll be no anti-Semitic dolls in my house!" That was the closest she ever got to a religious school education. Her first Storybook doll was Miss Mexico.

"So do you still have them?" Elaine asked.

"Forty-two of them," Mary answered, deliberately provoking her cousin. "And they're staying exactly where they are now. In my room."

Elaine looked wounded. "It's not like I want to keep them. I'd just be borrowing them until you have children of your own," she said, snidely.

"That's a wonderful idea," Vera chimed in.

"No," Mary said.

"What possible value could they have for you?" Elaine challenged.

"They have considerable value," Cynthia chimed in. "Some weeks back a woman brought her Storybook doll collection to the Antiques Road Show, and the dealer said that the ones in prime condition were worth about $300 each."

Elaine shot her mother-in-law an angry look. Paul let out a low whistle.

"That comes to over $12,000," Paul calculated.

"But you never even *liked* dolls," Elaine said to Mary. Mary ignored her. "Of course, later on when I was older, I understood *why*."

"Then maybe you'd like to explain it to me," Mary said.

"Can't you connect the dots?"

"Apparently not."

"Well, you never liked anything *normal* girls did, like dolls and playing house. You liked rough stuff, like cops and robbers and jumping off of buildings."

"What's your point?"

"It all explains why you were never able to sustain a long-term relationship with a *man*."

The only sounds to be heard in the room were Elaine's labored breathing and air whining through Mary's blocked nasal passages. It was Sylvia who finally broke the silence.

"Are you suggesting that my daughter is a lesbian?" Elaine smirked. "It just so happens that Mary is currently having a tempestuous love affair with Chicago's most eligible bachelor—a leading *male* surgeon at Northwestern Hospital. There are nights when she doesn't even come home; furthermore, there's more femininity in Mary's little pinky than there is in your whole fat body!"

Paul whispered in Elaine's ear. "I think you owe Mary an apology."

"Whose side are you on anyway? Besides, I'm not asking for me. I'm asking for Ashley," she shouted back.

"Who's Ashley?"

"Our daughter!"

"Our daughter doesn't have a name yet."

"I like the name Ashley. I'm trying it on for size."

Vera jumped into the fray. "Ashley? After whom?"

"Stop with the 'after whom' business already! Why does it always have to be *after* somebody? Why can't I just name my baby some name I like instead of after a dead person I never knew?"

"*Our* baby," Paul corrected.

Mary stood. "I'm sorry, but I have to leave now. I'm on the early shift tomorrow. Thanks for everything. It's been lovely."

"But we haven't had dessert yet," Vera wailed. "And Paul hasn't opened his gifts."

"Are you ready, *Mom?*" Mary asked. Sylvia's heart soared, and she got up quickly from the table.

"You're not going, too, are you?" Vera asked. "Al can drive you home."

"I'm leaving with my daughter," she answered. "Furthermore, I won't be back until Elaine apologizes to Mary."

"I have to leave, too," Cynthia said.

"Now isn't that just too lovely? It's Paul's birthday and my cousin, my aunt, and my M.I.L. are leaving."

"Your *what?*" Cynthia asked.

"M.I.L That's texting for mother-in-law."

Al got up. "Your F is going to B," he announced, leaving the room. Only Vera, Elaine, and Paul remained.

"Do something!" Elaine ordered Paul. "This isn't coming out right."

"I'm a geologist, not an alchemist. I can't turn shit into gold."

Mary and Sylvia stood outside on the sidewalk, Mary's arm wrapped awkwardly around her mother's shoulder.

"You know what you've done."

"Yeah, cut off 90% of what little social life I had, but it was worth it."

"That was quite a lie you told—about me and Simon."

"He'll be back. I'm sure of it."

They walked towards the car together.

"I found an apartment I like," Mary said. "I've signed a lease."

"I'm glad."

"You're not afraid to live alone?"

"I won't be alone. I've rented your room."

CHAPTER THIRTY-THREE

Irene, Mel, and Susan

"Selfishness is not living as one wishes to live.
It is asking other people to live as one wishes to live."

Oscar Wilde

MEL was making an effort to please Irene—suggesting they eat out and going to exhibits, like this morning's at the Art Institute. He was even wearing Snore-X to bed at night, despite the ugly welt on his lower lip. His personal habits, however, continued to annoy her, and he had even managed to add a new shtick to his repertoire. Twice she had caught him using her toothbrush. She wondered if this was some kind of subconscious passive-aggressive vendetta, but there was no need to get upset, she told herself. She was in a win-win situation. Her only concern was that Bambi and Charles were getting sloppy. If she saw them together as much as she did, what had others seen?

"This way," the hostess said, leading them to the back of the restaurant.

"Enjoying yourself, Renie?" Mel asked.

"Yes. The exhibit was wonderful. How did you like it?"

"It was OK. You know art's not my thing, but as long as you liked it."

That's when Irene saw her daughter Susan coming their way. In retrospect, she should have guessed. DiMicio's was a favorite of Susan's. She must have contacted Mel at work, suggested they meet for lunch, and made him promise not to tell. As Susan bent to kiss her, she wondered how much this lunch was going to cost.

"Hi, Mom! You're looking wonderful!"

"You, too, dear. Are you having lunch with us?"

"Yes, Mel and I decided to surprise you. I hope it was OK," she said, winking at Mel.

The waiter took their orders and left.

"How's work?" Susan asked.

"The usual grind."

"And you, Mel?"

"Numbers never change. That's why I like them. Predictable and dependable. But you're the one with the heavy agenda now, Susan, with the big event just around the corner."

Irene half-listened to Susan's description of the wedding dinner, the table settings, the menu, the flowers, and all the other decisions that had been made without asking for her input. Susan described her bridal gown, the bridesmaids, the matron-of honor's, and the flower girl's dresses—the latter two, she knew, bones of contention in Nancy's home.

The waiter returned with their drinks.

"And I put this incredible dress on hold for you at Nordstrom's, Mom. It's a size twelve, and I think will be perfect for you—unless, of course, you've already found something." She nodded although she had no intention of going to Norstrom's to look at some $500 dress her daughter who was so good at spending other people's money had put on hold for her. Susan touched her arm, lightly. "And, Mom, you've got to talk to Nancy about the shower she's giving me. You know how small her house is, and I've got twenty people on her list. She simply *has to* move it to a restaurant." Irene was going to tell Susan that Nancy did not have that kind of money when she felt Mel's hand on her knee, squeezing it. She flicked it off. "And did I tell you that Matt's parents offered to pay for all the food and flowers?" Yes, Susan had told her, and Susan very well remembered that she had. "We're paying for everything else, and we've been very frugal, cutting corners wherever we could." Susan didn't cut corners, Irene thought. Susan *added* corners. "That's why we decided to go with a DJ instead of a live band; after all, what's really important is the ceremony and having our friends and family with us, right?"

Yes, Susan was a real family person, Irene thought. She and whatshisface had been engaged for three months, and she still hadn't met his parents, although they lived an hour away. "Of course, dear." Susan turned her attention to Mel.

"Do you even *remember* the music at your sons' weddings?" Susan asked. Ah hah! That's where she was going, Irene realized. She was being set up for a live band. She tried to get Mel's attention, but he was too taken with the beautiful young woman sitting next to him, showering him with attention.

"As a matter of fact, yes. They both had live music. I remember Alan's in particular because they played enough slow music so we old farts could dance. It was a great band. Memorable, you could say."

Susan sighed, loud and long.

"Oh, dear, you make it sound as though having a live band *did* make a difference." She was good, Irene thought. A seamless performance for anyone who didn't know her. "But $2500 *is* a lot of money for a couple of hours. Don't you think?" She gazed at Mel with her baby browns.

Mel patted her arm. "I never gave it much thought before now, but you're right. It *did* make a difference." She tried to stop him, but it was too late. "Tell you what, if that band is still available, your mother and I will be happy to pay for it."

"You will? You really will? Mom? Mel?"

"Sure," Mel answered. "How often does a person get married?"

"Oh, my God, this is so wonderful! I can hardly wait to tell Matt." Susan looked at her watch. "Oh, no. It's almost one, and I've got an appointment around the corner for a manicure and pedicure." Mel looked disappointed. "Oh, and I almost forgot. You're both invited to Matt's parents' home for dinner Sunday. I hope you can make it." Irene nodded, silently. "Mom, I'll call you during the week to see how the dress fits. And thanks to both of you for everything." Susan bent and whispered in her ear, "Now I *know* you love me."

They watched her leave.

"Beautiful girl," Mel said. "You must be very proud of her. My boys are great, but you know what they say. You have your sons till they marry and your daughters forever."

"How *could* you?" she asked.

"How could I what?"

"Promise her $2500. Do you know how long it takes me to save that much money?"

"I never intended for you to pay it. I said 'we' because I didn't think she'd take money from me; after all, I'm almost a stranger to her."

"She'd take money from a blind man. That's number one. Number two, you let her blackmail me."

"Blackmail? Say, that's pretty dramatic, Irene. Even for you. This is your daughter. Give her some credit."

"Think about it, Mel. It was only after you promised her the $2500 that we were invited to meet Matt's parents. They've been engaged for three months, and his parents live an hour from here." He squirmed. "And there are things you don't know; things I've never told you because I'm not proud of them, but here's a short history on Susan and money. She dropped out of school at the beginning of her senior year in college and ran off with a rock guitarist named Tio Frito. They lived on the balance of her college fund, and she never called or wrote. I didn't know where she was. I was frantic. I hired a private detective to find her. He cost me about $3,000 and depleted what little personal savings I had. Eighteen months later, she tired of Tio Frito and came home, repentant. She wanted to go back to college, she said, but her education fund was zero so I took out a loan, which she promised to pay back after she graduated. But she didn't graduate. She dropped out of school again to open a gift shop. I stupidly co-signed a note with her at the bank to help her start the store. After eighteen months, she met a Moldovian poet and left the country. I was stuck with the store, the inventory—which I had to liquidate—and the bank loan."

"I don't feel so good, Renie. Let's give up the play and go home. What do you say?"

"I say no. I'm going and without you. Where are the tickets?" He handed them to her. "And after the play, I'm going to dinner, and after dinner, I'm going to a movie, and after the movie, I'll be home. Don't wait up for me."

* * *

When Mel woke up the next morning, Irene was already in the kitchen. This change in their routine upset his equilibrium, as well it should have. He sat, quietly, waiting for whatever was about to happen, to happen.

"Juice?" she asked.

"Sure."

She poured his orange juice into the dirty milk-coated glass he had left in the kitchen sink the night before. "Toast?" she asked. He wasn't so sure. She served it to him on a plate coated with a layer of cheese that she found in the sink. Then she hit the replay button on the answering machine and turned up the volume.

"Hi, Dad. It's me, Alan. Just wanted you to know I'll be arriving on Tuesday at six in the evening and will be staying with you through Saturday. Looking forward to seeing you and meeting Renie."

Mel looked up at Irene with the eyes of a misbehaving cocker spaniel.

"I guess I forgot to tell you that I invited Alan to stay with us while he's in town."

"*Tell?* Whatever happened to ask?"

"*Ask?* Hey, I thought when I moved in we agreed this was going to be *our* place, not yours or mine, but *ours*. I rented my condo for a year, remember? I have no other home, and Alan is my son. You think I should send him to a hotel? I wouldn't do that to either of your daughters."

That was probably true, she thought, but then he wouldn't be the one cleaning up after them. It was easy to be good natured and generous when someone else was doing the dirty work.

"Mel, it's not working out, and we both know it." From the look on his face, he hadn't. "I'd like you to move out—while we're still friends. You're welcome to stay here, of course, until you find something. I'll fix up the bed in my office for you."

"You know what your problem is, Irene?" She wondered what happened to Renie. "You're afraid of intimacy."

"If by intimate you mean listening to daily BM reports, you're right. I don't want to be intimate."

"You're a hopeless romantic, but I'm not going to stay where I'm not wanted. I'll start looking for a place today."

CHAPTER THIRTY-FOUR

Sylvia at The Sharper Image

"Work: a high human function: the most dignified thing in the life of man."

David Ben-Gurion

After Rio trained Sylvia on the registers and before he introduced her to David and Larry, the two salesmen on the floor that morning, he warned her about LILAC.

"LILAC," he explained, "stands for Last in, Last At Customer. Ignore it. It's an employee scam. There's no such policy. You take your customers as they come, and don't worry about the other employees. They're not going to like you no matter what you do, but you're in good company. They don't like me either."

Armed with cleaner and rags, Sylvia began at the back of the store, spritzing, wiping, and organizing, a beatific smile on her face. So much more satisfying, she thought, than cleaning a clean place, where the improvement was so minimal even she couldn't see the difference. But here, everyone could see and admire the fruits of her labors.

David and Larry leaned against the dirt-stained wall: one eye on Sylvia, the other on the door.

"First Molly. Now Sylvia," David said. "What can Rio be thinking?"

"Maybe ownership is planning a new chain of stores—to be called The Duller Image, and we're the pilot."

They hee-hawed.

"And all that cleaning. What's the point? It just gets dirty again."

More hee-haw.

"Do you think Rio told her about LILAC?"

"Probably not, but not to worry. That old lady will never make a sale."

"That's what we said about Molly."

"Yeah, you got a point there. I'll tell her." Larry sauntered over to where Sylvia was wiping off dusty boxes and arranging them in a pyramid. "Hey, Sylvia." She stopped. "We need to tell you about staff seniority and how it works. See, the first hired gets first dibs on an incoming customer. Second hired gets the next customer, and so on and so forth. So since you're low man—-heh heh—on the totem pole, you get a customer only after David and me are already working with someone. And if you're here in the afternoon, you'll be fifth in line after us and Bucky and Molly."

"Sure," she answered, crossing her second and third fingers behind her back, which everyone knew neutralized a lie.

Larry went back to his post. An elderly woman entered, looked around the store, and aimed for Sylvia. Sylvia led her to the personal products section. Minutes later, she rang up a sale. David and Larry were on top of her.

"I just explained to you about seniority," Larry complained. "You stole my customer."

"I told her, but she didn't want a boy. She wanted a woman. She was buying a personal item. Better me than no sale at all."

"She's a loose cannon," David said to Larry.

"That's why I don't like old people. They don't think like regular people. They're unpredictable."

Instead of returning to their piece of wall, Larry and David walked the aisles, tentatively touching display tables as they passed.

Sylvia saw the Hunter enter the store. She knew a Hunter when she saw one because she was a Hunter, too. Hunters needed special handling. You never approached one too early in their quest or you risked antagonizing and losing a sale. You waited for the Hunter to signal you. Sylvia kept one eye on the Hunter as she attacked another dusty table.

The Hunter surveyed the store.

There were two kinds of hunters: linear and circular. Circular Hunters made concentric circles around a store, even if they knew what they wanted; while Linear Hunters zeroed in directly on what they were looking for, providing they knew where to find it. This was a Circular Hunter, Sylvia realized.

She watched Larry approach the Hunter. He was on his way to losing the sale and alienating the customer. The Hunter snapped at him, and he retreated to the safety of his wall. A few minutes laer, David sidled up to her, offering his help. Sylvia could almost hear the Hunter roar. David scurried away.

Sylvia organized a display of lighted globes on the now-clean table and waited. The Hunter looked up, and Sylvia hurried to her side.

"May I help you?" she asked.

That was her second sale of the day.

"You took that customer from me," Larry accused.

"I took nothing from you. You lost the sale."

"Before you showed up," he hissed, "there was peace on earth, good will towards all here. You've destroyed that." Sylvia was unmoved. "I think you ought to know that David and I don't like you."

"Get in line," she snapped.

"We think you'd be more at home at Lane Bryant."

A customer entered and both Larry and David rushed her.

"Sylvia?" Rio was at her side, a videocam in hand. "I'd like to ask you a few questions." Sylvia fluffed up her mop of gray hair. "To begin, would you like to describe to me exactly what you're doing?"

"Cleaning."

"Cleaning," Rio repeated, with a swoon. "And what are you using?"

"The usual. Rags, cleaning solution, and a lot of elbow grease."

"I've never heard of Elbow Grease. Where do you buy it?"

She laughed at him. "It's an expression. It means using muscle."

"Oh. So do you have any particular thoughts on cleaning you'd like to share; such as, its benefits?"

"You serious?" she asked. He turned off the videocam.

"Yeah, I'm serious. So what's it good for?" He turned the camera on again. Sylvia smoothed out her oversized tunic.

"Cleaning is good for lots of things. First of all, idle hands are the devil's work." He loved it when she apotheosized. He might include an appendix in the paperback version, devoted strictly to clichés and aphorisms relevant to retail. "Two, dirt doesn't sell. And, three, cleaning kicks up molecular energy which in turn attracts customers." Rio turned off the camera.

"You're putting me on," he accused.

"I am not. This is science. You've heard of Kirlian photography?" He hadn't. "There's an electromagnetic field around all things, animal, vegetable, and mineral, and when they're touched, their molecules are moved, and that molecular movement attracts customers because moving molecules causes vibrations."

"La da da da, la da da," Rio answered, intoning the theme from *The Twilight Zone*.

"You don't believe me? I'll prove it to you. Give me the slowest moving item on the floor, and I promise you'll sell three of them before the end of the day."

The challenge was on. Rio looked around the store.

"We haven't sold any climate control collars in six months. If we sell three today, I'll increase your commission by 5%, but you can't put them in the front of the store, where we all know there's more traffic and greater visibility. They have to stay right where they are now—on the same display table."

"You're on."

Sylvia couldn't remember when she'd had more fun. She wiped clean each climate control box, kicking up their magnetic fields. She cleaned the display table and arranged the boxed collars in an attractive display. Three hours later, as she was getting ready to leave for the day, she passed Rio's office and overheard him talking to Larry.

"Get rid of Sylvia? Are you crazy? In the four hours she's been here she's cleaned most of the store, reorganized and restocked inventory, sold three dead climate control collars, and had sales of almost $500. Fire her? On the contrary, I wish I had a dozen more just like her!"

CHAPTER THIRTY-FIVE

Rochelle, Jonathan, and the Butterfly

"The heart has its reasons that reason knows nothing of."

Blaise Pascal

IT was almost six in the evening when Rochelle stepped back from the easel and studied the finished painting. It was good, she thought. No, it was better than good. It was excellent, and if B.J. didn't like it, she might be able to place it in a gallery. She signed her name, cleaned her paint brushes, and went downstairs to prepare fresh sugar water for the Butterfly. The phone rang.

"I've been hit by a twenty-year-old pothead!" Mark was almost incoherent. "My car is totaled, but I'm OK. Every intersection is a virtual war zone. Yellow doesn't mean proceed with caution anymore. Yellow means increase your speed so you can beat out red—not that red means 'stop.' Not anymore. The only stop you can count on today is the stop that happens after you've been slammed into by another car, which is what happened to me, and I've got a business meeting in a half hour, and I'm going to be late. Can you come get me?"

"Now?"

"Yes, now."

"I'm supposed to meet Irene for dinner. I was just getting ready to leave the house."

"Where are you eating?"

"La Hacienda."

"Perfect. Pick me up first, and I'll drop you off there. Then Irene can take you home, and I'll bring your car back in the morning."

"I'm babysitting tomorrow at eight o'clock. I need my car before eight."

"You'll have it, I promise. Now come get me. I'm at the southwest corner of California and Touhy, and if you don't dawdle, you could be here in about twenty minutes." He hung up the phone.

The Butterfly flew at her and dug its sticky feet into her hair.

"The truth is you never liked Mark and don't think I don't know why. You and Daddy were no better than the children, competing for my time and attention."

The Butterfly fled the room.

* * *

By the time Rochelle reached Mark, the tow truck had come and taken his new Acura to the garage. He motioned for her to move into the passenger's seat.

"I can't believe you're eating at La Hacienda," he said. "They have the worst Mexican food this side of the Rio Grande." She wondered why she had ever taken his pronouncements to heart. Except for the size of the bill, he couldn't tell the difference between a meal at Bob Evans or the Four Seasons. "I thought you had better taste than that."

"Guess you were wrong," she answered, snidely. He looked surprised. Snide was not her style. "What's this important meeting all about?"

"Some guys are going to convert their apartment buildings into condos and may want our office to handle the sales."

He sounded convincing, but she knew he was lying. He was wearing Paco Rabanne after-shave cologne, a dead giveaway he had a date—with a woman. "Don't forget. I need my car before eight tomorrow morning."

"When are you going to tell them you're out of the day care business? I know you think they'll stop loving you." She didn't answer.

"Do they even thank you?" He knew they didn't. "Wait until you need *their* help. They won't remember who you are."

"You, on the other hand, are at the other end of the spectrum. When was the last time you saw your children or your grandchildren? Jonathan doesn't even know who you are."

"That's ridiculous."

"Is it? I told him it was Grandpa Mark's birthday in two weeks, and he said he didn't have a Grandpa Mark—just a Grandpa Dave."

"He said that?" She enjoyed watching him squirm. "Maybe I'll call him this weekend and take him out for lunch." He pulled into the parking lot of La Hacienda, and reached across her—to open her car door. On the way, he copped a feel. "I could bring the car back at *seven* tomorrow morning. That would give us time for a quick roll in the hay."

Since their divorce, they had made love on the average of once a month, and in all that time, he had yet to buy her a meal. Or a drink. She'd become a cheap lay, she thought. "Eight o'clock. Not a minute earlier," she answered, getting out of the car.

* * *

Mark pulled into Rochelle's driveway a little after ten that night and turned off the ignition. He was feeling sorry for himself. After suffering through three hours of childish dribble and forking out $100 for their dinners, he'd come up empty-handed. "Such fun," she'd tittered at the door to her apartment. "We *must* do this again some time." When he suggested he come in for a night cap, she offered him her hand to shake.

The truth was he wasn't scoring like he had—not with the under-forty crowd. If someone were to ask him which decade of his life had impacted him the most negatively, he'd have to say it was this one— his sixties. He thought of it as the Decade of Invisibility. Before this, women of all ages, sizes and shapes could see him, no matter where he was or what he was doing. But now they didn't. He'd suddenly gone from visible to invisible; yet he couldn't tell you when it had happened. You'd think a moment of such magnitude would announce itself with thunder and lightning.

He turned on the inside car light, looked at himself in the rearview mirror, and smoothed down his thinning hair. The irony of it all, he thought, was that he was a better man now than before—more emotionally supportive and sexually sophisticated. So what if he'd been able to come three or four times a night when he was in his forties? Now he could make *them* come three or four times a night, and no thirty-year old man could—or would—do that! He'd also developed listening skills that younger men didn't have—and didn't need, he thought, wryly. What was it Juliette had said? "I've never been out with anyone who listens better than you." But he was getting tired of listening to nonsense from half-grown women whose world views began and ended at their pierced navels, especially when all he got for his suffering was a handshake. Oh, they liked the expensive dinners alright, and being able to talk ad infinitum and ad reguritum about themselves, but what they liked even better was a thick head of hair, a flat belly, and a thirty- or forty-year-old face on the pillow next to them the next morning.

The fifty-and sixty-year-olds, however, still saw him as more than a meal ticket. They called him at home and at work and made pests of themselves, pretending to be in the market for a new home or condo—not that he'd been above bopping one or two of them in an empty bedroom—but they looked their age, older than Rochelle, who looked twenty years younger than she was and was still a great piece of ass, he thought, getting out of her car and unlocking the front door.

* * *

It was 7:30 in the morning when Rochelle went downstairs. The coffee pot was still warm.

"Mark?"

She looked in the garage and down the driveway. He was gone and so was her car. He'd promised to call a cab. I am a fool. I am used and abused, and I never seem to learn, she told herself, and if I don't put an end to it, my tombstone will read: LIVED FOR OTHERS, DIED ALONE. The Butterfly, still angry at her for having been shut out of the bedroom the night before, flew past without stopping. First she called the police; then Sylvia's locksmith, who promised to be at the house within the hour, and at eight o'clock Bette arrived with Jonathan.

"He can't go out today," she instructed. "He's got a sniffle and it's still raining."

Jonathan looked around. "Where's the butterfly?" he asked.

"That's all he talks about. Is there really a butterfly here?"

"Uh huh." Bette handed her a small grocery bag. "What's this?"

"A brisket. We've got last minute company coming for dinner, and I figured since you're home anyway, you could bake it for me; besides, your briskets always come out better than mine."

"But I have to stuff and seal two hundred envelopes for the Art Guild today."

"I don't know why you let yourself get suckered into all these volunteer activities. People take advantage of you," Bette informed her. "If you put the brisket in the oven right now, you'll be able to work on the envelopes while it's baking, and Jonathan can help you seal them. It's better if he does the licking because there's ten calories in every envelope you glue, and he can use a few extra pounds."

Jonathan returned to the kitchen. "I can't find the butterfly, Gramma. Where is she?"

"I'm not sure it's a good idea exposing him to some of your strange ideas," Bette said, giving Jonathan a kiss good-bye.

"What time will you be back?"

"About one. The meeting should end at noon, and then some of us are going out for lunch. Oh, damn! I forgot the carrots. Do you have any? And maybe you could add a few onions, too?" She followed Bette to the front door. "And potatoes, if you have some."

After preparing the brisket, Rochelle called Jonathan into the kitchen to help her stuff and lick envelopes. He came, complaining.

"I've looked everywhere for her. Is she hiding?"

"She's shy. I'll stuff, and you lick and seal."

"What do butterflies eat?"

"Nectar."

"What's that?"

"Sugar water."

"Does she come when you call her, like a dog?"

"Yes."

"What's her name?"

"Bess."

After licking four envelopes, Jonathan stopped.

"My tongue's dried out," he said. She could give him a sponge and a bowl of water, but the results would be disastrous. "Does the butterfly sleep with you like Sparky sleeps with us?"

"Yes."

"Do you think the butterfly will like Sparky?"

"I don't think so." Jonathan looked worried. "Is that a problem?"

"Mommy and Daddy are going to Europe this summer, and Sparky and I are staying with you." A headache settled between her eyes. "I'm bored, Gramma. I want to go outside."

"I'm bored, too, but you can't. It's still raining, and you have a cold. I'll give you a penny for each envelope you lick."

"Pennies can't buy anything. How about quarters?"

"I don't think so."

"Then I'm not licking anymore. My tongue hurts."

"I'll put on one of your videos."

While Rochelle was in the family room, the phone rang. Jonathan ran to answer it.

"No, you're not my Grampa," she heard him say. "I only have one Grampa, and his name is Dave, and I'm not allowed to talk to strangers." She grabbed the phone from him.

"Yes?"

"Would you like to guess where I am? No, let me tell you. I'm at the police station. It seems someone reported your car stolen."

"That someone was me."

"I want you to talk to the sergeant."

"On one condition. You bring my car back here right now and then take a cab to wherever you're going." Mark didn't answer. "Call me later when you've made up your mind."

"OK, OK. I promise."

"And I swear if my car isn't in my driveway in thirty minutes, I'll put out another APB on you."

God, that felt good, she thought, hanging up the phone. She had confronted, and the sky hadn't fallen in. She had confronted, and she had won. Adrenaline was shooting through her body, and she felt strong, like there was nothing she couldn't do.

"Jonathan?" He wasn't in the kitchen or the TV room. "Jonathan?" She hurried upstairs. She found him lying on her bedroom floor, staring into a closed glass jar. Inside the jar lay a motionless Butterfly. She grabbed the jar, unscrewed the lid, and gently removed the Butterfly. She lay her lifeless body in the palm of her hand and blew on her gently, but it was too late. Bess was dead. Tears streamed down her face.

"Don't cry, Gramma. It's only a butterfly."

She dug her nails into her grandson's scrawny four-year-old arm and dragged him across the floor to her dresser. He screamed and kicked, but she held onto him with one hand, and with the other removed a small porcelain box from her top dresser drawer. She laid the Butterfly's lifeless body inside it.

"That's my mommy's box!" Jonathan screamed at her. "I heard you promise it to her!" She dragged him into the foyer and down the stairs. "Where are we going?"

"To bury the Butterfly and give her a proper funeral."

"I don't want to, and you can't make me!"

"Think so? Just watch!" He tried to stop her by dragging his rubber-bottomed Nikes into the carpet, but down the stairs they went—thump, thump, thump.

"And I can't go out. It's raining. I have a tempature, and I could die!" he screamed. "Dja hear me? If I go out, I'm gonna die! You heard what my mommy said! I'm not supposed to go outside!" Thump! Thump! Bump! Bump! Down the stairs he came, like a dead weight. "I didn't mean to kill her," he cried, beginning to take the situation more seriously. "I just wanted to take her home with me."

"What makes you think that what's in my house is yours for the taking? Do you see me going to your house and taking *your* things?"

She forced him into his raincoat, slapped his rain hat on his head, and threw a poncho over herself.

"When my mommy finds out what you did to me, you're gonna be in big trouble!"

"Who gives a shit?" Rochelle answered, setting the porcelain box inside an empty shoebox and leaving the house with Jonathan in tow. The rain was coming down even harder now. She tucked the shoebox under her arm, and with her free hand grabbed the shovel that was leaning up against the wall.

"Maaaaaaaaaammmmmmmmmmmmmeeeeeeeeeeeeeeeeeee! Daaaaaaaaaaaaaadddddddddddddeeeeeeeeeeeeeeeeeeeeeeeeeeeee! Gramma's trying to kill meeeeeeeeeeeeeeeeeeeeeeeeeeeeeeee!"

She dragged the struggling child across the yard and to her mother's transplanted butterfly garden. She set the shoebox down, and with one hand, quickly dug a hole in the wet dirt.

"Put the box in the hole!" she ordered.

"You can't make me! You're not the boss of me!"

"Then don't. I will." She set the box in the hole and shoveled dirt over it.

"You promised that box to my mommy. I heard you, and you're breaking your promise. You're a liar, and I'm gonna tell on you and you're gonna be in big trouble!"

She started laughing. It was a good laugh, she thought, and it felt good to laugh. She had let these people take everything from her, including her laughter. "Now throw dirt on the grave. It's a tradition."

"I don't have to!"

"Then I will." She scooped up a handful of dirt, but it was muddy and stuck to her hand. She would come back later, when it had stopped raining, the dirt was dry, and she had a marker for the grave. "Now we're going to say a short prayer."

"When my Mommy finds out you buried her box, she's going to punish you."

"Here's how it works, Jonathan. The box is your mother's after I die. Once I'm dead, you can show her where it is and dig it up."

He looked up at her with big dark eyes. "How will I know you're dead?"

"I'll be underground, like the Butterfly. We don't bury the living. Now repeat after me: *Yitgadal vyitkadash shameh rabah.*"

"I'm cold!" he wailed. "I wanna go home!" Water was dripping off his long, thick lashes and running down his chin and neck. He was starting to look like an adorable four year-old again, she thought, and some of her anger washed away.

"Jonathan, *Yitgadal vyitkadash shameh rabah.*"

"I can't. It's too hard." There was another clap of thunder.

It would take forever, she thought; unless . . . "OK. I'm saying it for both of us. *Yitgadal viyitkadash rameh rabah . . .*"

"Jonathan! Oh my God, Jonathan!" Bette was racing towards them, arms outstretched, her thick curly hair spiraling off her head and mascara running down her face. She looked like the head of Medusa. "My baaaabeeeeee!" she screamed, running at them. Jonathan took his cues from her.

"Maaaaaaaaaaameeeeeeeee!" he screamed back. Bette scooped him off the ground and into her arms. "Save me, Maaaaaaaaameeeeeeeeee. Granmma's trying to kill me!"

Bette looked at the ground, the shovel, and the mud. "What in the hell is going on here? Have you lost your mind?" Jonathan stopped crying. "You *know* he has a cold and a temperature, and you bring him outside in this weather? *Are* you trying to kill him?" Rochelle walked towards the house and Bette followed. "Where do you think you're going? I'm talking to you!" Rochelle hung up her poncho and calmly set her wet shoes on newspaper. "And what's wrong with the front door? My key didn't work so I had to come around back, and thank God I did!" Bette took Jonathan's wet clothes off of him and dried him with a towel. "What were you doing out there anyway?"

"We were burying the butterfly," Jonathan answered, now a proud advocate of burying dead insects.

"Burying *who*?"

"The butterfly. That's who. And Gramma put her in that pretty little box she promised you, the one with the elephant on it."

"You buried an insect in Limoges?" Bette asked. "Now I *know* you're crazy. That box is worth about $250."

"How do you know?"

"Because I took it for an appraisal some months back." Rochelle felt sick. She wasn't dead yet, and they were counting up the spoils. "I pray to God this experience hasn't permanently damaged Jonathan's psyche." She went into the kitchen, and Bette followed, pulling Jonathan behind her. "I'm not sure I can trust you with the children anymore. I mean there's no telling what you might do next."

"I agree," Rochelle answered, calmly. "You and your sister should *not* trust me with your children."

"Are you trying to be clever?"

"That's impossible. Haven't my children already established the fact that I'm not very smart? So here's my advice to you. Quit your job, stay home, and raise your own children so twenty years from now you'll be sure that any damage done their psyches was *your* doing and not mine." Bette's silence gave her strength. "Do you realize there are weeks when I see more of your children than you do? Raising your children is not how I want to spend the last ten to twenty years of my life. There are things I want to do for me."

"Like what? If you weren't caring for your grandchildren, you'd be like Barbara—flitting your time away at a country club playing golf, or sitting on civic boards. You should *thank* us for giving you something productive to do with your life."

"This discussion is over. I will decide how I spend my time—not you—and if I decide to piss it away, I will. Now pay close attention. I am no longer babysitting for you or your sister!"

"You can't quit without giving two weeks notice."

"That's for paid professionals, and I've never been paid a red cent, let alone get a thank you.

"Changing caregivers before age seven can severely damage a child."

Bette had the tenacity of a Gila monster, she thought. "If their psyches are that fragile, then they definitely need a stay-at-home mom. I stayed at home with my children, and look at the size of their egos. They don't come any bigger!"

"But what about this summer? You promised to babysit."

"You'll have to find someone else, and that's final." Rochelle could see that Bette was revving up for a final attack.

"Take a good look at your grandmother, Jonathan. I don't know when you'll be seeing her again."

"Some concern for his psyche," she said. Jonathan ran towards her, wailing.

"You're still my Gramma, aren't you?" She lifted him up and pressed him against her.

"Of course, I'm still your Gramma, but you'll be seeing much less of me . . . and more of your mother, I hope."

"I didn't mean to kill the butterfly."

"I know you didn't, and who knows? Maybe she'll come back again, but don't forget. All living things need air to breathe; otherwise, we die." She looked out the living room window. The rain had stopped, and she could see the beginning of a rainbow.

"Jonathan, I'm waiting for you!" Bette said. Rochelle put him down. "We'll have to talk to Dad about your condition. Imagine burying a $250 porcelain box in the backyard."

"You're too preoccupied with Things."

"Easy enough for you to say, surrounded by a houseful of beautiful things."

"It was easy for me to say when I wasn't."

She locked the door behind them and looked around at the beautiful things. Bette didn't know about the Things; not yet, and if she were lucky, she never would. The Things were like drugs. They made you think you were happy, and if you weren't, then you thought you could be if you just bought that one more Thing you didn't have. The truth was that if you wanted to be free, you had to get rid of the Things because Things made demands on you, like time and money for cleaning and repairing, and insuring. They cluttered your life, confounded your thinking, and kept you so Thing-focused you couldn't see what was really important. The Things also kept you close to home because someone had to watch over them, and that someone was almost always a woman. Making Woman the keeper of Things had been a clever male strategy, devised to keep women in their place; not that men didn't have their Things, too, but their Things weren't cumbersome, like furniture and cookware, and appliances, which rooted a person to the ground. Men's Things were moving Things, like trucks and cars and motorcycles and boats, Things that enabled them to get away.

> Peter, Peter Pumpkin Eater
> Had a wife and couldn't keep her
> He put her in a pumpkin shell
> And there he kept her very well.

Mark had taken nothing but his car and bike when he left. At first she thought it was guilt that led to his dramatic announcement—"I want nothing from the house"—but that wasn't it at all. Mark wanted to travel fast and light, unencumbered by all the Things that now loaded her down. Things didn't add to your security. They added to your insecurities because once you had them, you wondered if you were loved for yourself or your Things. Would her children love her less after she sold the Picasso sketch and the Van de Rohe chair at auction? Would she even hear from them again when she was living downtown in a one-bedroom condo, unavailable for babysitting? Would she go, as Irene suggested, from useful . . .to... inconvenient . . .and, finally, to irrelevant?

The only way to find out, she decided, was to get rid of it all, and the first Thing to go would be her made-to-order extra-long, king-sized bed, built to accommodate her 6'2" 200-pound ex-husband who liked to hump her when he was between babes. She picked up the phone.

CHAPTER THIRTY-SIX

Irene, Bambi, and Charlotte

"My only books were women's looks, and folly's all they've taught me."

Thomas Moore

IRENE and Bambi were at the conference table in Irene's office, planning the fall back-to-school campaign, when the office door flew open and a 5'10" 170-pound Viking stood in the doorway. Charlotte Williams, the CFO's wife, loomed over them, nostrils flaring, ready to charge. She looked from Bambi to Irene and immediately back to Bambi.

Twenty years earlier, Irene thought, she would have been considered a contender.

"Who's that?" Bambi whispered in her ear.

"Your lover's wife. Charlotte."

"So there you are, my little Barbie!" Charlotte bellowed, pointing a blood-red nail at Bambi.

"Bambi," Bambi corrected. "Not Barbie."

"This is no time to edit," Irene advised. "She means to kill you."

"Bambi, Barbie, Tiffany, or Muffy. Who gives a royal fuck? When I get hold of you, you bitch, I'm going to pour boiling oil down your cunt!" Bambi bounced onto her feet and danced up and down the length of the conference table, her eye on the open doorway, currently blocked by Charlotte's mammoth hulk. Bambi moved to the front of the table, feinted forward, then backward, baiting Charlotte to come and get her, but Charlotte, fists held high, stood fixed in the doorway. Bambi inched closer ... and closer ... and when she was only an arm's length away, Charlotte lunged for her, leaving the doorway unguarded. Bambi, fleet of foot, escaped.

"You can tell that slut when you see her she's wanted in Human Resources immediately. This is her last day on the job!"

Irene closed her office door and cried—not for Bambi, who was young and pretty and intelligent enough to make it up the corporate ladder without opening her legs—but for herself. Not only was she sure she had just lost her early retirement package, but now she'd have to work even harder—doing her job *and* Bambi's—until she read through a hundred job applications, interviewed dozens of incompetents, and picked and trained her new Bambi, who, in the end, would never be as quick and conniving as this Bambi.

Bambi was back in her office in less than an hour.

"They gave me three choices," she said, tearfully. "The first was to leave immediately and take the job they'd arranged for me at the *Sun Times*. The second was to leave immediately with two weeks severance pay, excellent recommendations, and find my own job, and the third was to leave immediately without severance pay, without recommendations, and without a job. I took the job at *The Sun*."

Irene wrapped a motherly arm around Bambi, and the two wept together.

The *now* most beautiful human experience in the world, Irene thought, was having enough money in the bank so you could afford to quit your fucking boring job!

She left work at the end of the day reconsidering her situation with Mel. Maybe she had been too hasty giving him the heave-ho. He had, after all, demonstrated—for the short term—a willingness and ability to change. After mahjongg tonight, she decided, she would have a heart to heart with him. Maybe they could reach some new accommodation with each other.

She got on the bus, scoped the crowd, and took the empty seat next to an elderly Chinese woman.

"I had a rotten day," she told her. "I was about to retire early because the woman who wanted my job was sleeping with the CFO, and he was going to arrange it, but then the CFO's wife found out about the girlfriend and had her fired so I've lost my early retirement.

I was this close." She held up her thumb and index fingers, an inch from each other.

"Stop whining!" the woman answered. "You, at least, have something to lose. Not everyone does."

CHAPTER THIRTY-SEVEN

Mahjongg at Irene's

"Do not go gentle into that good night,
Old age should burn and rave at close of day."

Dylan Thomas

W HEN Irene entered her apartment and didn't hear the TV, she knew something was wrong. She half-expected to find Mel dead on the living room floor, electrocuted by a freak exchange of current passing between his electricity-packed silk robe and her old TV, but he wasn't there. And he wasn't in the bedroom . . . or the bathroom . . . or the kitchen. He was gone and so were his clothes, toiletries, and containers of Metamucil, liposomes, glucosomine, ginkgo, Tylenol PM, and Colostrum Plus.

The girls arrived at eight, and although Sylvia was the last one through the door, she was the first to notice. She sniffed the air.

"Mel's gone, isn't he? I don't smell him."

"Looks like," Irene answered, tight lipped.

"Gone as in gone down the street for a cigar, or gone like in gone and lost forever?" Barbara asked.

"Gone forever," Irene growled.

"But isn't that what you wanted?"

"Yes, but that was before the CFO's wife found out about her husband's affair with Bambi and had her fired." She didn't give them time to think. "The game's set up. Let's play mahjongg."

The only sound to be heard for the next few minutes was the familiar clicking of tiles knocking up against each other. They built walls, pulled tiles, and set them on their racks.

Barbara broke the silence. "Richard's moved back in."

"And you *let* him?" Irene spoke for them all.

"Things are different now."

"Richard will never change."

"I know, but *I* have." They rolled their eyeballs. "I'm different. Trust me."

"You look the same," Rochelle said drolly.

"It's down deep, where you can't see," she answered, smiling.

"You're a glutton for punishment," Irene accused, throwing out the first tile. Sylvia pulled a tile from the wall and tapped it repeatedly against her water glass. "For God's sakes, Sylvia, stop it!"

Sylvia dropped her mahjongg tile in her glass. "Mary's moved out," she said.

What shocked them more than this piece of news was the enigmatic smile on Sylvia's face.

"For someone who's convinced she's going to choke to death if she lives alone, you look downright happy," Rochelle remarked.

"I am. It's the right thing for Mary. She needs a place of her own. As for me, I won't be alone. Molly is moving in."

"Who's Molly?" they asked in unison.

"I told you about her. She works at The Sharper Image, but in the fall she'll be teaching high school math."

"You can't be serious. You just met her. She could be a drug addict. Or a serial killer," Barbara warned.

"I know all I need to know."

"Which is?"

"For one thing, she smells good. And for another, I make her laugh." They circled their index fingers in the air around their ears— the understood sign of insanity. "You think that's nothing, making someone laugh? When did I ever make one of you laugh?" She was right about that, they thought. There was nothing funny about Sylvia. "You'll meet her later. She's picking me up here tonight, after her meeting, *and* . . ." How much more could there be, they wondered. "I have a job. I'm working part-time at The Sharper Image. I didn't want to tell you right off—in case I got fired—but I've been there a week

now, and Rio likes me. Actually, it's more than that. Rio needs me."
She paused. "It feels good, being needed."

"A toast to Sylvia." Irene raised her water glass. They followed suit,
even Sylvia. "To Sylvia, living proof that there's life after . . .after . . ."

"After death," Sylvia finished.

Rochelle raised her hand. "My turn. My house is on the market,
and I'm out of the daycare business."

They were out of their chairs, hugging and kissing each other.

"What finally did it?" Irene asked. "What made you kick ass?"

They killed something I loved, a beautiful thing, smothered it to
death." She hesitated. "I couldn't let her die in vain."

"Like a sacrificial lamb," Irene said.

"Yes, but smaller."

The doorbell rang.

"Be right back," Irene said.

Irene put an eye to the peephole. Mel stood on the other side of
the door, dressed in a crisply ironed pair of khaki pants, a light blue
Oxford button-down shirt, and a natty sports jacket. In one hand he
held a plastic bag; in the other, a gold chain. Dangling from the chain
was a key. She opened the door.

"First take my robe," he said, handing her the bag. "Burn it. And
this is for you." He gave her the chain. "It's the key is to apartment
20A upstairs. I've sublet it for the next six months while the owner
is in Europe." He paused. "Listen, Renie. I know I've got a lot of bad
habits, and it's not easy for me to change, but I want to try again; that
is, if you're still willing." She reached for him, and he held her tightly.
He smelled good, she thought. He'd used an after-shave lotion, like
he did before he moved in. "Maybe you'd like to use the key later
tonight—after the girls have left?" He winked at her.

"Sounds good," she answered. She watched him swagger down
the hall towards the elevator and wondered if married but living in
separate apartments might not be another one of the world's most
beautiful human experiences.

"That was Mel," she said, returning to the living room. She swung
the key at them. "He's taken a sublet upstairs, and this is the key to
his apartment." Barbara grabbed hold of the chain.

"That's an eighteen-inch 24-karat gold cobra chain, which runs in the neighborhood of $1,500." Barbara's cell phone rang. Before answering, she checked the caller I.D. "Helloooo," she trilled, in a voice they'd never heard before. "Yes. I think I can...OK . . . see you in five minutes." She turned off her cell phone. "That was Richard. He wants me to meet him downstairs. I hope you don't mind."

"You're leaving us for Richard?"

"I don't want to discourage him. He's trying."

"Very trying," Irene quipped.

"Trust me when I say he's like a new man."

They waited until they heard the front door close.

"She would never leave us for Richard."

"You're right."

"Then who?"

"Whom," Irene corrected.

They hurried to the living room window and waited for Barbara to appear on the sidewalk below. As she did, a man exited from a car parked at the curb and ran to meet her. They wrapped their arms around each other and kissed, passionately.

"That's not Richard," Rochelle said. "Who do you think he is?"

Sylvia knew. "That's J.W., the private detective I had her call."

The doorbell rang again.

"*Now* what?" Irene asked.

"That's probably Molly."

Irene looked through the peephole. An attractive but mannish-looking woman looked back at her. She opened the door.

"I'm Molly." She grabbed Irene's hand in an iron grip. "And I'm here to pick up Syl."

"Come on in. I'm Irene."

They returned to the living room. A blushing Sylvia introduced Molly to Rochelle.

"Great game, mahjongg," Molly said, eyeing the set. "I used to play when my mother needed a sub."

"You're Jewish?" Sylvia asked, shocked.

"No, Army brat. Lots of military wives play mahjongg."

"Maybe you'd like to sub for us sometime," Irene suggested, thinking that a fifth would give them greater flexibility, and from the look of things, they were going to need it.

"Say, I'd like that." Molly looked anxiously at Sylvia. "I hate to do this, Syl, but I had to double-park, and if we don't leave fast, my car could get towed."

Molly laid a familiar hand on Sylvia's arm and guided her out of the room. Sylvia moved faster than they'd ever seen her move before.

"Do you think she knows?" Rochelle asked Irene, after she heard the front door close.

"Definitely not."

"Should we tell her?"

"Definitely not. She's never looked happier. Or prettier. Besides, she'll find out for herself soon enough."

"Well, two can't play mahjongg so I may as well head home and start packing. And you can put your new key to good use."

They walked to the front door.

"You came with a carful but going home alone," Irene remarked.

"You make 'alone' sound like a pejorative. It isn't. 'Alone' is the beginning of life."

THE END

About the Author

Carol Mizrahi has had a diverse career. From awards for high school poetry . . . to gainful employment as a verse writer for Gibson Greeting Cards . . . to Iowa's Writer's Workshop in Fiction . . . to three non-creative masters and doctoral theses . . . to sixteen years as the owner and manager of a fine used bookstore . . . to an (unsung) libretto . . . and a (non-produced but contest-winning) screenplay, Carol has never stopped writing. Maybe she should.

Mizrahi lives in Champaign, Illinois, with her husband and seven goldfish.